"This warmhearted book is fast-paced, with realistic dialogue and a captivating plot."
—*Mystery and Suspense Magazine*

FOREVER FUDGE

"Nancy Coco paints us a pretty picture of this charming island setting where the main mode of transportation is a horse-drawn vehicle. She also gives us a delicious mystery complete with doses of her homemade fudge . . . a perfect read!"
—*Wonder Women Sixty*

OH, FUDGE!

"*Oh, Fudge!* Is a charming cozy, the sixth in the Candy-Coated Mystery series. But be warned: There's a candy recipe at the end of each chapter, so don't read this one when you're hungry!"
—*Suspense Magazine*

OH SAY CAN YOU FUDGE

"Beautiful Mackinac Island provides the setting for a puzzling series of crimes. Now that Allie McMurphy has taken over her grandparents' hotel and fudge shop, life on Mackinac is good, although her little dog, Mal, does tend to nose out trouble . . . Allie's third offers plenty of plausible suspects and mouthwatering fudge recipes."
—*Kirkus Reviews*

"WOW. This is a great book. I loved the series from the beginning, and this book just makes me love it even more. Nancy Coco draws the reader in and makes you feel like you are part of the story."
—**Bookschellves.com**

TO FUDGE OR NOT TO FUDGE
"*To Fudge or Not to Fudge* is a superbly crafted, classic, culinary cozy mystery. If you enjoy them as much as I do, you are in for a real treat."
—**Examiner.com** (5 stars)

"We LOVED it! This mystery is a vacation between the pages of a book. If you've never been to Mackinac Island, you will long to visit, and if you have, the story will help you to recall all of your wonderful memories."
—*Melissa's Mochas, Mysteries and Meows*

"A five-star delicious mystery that has great characters, a good plot, and a surprise ending. If you like a good mystery with more than one suspect and a surprise ending, then rush out to get this book and read it, but be sure you have the time, since once you start, you won't want to put it down."
—**Mystery Reading Nook**

"A charming and funny culinary mystery that parodies reality-show competitions and is led by a sweet heroine, eccentric but likable characters, and a skillfully crafted plot that speeds toward an unpredictable conclusion. Allie stands out as a likable and engaging character. Delectable fudge recipes are interspersed throughout the novel."
—*Kings River Life*

ALL FUDGED UP
"A sweet treat with memorable characters, a charming locale, and satisfying mystery."
—**Barbara Allan**, author of the Trash 'n' Treasures Mystery Series

"A fun book with a lively plot, and it's set in one of America's most interesting resorts. All this plus fudge!"
—**JoAnna Carl**, author of the Chocoholic Mystery Series

"A sweet confection of a book. Charming setting, clever protagonist, and creamy fudge—a yummy recipe for a great read."
—**Joanna Campbell Slan**, author of the Scrap-N-Craft Mystery Series and the Jane Eyre Chronicles

Books by Nancy Coco

The Oregon Honeycomb Mystery Series
Death Bee Comes Her
A Matter of Hive and Death

The Candy-Coated Mystery Series
All Fudged Up
To Fudge or Not to Fudge
Oh Say Can You Fudge
All I Want for Christmas Is Fudge
All You Need Is Fudge
Oh, Fudge!
Deck the Halls with Fudge
Forever Fudge
Fudge Bites
Have Yourself a Fudgy Little Christmas
Here Comes the Fudge
A Midsummer Night's Fudge
Give Fudge a Chance
Having a Fudgy Christmas Time
Three Fudges and a Baby

Three Fudges and a Baby

Nancy Coco

Kensington Publishing Corp.
www.kensingtonbooks.com

This one is for Ashley and Mike. Thank you for taking care of me so that I could write these books. Your care, understanding, and love have enriched my life more than you will ever know!

Chapter 1

Don't tell my boyfriend, Officer Rex Manning, but Mackinac Island might just be the love of my life. It's April and I'm prepping for my third season on the island. The Historic McMurphy Hotel and Fudge Shop had made it through nearly one hundred and fifty winters on the island. I felt pretty proud about the fact that I had made it through my second with flying colors.

The fudge shop sales soared with my best-in-show fudge flavor driving most of the online sales. Who knew dark chocolate mint would be popular?

"Morning, Allie," my general manager, Frances Devaney, said as she walked into the hotel promptly at eight a.m. "It's going to be a gorgeous day. They say it might even get up to seventy degrees."

I glanced out the front window. "That would be a heat wave for this time of year. But I'll take it because it could snow tomorrow." Frances chuckled.

Main Street Mackinac was busy as more and more shop owners trickled back into town to open and get ready for the "fudgie" season. We love to call the tourists who came to spend time in the beautiful parks and the Victorian era no-cars-allowed feel of the island fudgies. I saw my best friend, Jenn Carpenter, who shared my office for her event planning business, reaching for the door, I opened it and waved her inside.

"Don't say I look positively radiant, or I will slug you," she said. Her cheeks were red as she waddled in. "This baby was supposed to come two weeks ago. I'm no longer worried about the pain of childbirth. I'd just like to see my toes again."

Jenn's pregnancy felt like it had gone on for years, but in fact it was just over nine months. She was one of those lucky women who looked even prettier while pregnant. She held her back and sat in a wingback chair near the front door. I had designed a seating area with a cozy gas fireplace and a wonderful view of Main Street. There was no need for a fire today.

"Hello, Jenn." Douglas Devaney, my curmudgeonly handyman and Frances's new husband, walked toward the front door. "You look—"

"Don't say it," I warned and put up my hand in a stop gesture.

"What? I was going to say she looks—"

"Ready to pop?" Jenn said from her perch on the edge of the chair. She told me last week that if she sat back, she would never be able to get out of it due to her current low center of gravity.

"I was going to say, lovely as ever," Douglas said. "What is wrong with that?"

"Nothing," I answered. "Absolutely nothing." I hurried to the coffee bar behind the fudge shop and grabbed a bottle of water for Jenn.

"I'm sorry," Jenn said to Douglas. "I'm just so crabby these days."

"That's understandable." Douglas scooted the foot stool over so that she could prop her feet up. "Are you sure you should be working?"

"Sarah, my midwife, said it's good to move around as much as possible," Jenn said. "Although I feel more like I'm waddling than walking. That and I have to get out from under Shane. That man drives me crazy with his hovering. Just last night I woke up to find him watching me with the go bag at the foot of the bed."

"How does he handle going to work in St. Ignace and leaving you here on the island?" I asked.

"Oh, he's not going to St. Ignace. No, no, he's built a small lab in the shed, complete with an evidence cage and chain of custody logs."

"That had to be expensive," I said.

"You don't want to know." She shook her head. "But he got it okayed by the county so there's that."

"How'd he manage that?" Frances asked.

Jenn shook her head again. "His father is good buddies with the governor so that might have helped him."

"Then you have definitely decided to have the baby on the island?" I asked.

"Yes," she said and rubbed her belly. "Sarah has permission to set up at the clinic, and I have a doula, Hannah Riversbend. She's been working with us through the birthing classes and such. In fact, she's supposed to be meeting me at the Coffee Bean." Jenn held up her hand. "Before you say anything, I'm not drinking coffee. They have this nice triple-berry herbal tea. Anyway, I'm supposed to head over there, but I thought I'd stop for a moment and take a load off."

"I'm done stocking the fudge shop," I said. "Why don't I go with you? I would love to meet your doula." I unbuttoned my baker's coat and pulled off my baking hat. "As long as you don't mind my going smelling of sugar."

"Sure," she said. "You know I love the smell of sugar. But I'm going to rest a bit if you would feel better about changing first. I can text Hannah what's going on."

"Great," I said. "I'll just be a minute. Besides, that way if we run into Rex, I look less like the walking dead."

"You know he doesn't mind how you look," Douglas said.

I shook my head and scurried up the stairs; my Bichonpoo pup, Mal, raced ahead of me. It took less than ten minutes for me to wash up and change. I even brushed out my wavy hair and pinned it up into a top bun, which I hear is all the rage for busy women these days.

I came down wearing jeans, a pink polo with the McMurphy logo on it, and my favorite pair of black flats. Mal loved it when I hurried. She would dance around picking up on my excitement.

"You can't come with us," I said to my pup as she raced down the stairs and watched me descend, her stub tail wagging. "It's still too cool for Jenn to be sitting outside and the Coffee Bean doesn't allow dogs inside."

Mal sat and cocked her head to the side and just kept looking at me like I spouted nonsense.

"Oh, let's take her." Jenn rose awkwardly from the chair. "Sarah said sitting out in the sunshine was good for the baby. Plus, I have my sweater."

"Are you sure?"

"Positive." Jenn waddled toward us at the back of the lobby. "Grab her leash, we'll cut through the alley."

I slid Mal into her halter and leash and opened the door for Jenn. The back alley was Mal's favorite spot. There was a small strip of grass between the alley and the fence of the neighboring hotel.

"How are you feeling really?" I asked.

"Do I look that bad?" Jenn asked as she held her low back and walked slower than I've ever seen her walk.

"Hey, only child here." I waved my hand. "I have no idea what you should look like at this stage of pregnancy. I asked because you don't complain about anything."

"Oh, I complain plenty," she said. "But only Shane gets to hear it because he helped this whole situation." She gestured toward her belly. "Not that I'm not excited for the baby."

"Oh, I know you're excited. You had your nursery done in October." We exited the alley and Mal turned left, not right toward the Coffee Bean. "This way, silly." I pulled her toward us, but Mal insisted that we had to go left toward Main Street. "I'm sorry," I said to Jenn. "She wants to go for a longer walk."

Jenn glanced down at her phone. "I texted Hannah we'd be running late, and she didn't get back to me. I see no harm in taking a detour. Maybe I can walk this baby out."

"Fine, we'll go around the block," I said. "You might want to text her and let her know where we are."

"Got it," Jenn paused and thumbed in her message, hit send, and we let Mal lead us to Main Street. The street itself held the usual bustle of handymen and shopkeepers, touching up paint and washing windows and prepping things for the season. Overeager fudgies spilled onto the island from the ferries, but mostly it was fishermen, hikers, and park enthusiasts. Thankfully, the sidewalks weren't crowded yet. Mal seemed to know which way we wanted to go and led us to the right. Joann's Fudge Shop hadn't opened yet. The ticket booth where people paid for horse-drawn-carriage tours around the island was also closed with a note that tickets were available at the visitors' center.

It was a pleasant walk as we turned right again and headed toward Market Street. Jenn stopped and pulled out her phone.

"Is there a problem? Is she there?" I asked.

"No problem, I was just checking. She hasn't answered yet."

"Huh," I said. "Maybe her phone died."

Jenn frowned at me. "She's a doula. Babies come at any time of day, so she needs her phone to always be working."

"Okay, well, hold on a second. Let me text Carrie and see if she's at the Coffee Bean waiting for us. If she's there, then Carrie can let her know we got delayed." Carrie was the owner of the coffee shop and unlike me, she knew everyone on the island.

"Okay," Jenn said and sat down on a small bench in front of a restaurant on the corner. "I need to sit for a moment anyway. It sucks being as big as a whale."

I texted Carrie and she got right back to me.

I haven't seen Hannah Riversbend today, Carrie texted. **But if I do, I'll let her know you got delayed.**

Thanks, I texted back and then glanced at Jenn, who looked tired from our two-block walk. "She's not there yet, we're fine."

Jenn frowned. "None of this makes sense. Hannah is reliable."

"Maybe she overslept," I suggested. It was only 8:45 in the morning.

"Hannah does not oversleep," Jenn said. "Her job is to be on call twenty-four-seven. I mean, what if I was to go into labor now?"

"Are you going into labor?" I asked, trying not to sound scared.

"No," Jenn said and sighed. She heaved herself off of the bench. "Hannah doesn't live far—just the next block over. I say we go and check on her."

"Are you up to it?" I asked. "Because I can totally go check while you go to the Coffee Bean."

"No, no, no," she said. "I'm going, too. I think something's wrong. She lives above a shop on Market Street. We can cut down the alley."

As we approached the mouth of the alley, a man wearing a hoodie barreled between us. "Hey!" I shouted. "Watch out for the pregnant woman." Mal barked fiercely and the man glanced over his shoulder for a second, then continued on his way. "Are you okay?" I asked Jenn.

"Yep," she said as she leaned one hand on the closest building. "I caught myself in time."

"Who was that? I mean, he was really rude. I want to follow him and give him a piece of my mind." I helped her straighten.

"Are you girls alright?" It was Monica Grazer, the owner of a nearby what-not shop. "I saw him nearly push you to the ground."

"I'm fine." Jenn sent us a reassuring smile. I still had ahold of her elbow.

"Do you know who that was?" I asked Monica.

Monica and I met at a Chamber of Commerce meeting last month. She had retired from a corporate marketing job and bought the shop last fall. Her brown eyes showed concern as if Jenn weren't telling the truth about being okay. "I think it was Vincent Trowski. I swear that boy gets ruder and ruder every time I see him. Are you sure you girls are okay?"

"We're sure," Jenn said. She glanced at her phone. "Still no answer from Hannah. I'm getting worried."

"Are you looking for Hannah Riversbend?" Monica asked.

"Yes, she's my doula, and she hasn't been answering my texts," Jenn said.

"I saw her just a bit ago," Monica said. "She was arguing with Matthew Jones. I have no idea what it was about, but it was pretty animated."

"Matthew Jones?" I asked.

Jenn shrugged. "He's a park ranger. Shane knows him from their softball league."

"Wait, Shane plays softball?" I asked. Jenn's husband was a skinny, science type with round glasses. He was also our local CSI.

"Why do you say it like that?" Jenn asked. "He's a really good pitcher."

"How did I not know this?" I asked.

"Because you spend a lot of your time making fudge and running the hotel." Jenn patted me on the shoulder. "It's okay that some of us have a life."

I frowned at her, and her eyes twinkled at me. I couldn't be upset because she looked happy when she teased me.

"Listen, you girls might be able to catch her," Monica said. "When she saw me, she stormed down the alley toward her place and Matthew followed. It wasn't that long ago."

Mal whined and pulled on her leash, telling me that she was done with our talking and was ready to go walking. "Thanks," I said. Jenn and I followed Mal down the sidewalk and into the alley. The shops along Main Street and Market Street often had two stories, with the shop underneath and an apartment or two above. Like my apartment, they often had exits facing the alley, keeping the street view of the shop from being marred by stairs.

Mal sped up as we entered the alley, dragging me behind. "Hey, slow down," I said. "Jenn can't walk that fast."

"Watch me," Jenn said and stepped up her waddle.

I watched her closely as we progressed down the alley. "I think that's Hannah on her stairs. Wait, is that Mella?" she asked and pointed to a calico cat sitting on the top of a set of wire stairs that led to an upstairs apartment.

I glanced at the stairs she pointed to. There was a young woman sitting on the stairs and my cat a few steps above her. "Looks like it," I said as we approached. I kept watch on Jenn to ensure she didn't fall.

"Wait. Stop." Jenn grabbed my arm a building away from the staircase.

"Are you okay?" I asked.

"Yes, I'm okay," she said, "but he's not." She pointed with her chin toward the bottom of the stairs while Mal strained at the end of her leash.

On the gray rocky alley floor was a young man, lying in a widening pool of blood. "Oh, dear," I said.

"Oh, dear is right," Jenn said. "Hannah? Are you okay?"

Hannah didn't answer as she sat two steps down from where my cat Mella sat licking her paws. "No," Hannah finally whispered and looked up at us with a gun in her right hand. Her hands were bloody and so was her blouse. Both hands rested on her lap as if she didn't realize what she held.

"Here." I handed Jenn Mal's leash. "Turn around. Seriously. You need to get as far down the alley as you can."

"But Hannah—" Jenn balked as she took Mal's leash.

"Has a gun," I said as calmly as I could. I glanced down at Mal. "Mal, take Jenn to safety."

Mal turned and immediately pulled Jenn toward the end of the alley we'd turned down.

Jenn looked like she wanted to protest, but Mal jerked hard, and Jenn took a step, turned, and hurried down the alley.

"Hannah," I said calmly. "You need to put the gun down."

She looked at me blankly. "What?"

"The gun in your hand," I said, and slowly stepped toward her. "You need to put it down."

"Gun?" She didn't seem to register my words. Mella took two slow steps down and wormed her way into Hannah's lap, knocking the gun out of her hand. The metal object rattled thickly across the end of the step and fell to the ground.

For a brief moment, I held my breath, praying that it didn't go off. When it hit the ground without discharging, I leapt into motion, diving under the stairs, grabbing the gun with the hem of my polo shirt. I rolled to the other side of the stairs and lay there for a moment. Hannah stared blankly, petting Mella, who had taken up residence in her lap. I got up and brushed the dust off of my clothes and carefully put the gun on a dumpster a good distance from Hannah.

I'm not familiar with handguns, but this one was stocky with a ridged grip. Carefully, so as not to startle Hannah, I walked over to the man, whose head was turned away from the stairs, and squatted down to check for a pulse. I didn't feel one and he was already starting to get cold.

Rex and Officer Charles Brown came dashing down the alley on their bikes. They stood them next to the building and stopped briefly to study the scene before coming any closer.

"EMTs are on their way," Rex said as he approached in his calm, steady strides.

"I don't think they can help," I said. "I have a gun that may be involved." Pointing to the dumpster, I watched as he slipped on gloves and squatted down much like I did, careful to avoid the blood. With a shake of his head, he silently communicated to Charles that they had another murder on their hands. Charles immediately went to a kit on his bike, then began to secure the scene with crime scene tape.

Rex studied the man, careful not to miss clues. Then he rose and walked over to me. "You picked up the gun? Why?" His blue eyes went flat cop, where everyone and everything was suspect—even me.

I swallowed as my heart rose in my chest. "Hannah was holding it when we got here."

He glanced at the woman who stared into space and kept absently petting Mella. "You said *we*. Do you mean you and Jenn?" he asked as he stepped to the dumpster, carefully took the gun, and examined it.

"Yes."

"Did you touch it?" he asked and sniffed the weapon. Then nodded, confirming that it had definitely been fired.

"I used the hem of my polo to pick it up after she dropped it," I explained. "I wasn't sure of her state of mind, and I thought it best to not keep the gun within reach."

He grunted as if to acknowledge what I said but did not agree or disagree with my thinking. You would think I'd be used to this by now, but it still shocked me to be treated as part of a crime scene, especially from the man I loved.

Charles came up with an evidence bag and took the gun from Rex. "We passed Jenn at the entrance to the alley," he said. "I imagine she called nine-one-one."

"And Shane," I agreed and hugged myself.

Rex went to the stairs and hunkered down to Hannah's eye level to try and talk to her; she appeared to be in a state of shock. I noticed that she barely acknowledged what was going on. All she could do was whisper the word *what*, no matter the question.

"Maybe it's a good thing we called for George," Charles said as the sirens of the ambulance—one of the few motor vehicles allowed on the island—pulled in from the opposite end of the alley.

I became aware of a small crowd of locals who stood at the edges of the crime scene tape, and the curtains moving from a neighboring window. "You might have a better witness than me," I said, and nudged my chin in the direction of the window. "They had to have heard the shot."

"I would be surprised if they did hear it and didn't run down to the alley to help," Charles said. "Stay put and I'll get your statement in a few minutes."

I agreed and watched as George Marron and Kathy Miller pulled a stretcher under the crime scene tape. Charles intercepted them, and they turned their attention to Hannah. The alley warmed up as the sun grew higher in the sky. My phone buzzed, and I grabbed it and saw it was Frances calling. "Hello?" I asked after hitting the answer button.

"I heard sirens and saw Shane riding fast down Main Street," Frances said. "Are you and Jenn alright? Did she go into labor?"

That thought made me smile. "Yes, we are fine. No, she didn't go into labor. We have a bit of a situation."

"Oh, dear," Frances said. "Another murder?"

"Yes, but this time it looks like we have our killer." I glanced over to see Rex take Mella out of

Hannah's lap and let George and Kathy do their work.

"Oh, good," Frances said with relief.

"Not good," I said.

"Why?"

"It's Hannah Riversbend." I spoke so low it was near a whisper.

"Oh, dear, the doula's dead?" Frances asked.

"No," I said. "Worse. We found her with the smoking gun."

Chapter 2

Fudgy Oatmeal Bars

I love these. They are a go-to recipe for when the kids come home after school.

Ingredients:
Top and bottom
 1 cup butter
 1 cup brown sugar, packed
 ½ cup white sugar
 1 tablespoon vanilla
 2 cups all-purpose flour
 2 cups quick-cook oatmeal
 1 teaspoon baking soda
 ¼ teaspoon salt

Fudgy middle
 12 oz. dark chocolate chips (semisweet
   will do in a pinch)
 14 oz. can sweetened condensed milk

2 tablespoons butter
1 teaspoon vanilla

Directions:
Preheat oven to 350 degrees F. Line a 9 x 13 baking pan with parchment first and then grease.

Set aside.

Melt the butter. In a large bowl, mix the butter, sugars, and vanilla until combined. Slowly add flour, baking soda, and salt. Once well mixed, add oats and mix thoroughly. Put ⅔ of mixture into the bottom of the pan and pat down until flat (leaving about 1½ cups for the top).

In a medium saucepan combine chocolate chips, sweetened condensed milk, and butter. Cook over medium heat, stirring often, until everything is melted and smooth. Remove from heat and add vanilla. Gently pour over the uncooked bottom crust and spread gently until even. Sprinkle remaining oat mixture on top and bake for 18–20 minutes until golden brown. Cool completely and cut into 2-inch squares. Makes 24. Enjoy!

George and Kathy put Hannah in the ambulance to transfer her to the clinic. She hadn't spoken a single word since they got there. Officer Lasko arrived earlier and went with Hannah. They had decided not to cuff her until they got her story, but that didn't mean she wasn't supervised.

I picked up Mella and checked her for any blood, but my wayward kitty seemed perfectly fine and content for me to pet her. After Shane checked on Jenn, and called Frances to ask her to see his wife home, he began the slow and careful process of collecting forensic evidence. Rex worked on the scene, taking note of who stood outside the crime scene tape and who lived nearby and might have heard something.

I stood beside Charles, who kept an eye on the crowd. I got a text from Frances.

Jenn is here at the scene with Mal, she wrote. **Even though Shane insisted that I take her far away from the scene, she didn't want to go home. Douglas and I convinced her to stay here.**

Great, I texted back. **Please take care of her.**

I will, she replied.

Knowing Jen was in good hands, I was able to put 100 percent of my attention on the scene. The poor deceased man turned out to be Matthew Jones. Shane positively identified him. It was strange for the ambulance to take Hannah to the clinic and leave the victim, but I understood why. Hannah was in a bad way. I would be, too, if my fiancé was dead—whether I shot him or not.

"You saw the killer, didn't you?" I whispered to Mella. "Was it Hannah?"

Mella ignored the question and closed her eyes. Not that I expected an answer. Although sometimes it would be nice if she could talk. My cat had adopted me by running into the McMurphy one day and not leaving. She and I had settled into a relationship where she mostly stayed with me, but then every now and again, she loved to take a walk outside. I was less concerned about her safety since the island was small and there were only two vehicles: an ambulance and a fire truck. Horse-drawn buggies and carriages were commonplace, along with bicycles, the odds of getting hit by a car were low.

We did have a few coyotes who had arrived in the winter over the ice that often bridged the island to the shore. I worried about them and last year there had been one or two that even ventured downtown. But the park rangers worked to discourage the behavior and this year none have been seen. It's why I let Mella out this morning before I showered. I'm sure she was feeling cooped up and I know she had friends to visit.

One time she had been gone a few days and I discovered she was a regular at Sheila's home and had stayed for a few days.

My cat didn't have any blood on her. That meant she hadn't been on the ground and then climbed the stairs after Matthew was shot. Rex was meeting with a couple of officers, but I couldn't hear what they were saying.

"What is he telling them?" I asked Charles.

"Most likely to canvass the neighborhood and knock on doors to see who was home, and who might have seen or heard anything," he answered.

At long last Rex turned to me and Mella. Charles nodded and left my side as Rex came over. "That poor man," I said with a shake of my head. "I take it the gun was the murder weapon?"

"That will be the coroner's job to determine," Rex said. "He just texted to let me know he'd arrived on the island and was headed this way."

"How will they transport the body?" I asked, looking around.

"The EMTs have safely delivered Hannah to the

clinic," he replied. "The doctor is treating her for shock. George should be back here momentarily. But he can't move the body until the coroner takes a look."

"I understand," I said. "He doesn't usually come out for these, does he?" I couldn't remember meeting him before.

"He was on his way to St. Ignace for a meeting when the call came in, and he texted to let me know he wanted to do this one in person."

"He must be up for election this fall," I mused.

Rex didn't even crack a smile. He was on full cop alert. "Tell me what happened."

I went over everything from the time we left the McMurphy until he arrived. "My biggest concern was that Hannah had the gun in her hand. I had Mal take Jenn away immediately. I assume that Jenn made the nine-one-one call and Charlene knew what to do"

"Hers was the second call," Rex said.

That news surprised me because we were the only ones in the alley. "Who called first? There was no one here when we arrived."

"The first caller was concerned because they thought they'd heard a gunshot or fireworks," he said.

"But Jenn and I were outside very near here and didn't hear anything," I said. "There were a lot of people out prepping shops for the season. Seems like we all would have heard a gunshot. Who was the caller? I mean Charlene knows everyone on the island."

"She said the voice was distorted, and it sounded like the person didn't want to identify themself."

"Strange." I frowned, wondering why whoever called it in didn't want to be identified. "Was it a man or a woman?"

"Don't worry about it. We'll look into that," Rex said. "What's Mella doing here?" I knew he wanted to pet my cat, and the instinct warred with his cop demeanor.

"I let her out this morning," I said. "We haven't seen a coyote downtown for a few months and she wanted out."

"Interesting," he said and made a note.

"Like I said, she was on the stairs above Hannah when we came on the scene," I said. "I don't know if she knows Hannah." I looked up at my location and the apartments around us. "She might have been visiting Mrs. Vissor. She lives near here."

"Okay." He closed his notebook. "Listen to me very carefully. Go home and stay safe. This case seems pretty open-and-shut."

"What are you going to do?" I asked, my frown deepening. "You can't arrest Hannah. She's Jenn's doula and she needs her."

"I'm going to follow police procedure," he said. "That means following the evidence and arresting a suspect. No matter who it is."

I opened my mouth to protest, and he stepped back.

"Go home, Allie, and be safe." Then he turned on his heel and headed toward the other officers.

I sighed long and loudly and turned away from the scene. My thoughts whirled. *If Hannah is arrested, that means Jenn needs a new doula.* I could probably solve that problem with a little research. I climbed under the crime scene tape and edged my way through the small crowd. As I reached the edge of the crowd a younger man in an expensive, well-tailored suit and tie nearly ran into me. "Excuse me," I said.

His brown eyes snapped. "Is that a cat? Did you bring a cat to a crime scene?"

"I didn't bring her, she was already here," I said.

"As a district attorney and a cat lover, I'd recommend you keep your cat inside for its own safety."

I started to say something when he raised his hand and cut me off. "I get that cats like to be outside. Look into a catio. Statistically cats who roam only live for three years."

"Um, o . . . kay," I said, taken aback. "Thanks?"

"You're welcome." He nodded his shaved head. His chocolate skin shined in the bright light. "Now, move out of the way for the coroner, we've got a dead body to examine." He turned and helped a more appropriately dressed, middle-aged man push his way through the crowd. He stopped in front of me. "Is that a cat? Why did you . . . Never mind. I've got work to do and I recommend you take that cat home before it messes up my work."

I stared after them, equal parts offended and mortified. I glanced down at my cat, who looked up at me and meowed. "I know, right?" The crowd let me through and I hurried toward the McMurphy. But then I turned back toward Main Street. When I hit the corner, Monica stepped outside her shop.

"What happened in the alley? Erin McDonald came into the shop and said that Hannah shot Matthew Jones. Is that true?" she asked.

"I don't really know, I wasn't there when it happened," I answered. In my short time of involvement with solving crimes, I had come to realize that they are quite often not so cut-and-dried. The last thing I wanted to do was to fuel any rumors that might make things worse if Hannah was somehow innocent. "Say, did anyone stop into your shop and tell you they heard a gunshot this morning?"

"No, the first I heard of it was Erin. Why?"

I didn't answer. "If anyone does, would you give me a call?"

"Sure," she said with her eyes wide. "Wait, so Matthew was shot? How awful, and Hannah did it? They seemed so in love."

"I don't know anything for sure," I hedged. "The coroner is there now."

"Oh, is that handsome new DA, Jamal Burns, here as well? I heard he was seen on Market Street." She patted her hair. "That man is gorgeous and usually very busy. I'm surprised he came."

"Me, too," I said, not remembering ever hearing of him before. But then I rarely interacted with anyone from the county. "How do you know him?"

"My sister-in-law is friends with his sister," she said. "He studied criminal law and public policy."

"Huh," I said, drawing my eyebrows together in confusion. "Why would the district attorney come to a crime scene?"

"I called my sister-in-law, and she told me he and the coroner were at a political luncheon."

"Wait, why would the coroner be at a political luncheon? Isn't he busy at the morgue or wherever?"

"Oh, no," Monica said. "The coroner is a political position. You must be thinking of the medical examiner. Coroners don't even have to be doctors."

"Huh."

She leaned in conspiratorially. "I heard Jamal has his eye on the governor's office, and he's single."

I shook my head and smiled. "I thought you were retired. Would you really want to be the first lady of the state?"

She laughed. "Not for me, silly, for my daughter, Angel. She would make a lovely political spouse. Just like Jackie Kennedy."

"Oh," I said. "Does she know that?"

"That poor girl doesn't know what is right for her. Thankfully, she has me to guide her. Well, there's a customer. Got to run!" She turned and greeted the pair of women making their way into her shop.

Mella meowed and I looked down at her. "My thoughts exactly."

Chapter 3

"Poor Hannah." Jenn paced our shared office. Maybe not paced but waddled around. "Matthew was the love of her life. And we both know that as soon as she's cleared at the clinic, she'll be taken to the police station and questioned for hours. It's horrible."

"She was holding the nearly smoking gun," I pointed out.

"And in shock," Jenn said. "I'm sure she didn't do it. That girl is the most caring and loving person. That's why I picked her. I must have interviewed at least a dozen doulas before I found her. I wanted her calm, caring energy in the room with me when I gave birth."

"I can help you find another doula," I offered, and turned my computer screen toward her. "I've been googling all the reviews of the local doulas."

Jenn sat down with a hefty sigh and leaned back so that she was nearly prone. "I already did that. In fact, I have a whole spreadsheet filled with notes on all the doulas."

"I'm sure you do," I muttered and turned my screen back to me. Jenn was always organized, and she researched everything. "Who was your second choice?"

"That's the problem," Jenn wailed. "I didn't have a second choice. It was Hannah by a landslide." Tears welled up in her eyes. "What happens now if the baby comes?"

I grabbed a tissue from the box and handed it to her. Then sat on the edge of my desk. "I can be there for you, and Sarah will be there." I tried to sound reassuring as she blew her nose. Then started to wail harder.

"I love you," she blubbered. Her voice was shaking. "But you don't know anything about having babies. I need Hannah's comfort and calm soul!"

I grabbed another tissue, handed it to her and awkwardly patted her on the shoulder. "We'll figure something out. I'll talk to Rex."

Jenn blew her nose again. "I'm sorry, I don't know what's come over me."

"You had a plan, and this blew things up," I said. "I get that. We can come up with a different solution."

"I don't want a different solution," she wailed. "I want Hannah!"

"Honey." I touched her arm. "Hannah shot and killed someone."

"She would never," Jenn said and grabbed a tissue, blowing her nose loudly. "I know her, and she would never." She looked at me, and from her expression she had a thought. "You need to find the real killer, Allie."

"I was there, and she had the gun." I tried to reason with my very pregnant friend.

"You didn't see her shoot the gun. We both know that." Jenn stood and started back to her waddle pacing. "We need to talk to her."

"She's in police custody," I said. "I don't know what you think we can do."

"You don't know that they have her already," Jenn said. "She might still be at the clinic."

"You want me to go to the clinic and see if I can talk to her," I stated.

"Yes." Jenn nodded fiercely. "Yes, I do. Oh, Allie, you'll do it, right? Please promise me you'll do it." A fresh set of tears welled up in her eyes.

"Okay, if I promise to look into it, will you go home and get some rest?"

"I have to put some finishing touches on an event this weekend," she said, and sniffed. "But I can't until I know that Hannah will be there when I go into labor."

"Okay." I stood. "Okay, I will see what I can do."

"Let's go to the clinic now and see if we can talk to her," Jenn said and headed to the door.

"No, no, no," I said. "You need to protect that baby. I'll go and I promise I'll do my best to help."

"Okay," Jenn said and narrowed her eyes. "But I can and will investigate this on my own if I have to."

"I'm taking you seriously," I said. "How you can help me is to go home and put your feet up. Then you can find out from Shane any details I might need as the investigation progresses. Deal?"

"Deal," she said, and I watched to make sure she wasn't crossing her fingers.

"We have to keep you and the baby safe," I said.

"Okay." Jenn sniffed.

"I'll walk you home, and then I promise I'll go

straight to the clinic. If she's not there, I'll check the police station."

"Fine." Jenn wiped her eyes, shoved her arms into her jacket and picked up her purse. "But I'll be texting you every ten minutes."

"I understand," I said, and grabbed my own jacket from the coat-tree near the door of the office. "Let's go out through my apartment. I don't want to have to explain to Frances what is going on."

We stepped out of the office and down the hall, where we entered my apartment. It was a small two-bedroom owner's apartment with a back door. I'd built stairs down from the fire escape so that I could take Mal out that way to go potty.

Mal and Mella greeted me at the door. Both seemed eager to go out, but I said no, and quickly closed them in when we exited the apartment.

"Are you sure you don't want to take Mal?" Jenn asked as she carefully descended the stairs, keeping both hands on the rails.

"I'm sure," I said. "If Hannah is still at the clinic, I can't take Mal in without special permission."

"And you don't want to give away the fact that you are there to investigate." Jenn finished the thought for me.

"Something like that," I said, and hurried to keep up as she steamrolled ahead of me in the alley toward her home. I hoped talking to Hannah would help.

After I walked Jenn home and was convinced that she would stay home with her feet up and rest, I headed to the clinic, which was just down Market

Street from the police department. It was the middle of the afternoon, maybe Jenn was right, and Hannah would still be there. She certainly needed to be treated for shock. As the day warmed the earth, the ground seemed to soften and cause flowers to begin to sprout. Mackinac Island was pretty no matter the season, and today the air held the promise of spring.

I entered the clinic and headed to the front desk.

"Hi, Allie," Esha White greeted me. She sat behind the desk in piano-decorated scrubs and a beautiful silk headscarf. Her cocoa skin shone against the pop of hot pink.

"Hi, Esha," I said. "How are you?"

"I'm good," she said, and stood. "I take it you're here to see Hannah?"

"Is she still here?"

"Yes." Esha walked to the door to the rooms and let me in. "She was in pretty bad shape shock-wise, and Doctor Simmons wanted to keep her overnight."

"I take it she's allowed to have visitors?" I asked as I followed her down the hall.

"No one said she couldn't," Esha said. "But you have to know that she has a police officer stationed outside her room, and she is handcuffed to the bed." Esha stopped and looked at me with serious eyes. "It's hard to see. She is such a wonderful and gentle woman."

"Thanks for the warning," I said. "And for showing me to her room."

We stopped in front of a very small room. Officer Smith sat in a small chair beside the door

and stood up when we approached. "You here to
see Hannah?" he asked.

"Yes," I said.

"She's not talking yet," he warned me. "I don't
think you'll be able to get much out of her."

"Thanks for the heads-up." I glanced at Esha,
who waved me inside. Then I pushed the door
open to find Hannah on a narrow hospital bed.
Her head was turned away from the door and her
left hand cuffed to the bedrail.

"Hi, Hannah," I said. "Jenn wanted me to check
on you." I took a chair and pulled it up next to her.
"How are you?"

She didn't answer and never turned her head.
Tears rolled down her cheeks.

"I see they have you on an IV," I chattered.
"That should help you with the shock. I know
they've given me an IV a time or two." That got her
to turn her face toward me. "Shock can be the
weirdest feeling. The first time it happened to me
I almost fainted, and I never faint."

She studied me and blinked as if she were wak-
ing up.

I reached out and took her hand. "It helps if
you're not alone." She closed her eyes and I let the
silence wrap around us. She had a slight tremor in
her hand, but she clung to me like a small child
and my heart went out to her. This didn't seem
like the actions of an angry murderer.

With her eyes closed she started talking. Her
voice was soft and low, and I leaned in to better
hear her.

"Matthew is dead."

I squeezed her hand and waited for her to

gather the strength to continue. "I don't know what happened. I . . . I was home when I heard a strange noise. I looked out the window and Matthew was lying in the alley." Her eyes opened and heavy tears welled up. "Oh, Allie, he's dead. My Matthew is dead."

With my free hand I grabbed a tissue from the box on the bedstand and handed it to her. She let go of my hand and took the tissue, blowing her nose. "I know this is difficult," I said and patted her shoulder.

"We were getting married." She choked up, her voice beginning to rise. "We had such a beautiful life planned."

"Oh, Hannah, I'm sorry for your loss. I know I would feel like I wanted to die if anything happened to my boyfriend," I said.

"If he's the one for you, don't wait. You just don't know. You never know when that chance will be taken away from you." She started crying harder.

I handed her a couple more tissues. "How did you get the gun?"

"What?" She paused mid-blow.

"The gun," I said gently. "When Jenn and I got there, you were holding a gun."

"I was?" She looked confused. "I . . . I remember running out the back door of my apartment and down the fire escape. I . . . I tried to stop the blood with pressure, but when I checked for a pulse, he didn't have one." She wailed the last two words.

"Okay." I patted her hand. "It's okay. Take a deep breath." She did. "Now take another and blow it out slow." She did. "Good. Now close your eyes and picture the alley," I urged gently. "Where was the gun?"

She squeezed my hand tight and closed her eyes. "Okay. I was kneeling and had pressure on the wound. I saw the gun . . . it was near his feet. Whoever shot him must have dropped it."

"Okay, good." Patted her hand and she squeezed tight.

"I was scared. I didn't know what to do. I kept one hand on the wound, figuring it was in or near the heart, and leaned into it while I grabbed my phone and tried to dial nine-one-one."

"Did you get to the operator?"

"No." She shook her head slowly and winced. "My hands were too slippery, and I couldn't get any of the buttons on my smartphone to work."

"Okay, that's fine," I said. "How did you get the gun?"

"I thought I saw someone in the alley, and I didn't know who it was. I was afraid it was the killer, so I grabbed the gun just as Matthew made this horrible sound and died." Her eyes popped open. "He just died. I couldn't do CPR. All I could think of doing was apply pressure. I just couldn't save him."

Tears formed in her eyes, and I grabbed the tissues again and handed her one.

"Then what happened?" I gently urged.

"I don't know," she said, shaking her hands. "It all went blank until I was here under warm blankets and Esha was putting in an IV."

"And you didn't shoot him?"

"What? No! I loved him. Why would I shoot him? Where would I get a gun?" Her eyes were wide with shock at the idea.

"It's okay," I said, and patted her hand. "I heard you and Matthew fought this morning."

"It was a stupid argument over how many people were on our guest list," she said and blew her nose. "Just stupid."

"But it got heated," I said, searching for how the police might look at it.

"Did it?" She seemed stunned by the idea. "Wait, who told you we were fighting? We were in my apartment. Who would know that?"

"You were seen arguing. Don't you remember?" I asked.

"No, I don't." She seemed truly surprised. "We fought, but then he left for work, and I was getting ready to meet Jenn when I heard the noise. None of this makes sense."

I sat back and squeezed her hand. "You're right. None of this makes sense."

Just then the door opened, and Shane and Rex stepped in.

"Oh, good, Allie, I'm glad you're here," Shane said. He set down his tech kit and pushed up his round glasses. "I need to check you both for gunshot residue."

Chapter 4

I let go of Hannah's hand and stood. "Wait, what?"

"You both handled the gun," Shane explained as he opened his kit. "I need to check you both."

I looked at Rex. "But I didn't shoot the gun. How would I have gunshot residue on my hands?"

Rex looked at me with compassion in his gaze. "When I got there you'd put it on top of the dumpster. How were you able to do that when your polo won't reach that high?"

"I used . . . oh." It was the only thing I could say when I realized he was right.

"When you touched the gun, you got residue on your hand," Shane explained while he tore open a swab package. "We need evidence. Hold out your hands."

I did as he asked and let him run the cool swab over my hands. "This is silly."

He put the swab into a plastic container and sealed it, then wrote my name and the date and time on it. "It's just precautionary."

"Do you need anything else from Allie?" Rex asked Shane.

"Are those the clothes you were wearing this morning?" Shane asked me.

"Yes, I haven't had time to change."

"I'll come by your place later and collect your clothes," Shane said.

"At this rate the crime lab is going to have more of my clothing than I do," I groused.

"Okay, Allie." Rex opened the door. "I need you to go home now."

"But Hannah needs a friendly face," I protested. Esha stepped into the open doorway.

"And she has one." Rex nodded toward the nurse. "Now go home. I'll talk to you later."

"Fine," I said and smiled at Esha as I passed by her. The clinic seemed cold and sparse as I quickly navigated the hall and headed outside into the cool sunshine.

Jenn was right, Hannah wasn't the murderer. I headed toward Monica's gift shop. It was important to understand why she'd told us that Hannah was fighting with Matthew.

Hurrying down the streets, I dodged the fudgies and pushed the what-not shop's door open. The bells jangled and Monica looked up.

"Allie." She came out from behind the counter and rushed to me, then looked around and said in a hushed tone, "I just can't believe that Hannah would do such a thing. She seemed like such a nice girl." She shook her head. "I guess you just never know about people. I heard you went to the police station, are you okay? Is Jenn, and her baby, okay?"

"Jenn's fine," I said and took a step back. "So am I, but I don't believe Hannah did it."

"What?" She cocked her head with a look of surprise on her face. "Craig Kowalski told me that you found her with the gun in her hand."

I didn't confirm or deny it, like Rex taught me. "Hannah says she was in her apartment when she heard the shot. She also told me they fought in her apartment, not on the street. Why did you think she did?"

"Welcome in," Monica said as a pair of fudgies entered the store. "Today's special is ten percent off of a purchase of fifty dollars or more." Then she gently took my arm and drew me around the counter. "I don't know why Hannah told you that. If that wasn't an argument, then I don't know arguments."

"Where did you see them argue?" I asked. "Was anyone else around?"

"I was on my early morning walk," she said. "I usually walk two miles a day. It's good for your health. Anyway, like I said, I was on my early morning walk when I heard them yelling at each other. It looked like they were walking back from the Coffee Bean because they were on Market Street with coffee cups in their hands. As I got closer, I heard Hannah say something like, how could you! And then she threw her coffee cup at him and stormed off. That really got him steamed and he took off after her. They turned down the alley and I continued on my walk. I figured it was a lovers' quarrel. You should never get mixed up with that. I didn't like the littering though. I picked up the coffee cup and tossed it in the trash can outside the Coffee Bean."

I knitted my eyebrows together and pursed my mouth in concern. Why would Hannah lie about that? "Was anyone else around who can corroborate this?" I asked.

"I'm not sure." Monica seemed startled. "I didn't look around, but the streets are usually empty that time of day."

"Okay," I said, and touched her arm to reassure her. "I figured. I only asked because I'm pretty sure Rex is going to want to talk to you and look for the coffee cup."

"Of course," she nodded. "I figured that you and Jenn told him what I said, and I suspected he'd ask me questions." The pair of shoppers headed toward the door. "Thanks for stopping in," she said. "The discount lasts all day, but do come back, it's a today-only special."

"Okay," the young woman replied while the man held the door open for her. "Thanks."

Monica turned back to me. "You know, I'm not sure if anyone else heard it. But I do know that Carol and Irma saw me toss the coffee cup. They were sitting in the Coffee Bean and waved at me from the window. I waved back."

"I see," I said.

"You know the argument could have started in the coffee shop," Monica said. "You might want to ask them if they heard anything."

"I will," I said. "Thanks, and I suspect Rex will come see you before the end of the day."

"As long as he doesn't chase away any customers, I'm fine with that," she said.

"Thanks for your help," I said to Monica as I walked toward the door.

"Anything I can do," she said. "It's just too bad. I really liked Hannah."

I stepped back out into the cool spring air and walked back to the McMurphy. My thoughts jumbled as I tried to make sense of both stories. They didn't match, which means one of the two was lying, but which one? Maybe the shock made Hannah forget the argument. But how do you forget killing your boyfriend? Why didn't anyone else hear the gunshot?

Chapter 5

Carol Tunisian, a dear friend and senior on the island, stopped by the McMurphy after my two p.m. fudge demonstration. To draw in customers, all the fudge shops offered two or three daily demonstrations on making fudge. My demonstrations were usually held at ten a.m. and then again at two in the afternoon.

I would pepper my demonstrations with stories of the island and the traditions of the McMurphy, handed down to me by my Papa Liam. I suspect that over the more than one hundred years that the McMurphy has been in the family, those stories have been embellished. But I think it added to the lore.

"I heard you and Jenn found poor Matthew," Carol said as she stirred cream into her coffee. She often helped herself to the hotel coffee bar. "It sounds like an open-and-shut case." She sipped the coffee and then shook her head. "I would have never thought Hannah was capable."

Carol moved toward the registration desk, where

Frances sat working on her computer and I stood, having just welcomed in a couple who were staying for the week.

"I'm not convinced Hannah did it," I said. Both Frances and Carol looked at me. "She says that she was upstairs in her apartment when she heard a noise and looked out her window to see Matthew lying in the alley. She rushed to his side and called nine-one-one."

"But she was holding the gun when you got there," Frances said.

"Yes." I nodded. "But she doesn't remember exactly why. She was in shock when she realized he was dead."

"But you just went to see her," Frances pointed out. "Was she still in shock?"

"She was struggling. They had given her an IV, probably with a sedative, and warm blankets," I said.

"And she still doesn't remember picking up the gun?" Carol asked.

"Keep this just between us girls," I warned. Frances always kept a secret, but Carol was iffy. Carol saw my hesitation and crossed her heart. I checked to see that she didn't have her other fingers crossed before I continued. "She thinks she picked it up so that no one else would get hurt by it," I disclosed softly. "Seriously, if she shot him, why would she just sit there with the smoking gun in her hands and wait for the police to arrive?"

"It does seem unusual," Carol said and sipped her coffee. "Unless she wants you to think she didn't do it, by acting the opposite of what you think a killer would do."

"What would a killer do?" Frances asked Carol.

"Why, run and dispose of the weapon, then wash up and head home to find an alibi," Carol said.

"Why would they wash?" Frances asked.

"Because they most likely had blood splatter on them and at the very least, they would have gunshot residue on them," Carol stated.

"But you can get gunshot residue on your hands just by handling a gun that has just been fired," I said. "Shane tested me for it because I got the gun away from Hannah. Well, with Mella's help, of course. But I picked it up with my shirt, then was silly enough to use two fingers to put in on the top of nearby trash bin."

"Wait, how did Mella help?" Carol asked.

I explained how she knocked the gun out of Hannah's hands.

"Smart cat," Carol said and turned to pet Mella, who sat on the desk licking her paws.

"Anyway, Jenn's very upset. Hannah is an integral part of her birth plan," I added.

"She is?" Carol tilted her head.

"Yes, she's Jenn's doula," Frances told her.

"What on earth is a doula?" Carol asked. "Back in the day, women went into labor and went to the hospital. Doctors and nurses took it from there."

"A doula is a trained professional who provides physical and emotional support and guidance during childbirth and directly after," Frances said.

"But isn't that the father's role?" Carol asked.

"I looked it up. A doula can often guide and team up to support the father in what to do to help and support the mother during childbirth," I said. "They help to keep the mother calm and comfortable. Besides, Jenn has a midwife, not a doctor.

She wants to have the baby at home if possible, or at the clinic. She doesn't want to have to go off the island."

"Well then, you have to prove that Hannah didn't do it," Carol declared.

"I don't think you can prove a negative." Frances went back to studying her computer screen. Our new housekeeping company provided their cleaning staff with a phone app that notified Frances when they finished cleaning a room. It was clever, really. Frances always knew which rooms were ready when guests checked in or returned for the day.

"What I meant was—" Carol started to say.

"I have to figure out who the killer really is," I said, "and I have to do it quick because the baby is already two weeks overdue, and Dr. Simmons keeps suggesting that Jenn let them induce labor."

"Alrighty then." Carol put her coffee cup on the reception desk. "We need to get to work!"

Frances eyed the cup and then Carol until Carol picked up the cup. "Sorry, I got excited."

"If we're going to find the killer"—I tapped my chin in thought—"we're going to have to know more about the victim. I met Matthew once. But I'm busy with work, I just don't really know too many people that well."

"It's a small island," Frances said, without looking up from her computer screen. "But we do run in different circles. It's no surprise, really, if you didn't know him."

"Did you know him?" I asked her.

"I taught his father in school." Frances was Papa's General Manager as long as I could remember and before that she was a teacher. "He was a nice bright young man who went into the family fishing business."

"Matthew or his father?" I asked, confused.

"His father, Larry Jones," Frances said. "If I remember right, he married a Lathrop girl. And I believe her name is Roxanne. They had three boys. But Matthew was the only one who didn't leave the island, except for college."

"Matthew studied forestry," Carol said. "He's worked as a park ranger for the last ten years." She shook her head. "Such a short life. Gunned down in your prime."

"Well, that's certainly a place to start," I said. "I know Joan Belfry. She's also a ranger. We used to play together sometimes when I was spending the summer with Grammy Alice and Papa Liam. I'll go talk to her after I get cleaned up."

"I'll ask the seniors if they know anything about Hannah and Matthew's relationship," Carol said. "Right after I refresh my coffee." She turned to the coffee bar.

"We should start charging her by the cup," Frances grumbled as she watched Carol over the top of her reading glasses.

"We don't sell coffee," I reminded Frances.

"Speaking of sales"—Frances's attention went back to her computer—"the crowds are going to be picking up again next month. Do you have any idea who you want as your assistant?"

"I've sent an email to my contacts at the culinary institute in Chicago," I said. "I said I was looking for a couple of interns who wanted to get some experience under their belt."

"It's good to get ahead of that early," Frances said. "There are lots of places looking for summer help. I think the pool of candidates gets smaller every year. Hospitality is a difficult industry, and the young kids today want work that pays a whole lot more."

"I don't blame them," I said. "But summers on the island are amazing." I sighed. "I wish I could pay more."

"It's really a shame Sandy was stolen by the Grander Hotel," Frances said with a shake of her head.

"She's doing well," I said proudly. "Her chocolate skills are amazing. I bet she makes more money than I do. She should anyway."

"Nonsense," Frances said. "Your candy skills are just as good, and you have the awards to prove it."

"I've been thinking about expanding to other types of candy," I said. "I know fudge is what Mackinac Island is known for, but it might be fun to try a few new kinds of chocolate candies."

"As long as you have the time, I say go for it," Frances said.

My phone dinged and I glanced down to see a text from Jenn. **Any news?** she asked.

No clues yet, I texted back. **Hannah was still in the clinic and uncharged when I left her. Rex should be holding a press conference later this evening. In the meantime, get some rest. I'm learning all I can.**

Please hurry, she texted. **My midwife is starting to agree with Dr. Simmons, which means I'll have to go off the island to have my baby.**

I'll do everything I can, I texted back. **Please don't be stubborn. Listen to your healthcare provider.**

She sent me an eye roll emoji.

"Is everything okay?" Frances asked.

I looked up to see her and Carol watching me.

"Jenn's doctor and midwife are starting to agree that she go off the island to induce her labor."

"Oh, no," Frances said. "I know how important it is for her to have the baby here."

"We'll have to move quick to solve this," Carol said. "I'll get started right away finding out what the seniors know. Then I'll set up a murder board and meet with you tonight. Tootles!" She hurried out the door.

"I don't know how I can turn around what looks like a cut-and-dried case in a matter of days, let alone hours," I said to Frances. "But I'm afraid if I don't Jenn will stubbornly wait until the last minute to have her baby and put them both at risk."

Chapter 6

Raspberry Chocolate Bars

Ingredients
Chocolate bar
    1 cup dark chocolate chips (melted until
      smooth)
    ½ cup butter
    ¾ cup packed brown sugar
    1 large egg
    2 teaspoons vanilla
    1 cup all-purpose flour
    ¼ cup cocoa (I prefer Hershey's)
    1 teaspoon baking powder
    ¼ teaspoon salt
    1 more cup of chocolate chips
Topping
    ½ cup softened butter
    1½ cups powdered sugar
    ¼ cup dried raspberry powder (often

found in the raisin aisle of your local
grocery store.

1 teaspoon vanilla
1 tablespoon raspberry jam
2 to 3 teaspoons milk of any kind but
  skim, as it won't have the same amount
  of body. (add until desired consistency)

Directions:

Bars: Preheat oven to 350 degrees F. Line
an 8 x 8-inch pan with parchment paper. In
large bowl use a mixer to cream butter and
brown sugar, add melted chocolate and beat
until combined. Add egg and vanilla. Then
slowly add flour, cocoa, baking powder, and
salt. Mix until smooth. Gently stir in the remaining chocolate chips. Pour mixture into
pan and spread until smooth. Bake for 30 minutes. Check for a jiggly middle; if jiggly then
bake 5 minutes at a time until middle is just
firm. Cool.

Raspberry Topping: Beat butter until smooth.
Add powdered sugar, raspberry powder, vanilla, and raspberry jam. Beat until combined.
Beat in milk, one teaspoon at a time, until
topping is spreadable. Spread over cooled
chocolate bars. Cut into 24. Enjoy!

Before I could change into street clothes and
take my first set of fudge-making clothes for evidence and do some more investigation, a small
crowd came into the hotel looking for fudge. I
went back to the shop straightaway and offered

them a pound of free fudge. They were kind and bought five more pounds for friends and family back home.

"Frances, can you watch the fudge shop?" I asked her after I'd helped the last one.

"Sure thing," she said without looking up from her computer.

I hurried up the stairs, pulling off my chef's jacket and hat. My pup, Mal, followed me up the stairs and into the apartment where Mella sat on the windowsill in a warm shaft of dwindling sunlight.

I took a quick shower, dried my wavy hair, and tossed on jeans and a long-sleeved T-shirt. A glance at the time and I saw it was nearly four thirty, and the park rangers closed the Visitor's Center at five. They left the parks open until sunset. If I was going to speak to Joan, I'd better hurry.

I slipped on my shoes and grabbed my jacket. Mal waited at the door for me, her little stump tail wagging. I paused briefly before deciding that I would take her with me. For some reason I had better luck finding clues when she was around. I slipped her into her halter and hooked her leash on. "We'll be back soon," I said to my cat, who opened one eye as if to say she didn't care. But I knew she would care if dinner was late.

I closed and locked the back apartment door and hurried down the stairs into the alley with Mal. It was a fast-paced walk to the Mackinac Island Nature Center, but we arrived before closing. "Hi," I said to the volunteer at the Welcome Center. "Is Joan Belfry around?"

"Yes," the volunteer said and smiled down at Mal, who had jumped up on her two back legs to see over the top of the desk. "She just finished her last class of the day. She should still be in the classroom down the hall and to the right."

"Thanks." Mal and I strode quickly down the hall. Joan was putting away materials when we arrived. I knocked on the open door. "Hello, Joan."

"Oh, my goodness, Allie." She seemed happy and slightly surprised to see me. Before we could talk, she finished putting away a handful of books. "What brings you out this way?"

"I wanted to see how you were holding up," I said and stepped into the room.

She straightened and walked toward us with a smile on her face. Her blond hair was off her collar and her state park ranger uniform still held the sharp crease down the middle and looked perfect at the end of the day. "What do you mean?" She knitted her eyebrows in confusion.

"Oh, no, haven't you heard?"

"Heard what?" She bent and scratched Mal behind the ears.

"About Matthew Jones," I said, and watched her face. She was still smiling.

"What about Matthew?" she asked. "He was off today. Did he get into trouble?"

"I don't know how to tell you," I said. "I mean, you work with him, I thought you'd know already."

"Know what?" She straightened and her smile disappeared. "You look serious. Is Matthew okay?"

"No," I said, and shook my head. "He's dead."

"What?" She looked at me as if I'd just lost my mind. "What do you mean he's dead?"

"He was shot and killed this morning," I said and pulled out a chair from under a long table and pushed her into it. "Sit before you fall down."

"I . . . I don't understand." She sat but still seemed confused. "I just talked to him last night. He was talking about his and Hannah's wedding plans. Oh, my goodness!" She stood and gripped my wrist. "Hannah! Is she okay? Wait, do they know who did it and why?"

"I hate to tell you this, but we found Hannah with the gun in her hands," I said.

"What!"

"I don't believe she did it," I said quickly.

"Well, of course she didn't do it," Joan said. "Don't tell me she's a suspect."

"I'm afraid so," I said. "Do you have any idea who else would want Matthew dead?"

"Certainly not Hannah," she said. "That's crazy."

"Was he having any trouble with anyone at work or anywhere else?" I asked.

"No, certainly not." She shook her head. "Matthew was kind to everyone, even that crazy girl he dated for like three months before Hannah."

"How long did Hannah and Matthew date?" I asked. "They're engaged, so they must have dated for at least two years, right?"

"Oh, no," she said. "I think they dated like six months before he popped the question. We talked about it. He was afraid he was moving too fast, but I told him my parents always said when you know, you know."

"Wow, six months seems like a really short time," I said.

"Well, they've known each other their whole lives. I think they were high school sweethearts, but then they went their separate ways after graduation. Matthew got his forestry degree at Michigan

State, and Hannah went away to some college on
the East Coast. Matthew came back to work on the
island right out of college, but Hannah got her
bachelor's in psychology, then her master's in
counseling before deciding to learn how to be a
doula.

"It took her another year to get certified and
then get her first clients. She returned to Mackinac for a summer sabbatical. They ran into each
other, and Hannah never left. Which is crazy because there aren't that many births on the island. I
think she also goes to Mackinaw City and St. Ignace to help her clients. In fact, Matthew told me
that one time she went all the way to Saginaw. Anyway, she sometimes has to leave for weeks at a time
when she's on baby watch."

"How did Matthew feel about that?" I asked, wondering if that was what they were fighting about
when Monica saw them. But then again, this fight
might've been over something else altogether, so
Hannah might not remember.

"Actually, Matthew was okay with it. He was
proud that she was able to help so many people."

"I see," I said. "What did Matthew do when she
was gone?"

"Oh, he worked double shifts," Joan said. "Sometimes he went out to the bars with his male friends,
but we never saw him around any girls."

"So, he only had eyes for Hannah?"

"Oh, yeah," she said with a chuckle. "That boy
was all in. He wanted to live with her until they
were both a hundred years old. He told me that he
pictured them being one hundred, lying in a nurs-
ing home holding hands when they died."

"What a lovely, romantic picture," I said, and gave her a soft smile.

Tears welled up in her eyes. She dashed them away. "Yes, well, that's never going to happen now, is it?" She finished straightening the room. I stayed with her, hoping I would be quiet comfort.

When she was done, she stopped and studied me. "I have a lot of questions."

"I don't have many answers, I'm afraid."

"Then I'll find someone who does." She pushed past me and headed straight to the front desk. I followed closely behind. "Victoria," she addressed the volunteer. "When did you come on shift?"

"I worked a full day," Victoria said. "Mrs. Ferguson was sick and asked me to take the morning shift. Why?"

"I'm afraid Allie brings us some difficult news." She waved toward me, encouraging me to fill Victoria in on the news.

"Matthew Jones was murdered this morning outside his fiancée's apartment," I said as gently, yet concisely as possible.

"What? Matthew was murdered?" Victoria stood. "Who would do such a thing?"

"That's what we're all asking, apparently," Joan said. She glanced at her watch. "It's close enough to closing time. Let's lock up. I'll call the district manager and let them know. I suspect we'll be closed the rest of the week out of respect."

"Oh, yes, of course," Victoria said, and closed down the computer and fumbled for her jacket and purse. "What happened? Do we know?" She looked frightened, her gaze darting from Joan to me and back.

"He was found shot to death," I said. "His fiancée, Hannah, held the gun that killed him."

"What?" Victoria covered her mouth in horror. "Why?"

"That's what the police are trying to find out," I replied.

Joan looked me square in the eye. "Do you think Hannah did it?"

"I'm not sure," I said honestly. "She told me that she picked up the gun without much thought because she didn't want anyone else to get hurt."

"There, see," Joan said. "She's innocent."

"But she never called the police." I held my hands out in a helpless manner. "Why did she pick up the gun, then sit down and wait for someone to find her? To find them?"

"As a park ranger, I can tell you that people do weird things under stress," Joan said. She held up her hand and ticked off her fingers. "There's *fight*, which means they react with anger. Then there's *flight*."

"Which means they run away, right?" Victoria said.

"Yes," Joan went on. "Then there's *fawn*, which means they try to placate anyone in the situation to diffuse the stress. And finally, there's *freeze*, which is exactly what it sounds like. People just freeze up."

"Do you think she froze when she picked up the gun?" I asked.

Joan pulled the keys out of the drawer and walked to the door, where she turned the sign from OPEN to CLOSED and stepped out. Victoria and I followed her. "Yes, it sounds like she froze. I think she had to be stressed out of her mind. Most likely when she touched the gun that killed Matthew, she froze."

"That would certainly explain why she didn't call nine-one-one," I muttered.

Joan locked up the center. "I certainly think that's a better explanation than she snapped and killed Matthew."

"I don't know." Victoria shook her blond head. Her blue eyes wide. "Have you ever watched that TV show, *Snapped?*"

"No." Joan and I said it at the same time as we headed down the sidewalk toward town.

"Well, the entire premise of the show—which is true crime—is that anyone can snap at any time and kill someone. Even someone they love." Victoria seemed proud of her answer. She was a young woman. I would have guessed she was maybe all of nineteen years old. Really out of place for a local volunteer before the season started. But then maybe I hung around with seniors too much.

"But really, can you imagine Matthew doing anything that would make the love of his life snap and kill him?" Joan asked.

"Oh, no, not Matthew." Victoria shook her head. "He was always such a good guy."

"See," Joan said to me. "It's ridiculous to think Hannah killed him. Now, where is she? Can I see her?"

"I think you'd have to ask the police that question," I said.

"When is the funeral?" Victoria asked. "I'd like to go. Matthew and I weren't close, but I did work with him."

"I don't know that either," I said, feeling help-less. "I imagine they took him to the morgue for an autopsy."

"I thought you said he was shot to death," Joan said. "Why would they need an autopsy?"

"To verify the gun caliber and to see if there are any other signs of a struggle or anything," I said. "At least that's what I would assume. Excuse me, ladies, I need to go check on a friend. Thanks for all your help." I turned at the corner that was a block away from Jenn's house.

"Well, I should say thank you for letting us know," Joan said. "But I'm not thankful for the news."

I just nodded. It was understandable. It must be terrible to lose a coworker.

Chapter 7

After I dropped my clothes at the police station, I knocked on Jen's door. "Come in," she said. "Have you learned anything?"

"Not much," I said. "You need to sit down and put your feet up. They look swollen." I took her elbow and guided her to the couch.

"I can't sit still," Jenn said, and rubbed her belly. "All I can think about is poor Hannah." I waited until she sat down, and I grabbed an ottoman and put it under her feet. "Has Rex arrested her?"

"I don't know," I said honestly. "Let me make you some chamomile tea." I headed to her kitchen. The home was an open-concept bungalow with a straight line of sight from the living room to the end of the kitchen.

"How can you not know?" Jenn called after me.

I picked up her kettle off the stove and moved into the doorway so I could see her. "Are you sitting?"

"I'm sitting. I'm sitting. My feet are up. Sheesh, you are as bad as Shane."

"All the pacing you're doing is going to make

that baby pop out sooner," I warned and moved to the sink, filled the kettle with water, lit the gas burner, and set the kettle on. I grabbed two mugs out of the cupboard and the tea off the counter and set them on the table. Then I joined her back in the living room. "I would normally say to go ahead and pace, since the baby is late, but you did say you wanted Hannah to be there when you gave birth."

"Exactly," Jenn said. "Rex simply cannot arrest her. I won't have it."

I gave her an intent look. "Wait, who do you want me to investigate for? A supposedly innocent Hannah? Or you, because you want me to clear a murderer so that your birth plan will go off without a hitch?"

"Now that's just mean." Jenn frowned and rubbed her belly. "Of course, I think Hannah is innocent."

I sat back and sighed. "I know. You're right that was mean. I'm sorry. I just don't see how I can help with the case, if we need to solve it today because you could have this baby at any moment."

She pressed her belly, closed her eyes, then blew out a long breath.

"Wait," I said, sitting up. "You're in labor, aren't you?" I eyed her, looking for any signs. There were tiny tight muscles around her mouth and eyes. "You're in pain."

"It's just Braxton-Hicks," she said, keeping her eyes closed. "I saw the doctor today and she said I'm only dilated to half a centimeter. My mother walked around for a week that way."

I put my hand over hers. "Promise me, you'll tell me when you go into labor. Okay?"

She opened her eyes.

"Promise me," I begged. "We need time for the midwife."

"It will take hours if not days," she said. "I've read the baby books and heard all the stories of thirty-six to forty-eight hours of labor, or more."

"Jenn!"

"Fine." She sighed. "I promise to tell you—"

"And Shane," I interjected.

"And Shane, the minute I go into real labor or my water breaks or whatever."

The kettle started whistling. I stood and walked to the kitchen. "Thank you." But while I made tea, I worried she wasn't being exactly honest with me. I carried both cups out to the living room. The warm beverage was great on a cool evening. Being in the park had made my fingers and toes cold.

"Here." I offered her a cup. Then I took a seat in the chair by the couch and blew into my tea to cool it off. "I went to talk to Hannah. She can't remember much, but thinks she picked up the gun to keep it out of anyone else's reach. The weird part is that she didn't call nine-one-one. She just froze to the point of almost being catatonic."

"I have no idea how I would react if I heard a gunshot and found Shane dead behind the house," Jenn said and took a sip of tea. "But I hope my first instinct would be to call nine-one-one."

I tasted the tea. It was fruity and floral. "When I first got here and found the dead guy in Papa's closet, all I wanted to do was run screaming down the stairs and outside."

Jenn raised an eyebrow at me.

"I'm serious." I took another sip of tea. "Do you want any cookies or anything?"

Jenn laughed and patted her belly. "I think I've eaten enough cookies for a year. The baby likes them. They really like strawberries and, weirdly, re-fried beans."

"They?"

"We still don't know the baby's gender, I say *they* for now." She smiled dreamily. "But soon we'll have either Abigail or Benjamin."

"Oh, I kind of like Bobbie for either a boy or a girl," I said. "I think it's cute."

"Me, too," Jenn said. "But Abigail is Shane's grand-ma's name and Benjamin is my grandfather's name. The family called him Benji, actually, but you get the drift."

"I do," I said.

"Okay, now spill." Jenn put her tea down. She leaned toward me as best she could. "Tell me every little thing you know about the case."

I spent the next half an hour going over every-thing from my visit with Hannah to Joan and Victoria. "One thing, I thought it odd that Victoria was volunteering when there were so many jobs open. Also, she's pretty cute. Do you think maybe she and Matthew were—"

"Oh, no." Jenn shook her head and leaned back. "Victoria Wells took a gap year before she goes to college to take care of her grandma."

"Oh, she's Mabel Wells's granddaughter?" I asked. Mabel was a regular at the senior center and she just got a hip replacement last fall and hadn't been out and about this winter.

"Yup," Jenn said. She closed her eyes and hugged her belly.

"You're exhausted," I said and stood. I picked up a throw blanket and pulled it over her. "Why don't you take a nap. I'll wash up the tea mugs and let myself out."

"Fine." Jenn opened her eyes and touched my wrist. "Please keep trying to solve this murder. I need Hannah at my baby's birth."

"I'll do my best," I reassured her, took the cups into the kitchen, washed them, and put them in the drainer. She was sleeping when I snuck back into the living room to get my shoes and jacket and let myself out.

The rest of the evening went by quickly, filled with the usual prep for the next morning's fudge making, and office responsibilities like checking the receipts and approving Frances's accounting work. I trusted Frances and didn't feel like I had to check her work, but she insisted I do it anyway.

"As the owner of the McMurphy, you need to be able to understand how the books are done and verify them against the receipts," she had said. "I'm not going to always be here, and even if you hire an office manager when I'm gone, you're going to have to train them. Which you can't do if you don't know how."

I got to bed late. The only time I heard from Rex was a simple text. **Good night.**

I texted him back. **Good night. I hope you get some rest.** Then sighed and turned off my light. But my thoughts had me tossing and turning. How the heck could I prove Hannah wasn't a killer?

Chapter 8

Later the next day, I went through the motions of fudge making, but my mind was still focused on freeing Hannah in time for Jenn's baby. With the daily fudge made, I filled the display cabinet and finished prepping for my ten o'clock demonstration, then left the fudge shop to take a break. Mal greeted me with a happy, two-legged twirl. I laughed and picked her up. "Hello, baby." I cuddled her and went over to the reception desk. "Frances, I haven't said good morning yet. How's it going?"

"Not bad," she replied. "The rooms are filling up fast for the season."

Behind me I heard the doors open, and I glanced over my shoulder to see who it was.

"Surprise! We're here," came a familiar voice. My mother and a well-dressed young man entered. I knew my parents had gotten over their troubled-relationship time. But still the thought that Mom had taken up with a younger man crossed my mind.

"Mom? What are you doing here?" I asked as she smothered me and Mal with a hug. Her perfume lingered on my chef's coat. "Did Dad come, too?"

"Well, hello to you, too, dear." She laughed, causing the heat of a blush to rise to my cheeks as embarrassment set in.

"Hi, Mom," I said. "You surprised me. Why didn't you call and let me know you were coming? We could have aired out the VIP room."

"We'll get to that in just a minute." My mother turned toward the young man, who dragged two luggage bags and an under-seat airline case, waving him over. "Allie, look who I ran into."

It was then that I realized who he was. "Brett?"

"Allie, good to see you." He pulled the luggage up to the reception desk and hugged me. Mal squeaked and he took a step back. "Who's this handsome fella?" Brett rubbed her ears and Mal fell in love. Sigh.

"This is Marshmallow," I said. "We call her Mal."

"Well, hello, Mal," he said and continued to pet her until her eyes closed. "You look great, Allie. You haven't changed one bit, except maybe a bit happier looking?"

I studied Brett. His hair was still sandy blond with brighter blond highlights, thick and well cut. His blue eyes twinkled. He was thin yet well-muscled under his blue polo, probably chosen to match his eyes, a pair of dark navy jeans, and boat shoes. Always the preppie, I thought. "Thank you," I replied. "You haven't aged a bit either."

"Allie, Brett works for a real estate investment group, and they're looking at a couple of properties on Mackinac. Isn't that great?" She smiled brightly at me and took hold of Brett's arm.

"Good for you," I replied. All I could do was hope Mom didn't want him to buy the McMurphy. Not that he could without my authorization.

"When I ran into him in Detroit the other day and he told me he was coming up to Mackinac, I simply had to come. Thank goodness I had some free time in my social calendar." She glanced at him adoringly. "He flew his own plane here. Isn't that wonderful? And I got to ride along."

"I remember you were interested in flying," I said. "You were even thinking about going into the Air Force to fly fighter jets at one time."

"Instead, my uncle got me private lessons and I went to Michigan State," he said.

Mom squeezed his muscular arm. "Brett has an MBA and a house in Birmingham." I raised an eyebrow. Birmingham was the ritziest suburb of Detroit. It took a lot of money to purchase their so-called *exclusive* homes, which I knew were way overpriced.

"I also have a house on Saint Thomas for when the winters get too bad. Nothing like warm, sandy beaches," he bragged.

"Glad you are doing so well." I glanced at my phone. "I'm afraid I have a fudge-making demonstration scheduled for fifteen minutes from now. If you'll excuse me, I have to get ready."

"Of course," he said.

Mom grabbed my arm. "Because Brett was kind enough to let me fly up with him, I told him he could have one of our best rooms."

"Of course, you did," I muttered.

"Sorry, darling, what did you say?"

I planted a welcoming smile on my face. "Of course, Mom. Frances, please do your best to re-arrange your room reservations and ensure these two get the best rooms."

Frances nodded and asked them to step up to the desk. I escaped to the safety of my fudge kitchen. And used the extra time to prep for this afternoon's demonstration as well. Funny how I decided I needed to replenish my chopped ingredients to mix into the fudge.

After the demonstration, I stayed an extra two hours in the fudge shop, deep cleaning, taking inventory, and selling fudge. Frances finally popped her head in. "You can't hide in here forever," she said, her tone almost laughing.

"I'm not—okay, maybe I am hiding," I said. "I can't believe that Mom sprang another surprise visit on me. It's like she's trying to catch me doing something wrong. And . . . I can't believe she brought Brett." I stuffed the last cleaning rag in the hamper, picked it up to take it to the laundry room, and walked toward the door of the now sparkling fudge shop.

"Okay, now you have to tell me who Brett is." Frances slid inside the door and held it closed. "I mean, your business is your business, but if I know more, perhaps I can help."

"Brett and I dated through high school. For a while, we kept in touch and would see each other whenever we could."

"Sounds like true love," she said and tilted her head in confusion. "What happened?"

"What happened was when he graduated, he asked me to marry him," I said.

"And you didn't because . . ."

"Because." I sighed. Really, I shouldn't have to disclose my *why*, but this was Frances and she meant well. "He wanted a stay-at-home wife with an eye for design, who would help make all his properties sparkle and shine and help him entertain guests."

"I see," Frances said, her big brown gaze thoughtful. "And you wanted . . ."

"To own and run the McMurphy," I said. "He knew that. Everyone knew that, including my mother."

"True," Frances said.

"Trust me, after two years that hasn't changed." I moved around her and opened the door. "Besides, I happen to be in love with Rex."

"Who's Rex?" Brett asked.

"Oh—" I was startled to run straight into Brett. At least the hamper was a barrier between us.

"Rex is Rex Manning," my mom said and made a face. "He's a police officer on the island and has two divorces behind him already."

"I see," said Brett.

"Do you?" I asked, letting some of my frustration show.

"Yes," he said jovially. "Look, I'm on Mackinac for business and thought it would be fun to catch up. In fact, your mom told me a lot about how well you're doing that I was convinced I needed to see you and see how you were. Like I said, you look happy."

Now I felt like a real heel. "I'm sorry," I said. "I've got so much on my mind right now."

"Allie found another murder victim this morning," Frances said behind me.

"Allie?" My mom looked horrified.

"Unfortunately, I did," I said.

"Wow, that's a kicker," Brett said, his expression one of respect. "Did you catch the killer?"

"Well, everyone seems to think we did, but I'm not sure," I said.

"Your mother and I were going to take a carriage ride and look at the properties," Brett said. "Do you want to come?"

"I'm sorry, I can't," I said as nicely as possible. "I've got laundry to do plus shower and such."

"Then will you join us for dinner?" he asked. "I have reservations at the Grander Hotel."

"Allie." My mom sent me the look. "Brett has come all this way."

"Sure," I said, and sent a weak smile. "Of course, when are the reservations?"

"They're at eight," Mom said. "Plenty of time for you to get presentable. Come on now, Brett, let's take that carriage ride." She put her arm through his.

"Better take a jacket," Frances said. "It might be April, but this is Michigan. The weather can turn in a heartbeat."

"Good call," Brett said. "Mrs. McMurphy, why don't we run up and get our coats. I'll meet you back down in about five minutes."

"Of course," Mom said.

"Allie." Brett nodded at me. "Mrs. Devaney."

We watched him take the stairs two at a time.

Mom turned to me. "Really, Allie, you're acting like I never taught you good manners."

"I'm sorry, Mom." I blushed.

"You better go get your coat. Brett will be down

here any minute," Frances said gently and led my mom away. I watched her stuff my mom in the elevator. Then I hurried up the other side of the stairs to my apartment.

Really, I thought. What more could happen today?

Chapter 9

I had just got out of my after-work shower when my phone began dinging relentlessly. I grabbed it and studied the texts as my wavy hair dripped down my back in a cold stream. They were from Jenn and Shane. It seems Jenn had gone into labor, and both were headed to the clinic and needed me. I glanced at Mal and Mella. "Well, babies, looks like I have a good excuse to skip dinner."

I rushed off to get dressed. Less than five minutes later, I wore jeans, a sweater, and comfy shoes. My hair was towel dried and I glanced in the mirror that was in the hallway and sighed. One look at this and Brett will know I'm not good material for a politician's wife. I smiled and for the first time was happy that my looks were more casual than my mother had hoped when she raised me. Hurriedly feeding and watering my pets, I grabbed a flannel jacket and my phone and keys. Then I closed and locked the back door behind me and hurried to the clinic.

"How's she doing?" I asked the minute I

stepped in. The night nurse, Maisy Two-feather, knew me well. Okay, it was a small island, and she knew everyone well, but I think me even more, with all the run-ins with crime I've had lately.

"She's in the emergency area," Maisy said without looking up from her phone. "Connie's prepping a room for her now."

"Thanks," I said, barely stopping before striding to the emergency area that consisted of one big room and three beds, separated by curtains. I went straight to the only area where the curtain was pulled around a bed. "Jenn?"

"In here," Jenn said.

I opened the curtains and stepped in to see Jenn in bed. Her belly was wrapped in a band attached to a machine. Shane stood beside her holding her hand. "Are you okay?" I asked. "Is it time?"

Jenn had tears running down her cheeks. "They said it's a false alarm," she said and sniffed. "I was certain it wasn't, and Hannah isn't here. The nurses won't even call the midwife."

"She's upset and they're going to keep her overnight," Shane said.

"I insisted that they call Sarah." Jenn brushed away tears. Shane pulled a fresh tissue from the box next to the bed and handed it to her. "But they said there was no reason to do that yet unless I wanted to induce labor. I need Hannah!" She wailed Hannah's name. "She would know what to do for me."

"I can call Sarah," I offered.

"I want Hannah!" Jenn wailed.

"Okay," I said.

"Take a deep breath," Shane offered gently. "Allie will help."

"You take a deep breath," Jenn snapped.

Shane looked at me helplessly.

I took Jenn's free hand. "I'll get Hannah," I promised.

Shane shook his head at me. "You can't promise—"

"I'll get Hannah," I said, leaning over and kissing Jenn's cheek. "Please try to rest."

Nurse Connie Stall opened the curtain, pushing a wheelchair. "The room is ready for you, Mrs. Carpenter."

"I'm going to go," I said. "I'll be back." Then I looked from Jenn to Shane. "I'll be back." I hurried out the door and went straight from the clinic to the police station. It was nearly eight and dark out, but the police station wasn't far from the clinic. I stepped into the office and my phone pinged. It was my mother texting me asking where I was. I started to answer when she called me. Rolling my eyes at her impatience, I answered. "Hi, Mom."

"Where are you, honey? We're waiting for you in the lobby."

"Mom, please tell Brett I'm sorry but—"

"No." My mom sounded upset and firm. "No, there is no reason you can't have dinner with your mother and an old friend. We've come all this way."

"Mom," I said, and turned away from the reception desk where the policeman on duty eyed me with interest. "I can't talk. Jenn is in labor, and I have to—"

"Congratulations to Jenn and Shane," Mom said. "But I'm sure they don't need you."

"Mom." I sighed. I didn't want to get into an argument with her. "I have to go." I pressed the end-call button and silenced my phone, putting it in my jacket pocket. Oh, I know it was rude, and I would be in so much trouble with my mom, but I had promised Jenn. "Hi," I said, walking up to the desk. "Is Rex here?"

"He's in the back," Officer Quinn Smith said. He was a young guy and was often either on foot patrol or sitting at the front desk.

"Can I go see him?" I asked.

"Sure." He pressed the button that unlocked the door to the back office.

"Thanks, Quinn," I said and opened the door as soon as I heard it unlock. Behind me he picked up the phone to let Rex know I was there.

"Allie." Rex rose from his desk when I entered the room. "What's going on?" He walked up to me and took my hand. "Is everything alright?"

"Jenn needs Hannah," I said. "She's at the clinic because she thought she was in labor. The nurses there said it was false labor and because she's upset, they decided to keep her overnight. Jenn doesn't believe them, and I promised her that I would get Hannah."

Rex frowned and sat me down in the chair next to his desk. He sat on the edge of his desk and crossed his arms. "She's the only suspect in Matthew Jones's murder. We have enough to hold her until she's arraigned."

"Rex, please trust me when I tell you that Hannah is innocent," I said.

"Yet you found her in the alley with the gun in her hand and her dead fiancé at her feet," he said. "Then you told me about Monica Grazer witnessing an argument between the two."

"Yes, but that's all circumstantial," I said. "I talked to Hannah. She thinks she picked up the gun to keep others from getting it. But when we got there, she didn't even realize it was in her hand. I think that picking up the gun made her realize what this meant, and she froze in shock."

"Allie," Rex started to say.

"Look, Jenn needs Hannah. I promised her that I would get Hannah."

"I can't let a murder suspect free because your best friend wants her there when she's giving birth."

"Fine." I stood. "Then you come with me and tell Jenn yourself that you can't let her have her doula because you have circumstantial evidence." I grabbed his hand and pulled.

"Allie, I'm not—"

"Oh, yes you are," I said, determinedly drawing him away from his desk.

"Okay, okay." Rex ran a hand over his bald head. "If, and I say *if* I let Hannah go to help Jenn, there will be a police officer posted at the door, and you will be responsible if anything happens. Could you live with yourself if Matthew's killer goes free or worse, hurts Jenn and her new baby?"

I swallowed hard, searching my heart. "Yes," I said, convinced that I was doing the right thing.

He studied me carefully. "You're serious."

I put my hands on my hips. "I'm very serious."

"Alright then, but she has to be back by her arraignment hearing and then *if* the judge sets bail, and *if* someone pays it, she can go home. Is that clear?"

"Yes." I nodded, fully understanding the chance

he was taking doing this. He could ruin his good standing on the island, or even his career, if this went south, but I stuck to my guns.

"Come with me." He took me back to the two small cells in the station. Hannah sat huddled on a cot in the left cell.

She stood when she saw me. "Allie?"

Rex motioned for the officer who watched the cell to unlock the door.

"Hannah," I said, and walked up to the bars. "Jenn thinks she's having the baby, but the nurse says it's only false labor and won't call the midwife."

"Oh, no," Hannah said.

The officer opened her cell.

"I promised her I'd get you," I said and glanced at Rex. "Rex told me he would release you into my custody, but we would have a police escort and you must be back here by your arraignment hearing."

Hannah looked at Rex. "My public defender hasn't notified me about that yet. When is the hearing?"

"Ten tomorrow morning," he said.

"I don't know." She shook her head. "If Jenn is in labor, I can't promise I will be finished by ten tomorrow. It's a first baby."

Rex's expression was stonelike. "Doesn't matter. You have to be at court at ten tomorrow morning or you will go straight to jail with no bail, along with Allie and most likely me." He crossed his arms over his chest. The officer holding the cell door open had wide eyes.

I felt my heart pounding in my chest. If I ended up in jail for real, my mom would definitely convince my father to take back the McMurphy and maybe even sell it. But I promised Jenn. I swallowed hard. "She will be there." I studied Hannah, waiting for her to decide. It was a lot. Right?

She seemed to make a decision. "Alright." She held out her hands to be cuffed.

"You can't cuff her," I said. "She'll need her hands to help Jenn."

Rex looked at the ceiling and huffed out a breath. "We'll uncuff her at the clinic."

"Will that work?" I asked Hannah.

"Yes," she said, and Rex cuffed her. We headed down the hall. Rex pushed the door open out into the foyer and headed to the reception desk.

"I'm signing her out," he told Quinn. "When Brown gets in for the midnight shift, send him down to the clinic."

"Yes, sir," Quinn said. "Is she sick?"

"She's a doula," I explained. "Jenn Carpenter is in labor."

"Okay." Quinn shook his head slowly. He looked at Rex. "What's a doula?"

"Look it up." Rex looked at me. "Is it cold out?"

"She can use my coat," I offered, and started to pull off the sleeves.

"No, mine," he said evenly and covered her shoulders with his police jacket. "Let's go."

We pushed out the door and headed toward the clinic, only to run into my mother and Brett.

"Allie," Mom said, clearly steaming mad. She was dressed in knee-high boots, a camel-colored turtleneck and brown tweed pencil skirt. Her brown wool dress coat hung open. "What is going on?"

"Mrs. McMurphy." Rex acknowledged her with a nod. His blank cop gaze stopped for a moment, taking in Brett in his shiny black dress shoes and gray wool Italian suit, blue dress shirt, and expertly tied silk necktie with navy and burgundy stripes. He had a black wool overcoat slung across his shoulders. His blond hair shone in the moonlight.

"I told you that I'm getting the doula to Jenn," I said calmly and firmly, then looked at Brett. "I'm sorry, but my best friend is going into labor with her first."

"Ah," Brett said with a charming smile. "I totally understand. Come on then, Mrs. McMurphy. It's a nice night, why don't we walk to the Grander." He took my mom by the elbow and gently moved her out of our way.

Rex strode firmly away with Hannah.

"Thank you," I mouthed to Brett and tried not to send my mom a look before hurrying to catch up. Rex walked in quick and determined steps. Hannah was two-stepping it to keep up.

When we arrived at the clinic, I burst in first. Maisy took one look at me, Rex, and Hannah and didn't even question us. "She's down the hall, first room on the right."

"Thanks," I said and hurried to the room. It was small but comfortable, with Jenn now in a hospital gown in a hospital bed, still hooked up to the belly band. She chewed on ice chips and looked at me. Shane rose from the easy chair beside the bed. I noted that there was a TV on the opposite wall that showed a slide show of outdoor photos and played soothing music. There was a window opposite the door. It was black, reflecting me and Rex and Hannah. Beside that was an open door to a restroom.

"I brought Hannah, as promised." I turned to point to the woman in handcuffs.

"Before I do this, I want to check with you and Shane," Rex said to Jenn. "Do you want a murder suspect in your birthing room?"

"Yes!" Jenn said definitely.

Shane looked a little more dubious. "I'm surprised you let her out."

"I'm taking full responsibility for her," I said.

"I'll have a policeman stationed outside your door," Rex said. "I recommend you lock the window."

Hannah stood there quietly, taking in everything. Her gaze moved from Jenn to the monitor, then around the room quickly and efficiently. But she didn't speak.

"Shane?" Rex asked.

"It's what Jenn wants," Shane said.

"Fine." Rex unlocked the cuffs. "I'll be outside until midnight and then I have Brown replacing me. Hannah must be at the courthouse by ten tomorrow for her arraignment hearing and for the setting of bail. No ifs, ands, or buts about it. Am I clear?"

"Crystal," Jenn and I said at the same time.

I truly believed that Hannah was innocent. Why, then, did I feel like I might have just made the biggest mistake of my life?

Chapter 10

The moment Rex was gone, Hannah went straight to Jenn and took her hand. "How are you doing? How's the pain level? How far apart are the pains? And where is the midwife, or at the very least the doctor?"

Jenn set down her paper cup of ice chips and pulled Hannah into a hug. She started crying and told Hannah what was going on.

I shifted over to beside Shane in the armchair and watched the doula do her magic. She made sure Jenn was relaxed and comfortable. Borrowed Jenn's phone and called the midwife.

"Yes," Hannah said. "Alright. Sounds like a solid plan." She ended the call and gave the phone back to Jenn. "Sarah said she is on the island and at her grandmother's house. She is coming down immediately."

"Oh, oh." Jenn grabbed Hannah's hand, her face contorting.

Shane came out of the chair and clicked the stopwatch app on his phone.

"Breathe." Hannah slowly and gently helped Jenn to breathe through the contraction, Hannah's hand on Jenn's belly. "Good, good," she said and smiled. "Now take a long, slow breath and relax." Jenn obeyed, closing her eyes and resting while I swallowed hard and addressed my worry.

"She's in real labor?" I said in a stage whisper.

"Sarah will tell us for sure," Hannah said. "I recommend that she only have ice chips for now until we see what's happening."

"But the nurse practitioner said that I was only dilated to half a centimeter," Jenn said. "She said I was not having my baby today."

Hannah addressed Shane. "Okay, daddy, I see you've been timing the contractions. How close together are they?"

"They went quickly from five minutes to one minute apart," Shane said. "It's why we headed to the clinic."

"I see," Hannah said. I admired her composure. It was as if her own life and worries were on hold as she focused on Jenn and Shane. She kept hold of Jenn's hand and turned her attention back to her patient. "On a scale of one to ten, how bad is your pain?"

"Oh, here comes another one," Jenn said and started puffing. I wanted to go into action, to help in some way, but there was nothing for me to do. I paced and listened to Hannah's calm voice and Jenn fighting the pain. "Whew—" Jenn said after blowing out a final breath. She rubbed her belly. "I would say the pain is a seven or eight," she said.

"Jenn has a high pain tolerance," I mentioned.

"She does," Shane agreed and shared his phone with Hannah. "See, forty-five seconds apart."

"Okay," Hannah said with a nod. Then she looked Jenn in the eyes. "I do have some special mamas who naturally have close contractions and don't fall into the usual patterns starting out far apart and getting closer."

"No, no, no!" Jenn started to cry. "No! This can't be false labor."

"It's okay. It's alright," Hannah said and patted Jenn's hand. She sent her a small, gentle smile. "There are choices that can be made once Sarah gets here."

That seemed to make Jenn burst into fresh tears. "But I don't want to induce. Please, if this isn't true labor, don't let them induce."

Hannah patted her hand. "We're a team and together we'll make the best decision for you and the baby," Hannah said.

I looked at Shane. He glanced at me. We were both helpless to change anything happening in the room. It was about this time that I realized Jenn had been absolutely right. I would not be nearly as good as Hannah was in this situation.

"Daddy, how long have you been here?" Hannah asked Shane. It was weird to hear her call Shane *daddy*, but I guess that is exactly who he was in this situation.

"He's been in the room with me for the last four hours," Jenn answered him.

Hannah looked at Jenn. "Is it okay if we give him a little break to stretch his legs and use the restroom? I'll be here with you the whole time and if you need him, I can send Allie to get him. How does that sound?"

It was clear Jenn adored Hannah. She relaxed

against her pillows. "Okay," she said and looked at me. "But Allie stays, right?"

"Yes," I said, and went to the other side of the bed and held her hand. "Of course."

"Shane?" Hannah motioned for him to take a break.

"Are you sure?"

"It's going to be a long night regardless," Hannah said and looked pointedly at the door.

"Okay, but text me the minute she says my name," Shane said.

"I will," I promised, and watched him hurry out the door with his phone in his hand.

"Now that he's gone," Jenn said. "Hannah, I know you didn't kill Matthew. I've asked Allie to investigate."

"Wait, what?" I asked. "I thought you were in labor."

"I am," she said, "sort of . . . at least I thought I was and then when the nurse said I wasn't, well I kind of fell apart a little." She made a wincing face.

"That happens," Hannah said. "Hormones are surging like crazy through you now."

"Is this . . ." I waved a hand over her blanket-covered body. "Is this all to get Hannah out of jail?"

"I doubt it," Hannah said and studied Jenn's face. "From what I can tell touching her stomach and looking at her contraction band, she is having mild contractions, but not as often as she lets on. Am I right?"

"Of course," Jenn said and sat up straighter. "Now, Allie, what have you discovered in your investigation?"

"You can't keep this up all night," I warned her.

"As soon as Sarah gets here, she's going to send you home and that means Hannah is going back to jail."

"Then you'd better talk fast," Jenn said.

I shook my head and Hannah swallowed a laugh.

I relayed everything, from Monica's insistence they were fighting to Joan's insistence that no one would ever want to see Matthew dead. "And she said he was even nice to that crazy old girlfriend of his that came in the other day."

"Crazy old girlfriend?" Jenn perked up.

"Oh, she must mean Angel Monroe," Hannah said. "Matthew told me she stopped by the park nature center."

"What's the story there?" I asked.

Hannah shrugged. "He dated her before we started dating. She broke up with him and he was fine with it. Turns out she was seeing another guy."

"Ouch," I said. "Unless they weren't in a steady relationship."

"Oh, he thought they were serious until she spelled it out for him," Hannah said, remembering. "He said he swore off dating for months until he realized the relationship was really all in his head. She'd never been serious." Hannah shrugged. "I asked his friends, and they told me Angel only used him to get the attention of the guy she really wanted, because that guy only looked at a woman if she was already in a relationship."

"Yuck," Jenn said. "I hate guys who do that. It's like the thrill of the hunt. It's all good until they best the other guy and steal the girl. After a few months they dump the girl and look for someone new to best."

"I don't know Angel, but I kind of feel sorry for her," I said. "How long was it before he dumped her?"

"Oh, don't feel sorry for her," Hannah said. "Angel gives as good as she gets. Any hint of this guy looking in another direction, she suckers some poor slob into paying her attention until her boyfriend declares her to be his one true love."

"A match made in heaven." I shook my head.

"It's why we all call her the crazy ex-girlfriend," Hannah replied. "Anyway, that all happened two years ago, and she lives in St. Ignace now."

"Then why did she go see him at the park center?" Jenn wondered out loud. "Oh, ow!" She clenched my hand. Hannah didn't skip a beat, gently walking Jenn through breathing, relaxing, and visualization. Finally, she blew out a long breath and closed her eyes.

"Should I get Shane?" I asked Hannah.

"No," Jenn insisted, her eyes popping open. "Go on, why did she go see Matthew after two years?"

"She wanted his help with some ridiculous plan to get her boyfriend to marry her," Hannah said.

"What kind of plan?" I asked.

"She wanted Matthew to take her to dinner two nights in a row in hopes that the news would get back to her boyfriend. Hoping he would realize that he either needed to step up and marry her or let her go." Hannah checked Jenn's pulse, holding her wrist with two fingers, and watching the second hand on her watch.

"Sounds like what she normally does," I said. "Why go back to Matthew now?"

"I hope he said no," Jenn said. Her expression was one of dislike. "I hate women who play games like that. If the guy doesn't want to commit, break it off. Even if he steps up now, it doesn't mean he'll stay later."

"Sounds like someone speaking from experience," Hannah said. "You're doing good, by the way."

"Thanks," Jenn replied. "When we arrived at the clinic, I really thought I was having contractions every thirty seconds. But now that I've had one or two more painful ones, I suspect those were just my muscles warming up." She ran her hands over her belly. "Should I get up and walk?"

"That would be a great suggestion," Hannah said. "Let's wait and see what Sarah says."

"I have to know, did he do it?" I asked Hannah. "Did he take her out to dinner?"

"He asked me what I thought about it," Hannah said. "I was out of town for a training class to keep my certification up-to-date, and I told him that I trusted him implicitly." She shrugged. "I guess we both thought what was the harm? He told her only one dinner as old friends and she was never to bother him again. That was it and she was to stay out of his life forever. It seemed like a sweet deal."

"He did it?" Jenn asked. "He trusted her enough to think she would stay away from him after that?"

"Yes." Hannah nodded. "He took her to dinner as an old friend and talked to her about how she was doing and what she wanted, what her dreams were." Hannah's expression took on a grin. "Then he proceeded to tell her all about me." She shook her head. "At the end of dinner, he hugged her, and they each went their separate ways."

"That's what he told you," I pointed out. "What if that's not what happened?"

"He wouldn't lie about something like that." Hannah's voice was no longer calm.

"Whether he would or not," I said, my mind whirling, "the prosecutor is going to use that as evidence that you had a motive to kill Matthew."

"A motive?" She sounded confused.

"Were there witnesses to Angel and Matthew having this friendly dinner?" I asked.

Hannah shrugged. "I suppose," she said. "I mean that was sort of the point, right? Still, he didn't go on a second date with her."

"Doesn't matter," Jenn said, rubbing her belly. "People are going to think that word got back to you and you two fought, and he threatened to leave you for her, and you shot him."

"I . . . uh . . . that's ridiculous," Hannah said, confusion deepening on her face. "Who would think that?"

"You'd be surprised," I said. "I heard there's a new county district attorney, and he's young with political ambitions and ready to make a splash."

"Wait." Jenn turned to me. "How do you know that?"

"Monica," I said. "Then my mom showed up at the McMurphy this afternoon."

"Your mom's here?" Jenn started to smile. "Don't tell me she 'surprised' you again." Jenn used old-fashioned air quotes around the word *surprised*.

"That's not the worst of it," I said. "She showed up with my old boyfriend."

"Trent?" Jenn asked, drawing her eyebrows together.

"No, Brett Summers," I said.

"Oh, no, not the guy you dated all through high

school and college who proposed to you at graduation," Jenn said.

"The one and the same," I muttered.

"How's he look?" Jenn's curiosity got the better of her.

"Better than ever," I groused. "Worse, I didn't even have time to wash the fudge out of my hair and off my face before she sprung him on me."

Hannah looked from Jenn to me to Jenn and back to me. "What has that got to do with me?"

"To begin with, Allie turned him down even though he planned like this really elaborate proposal."

"Oh, no, that had to be embarrassing." Hannah's eyes grew wide. "Did you, like, say no in front of everyone?"

"I said no."

"Why?" Hannah asked, her curiosity piqued.

"He wanted me to give up the McMurphy and Mackinac," I said. "My inheritance, my dreams, all to become his partner and keep his house, have his kids, mingle with his political associates."

"Wait, you mean, like the old days?" Hannah tilted her head.

"There're a lot of women who would kill to do that today," I said. "I had other priorities."

"And your mom just showed up with your old boyfriend?" Jenn asked, laughter escaping from inside her.

"It's not funny," I said, but I too started to laugh because Jenn was laughing hard. "In fact," I said between giggles, "I was supposed to go out to dinner with Brett and my mom tonight, but you went into labor."

"Oh, dear." Jenn laughed harder.

"I don't understand," Hannah said, looking from me to Jenn and back. "What's funny?"

"My mom—" I laughed harder. "My mom is . . ." I laughed harder. "Oh, my."

"Her mom has a heart of gold," Jenn said, laughing. "She's just certain she knows what's best for everyone." She laughed hard, causing her to snort, which had me laughing harder, until tears ran down our cheeks.

"I don't get why that's funny," Hannah said.

"Oh." I swallowed my laughter and dashed the tears from my eyes. "It's not. It's not funny, but sometimes you have to laugh or you will cry."

"Oh, ow, ow, ow!" Jenn said and clutched her belly. Hannah went to work keeping her calm and breathing. I let Jenn grab my hand and squeeze it until my fingers felt like they might be crushed.

Just as Jenn took a final long breath and relaxed, Shane arrived with the midwife in tow. "Sorry I've been gone so long, but I went to see if she was really heading this way. We met in the middle, and I walked her back here."

Sarah was probably in her mid-fifties and completely no-nonsense. She took off her jacket, tossed her long braid of black hair behind her back, and promptly kicked me out of the room.

I went out into the hall to find Rex leaning with his back to the wall, his arms crossed, and his gaze vigilant.

"You trust Hannah enough to not keep her in sight?" he asked.

"I don't know her," I said and sighed. "But Shane's in there and the midwife kicked me out. If she's going to try to go out the window, then I guess I'm screwed."

He was silent for a moment, and I grabbed a chair from the curtained room and carried it down to just outside Jenn's door.

"I don't need a chair," Rex said.

"It's not for you," I replied and sat down, resting my head against the wall. I closed my eyes for a moment and rubbed my sore hands. "I don't know Hannah, but Jenn trusts her." I opened my eyes and looked at him. "You should have seen how great she was in there. All calm and cool-headed. I really don't think she killed Matthew."

Rex took a deep breath and blew it out quickly. "The new DA thinks it's a slam dunk. He's pressing charges and likely to ask the judge to deny bail because of the seriousness of the offense. Look, there isn't a whole lot I can do about tomorrow's arraignment hearing."

I chewed on my bottom lip. "There's no way to prove her innocence by tomorrow morning, either. Which means she'll have to go back to jail."

"How's Jenn doing?" He changed the subject.

"Surprisingly better since Hannah arrived," I admitted.

We were both quiet for a moment. The corridor was empty enough to hear the humming of the lights. If you strained you could make out that there were people talking in the next room, but there was no way to hear exactly what they were saying.

Thank goodness. The last thing I needed was for Rex to find out Jenn really didn't need Hannah. At least not yet.

"You didn't tell me your mom was coming to visit," he said, breaking into my thoughts.

"She surprised me this afternoon," I said, trying desperately not to give in to the urge to bang my head against the wall. "She will always do what she wants, no matter what I might think or say."

"Who's the guy with her?"

"Oh, Brett Summers, we went to high school together," I said. It wasn't a lie and considering Rex asked me to marry him when my friend Harry got too close, I felt it was better to just leave it at that. "Mom says she ran into him the other day and he mentioned he was flying up to the island to look at a couple of pieces of property for sale. I guess he's in real estate now."

"She decided to come up and surprise you?" He looked at me with his blue, blue eyes ringed in thick black lashes, and raised an eyebrow.

"That's my mother," I said.

"Hmmm," he said. "You don't talk about your parents very often."

"I guess I feel like a bit of a disappointment." I blew out my breath. "Don't get me wrong, I love them, and I'm always happy to see them—given a little notice, of course. I don't really talk about them."

"You're lucky to have them," he said gently.

I straightened and looked at him. "You never talk about your family either."

"Don't have any living," he said. "I figured you would have sleuthed that out by now."

"I only look into murders," I said. "For the most part, I'm just a girl trying to make a go of her family business."

"Hm, I'll have to fill you in sometime," he said.

I opened my mouth to ask more questions when Shane popped his head out of the door. "Can you get the nurse?"

"Sure," I said and jumped up. "Any problem?"

"We need the nurse."

I hurried down the hall. Had things progressed farther than Jenn planned? I guess, only time will tell.

Chapter 11

The clinic was small, and the reception desk was part of the nurses' station. "Excuse me," I said. Both Connie and Maisy looked up at me. "Shane asked me to get you."

"Certainly." Connie stood. "I saw they called Sarah after all. I don't know why. She's just going to tell them what I already told them."

"They must have wanted their care team," I said as I followed her to the room.

"You don't need to go in." She stopped me at the door and went inside, closing it in my face. *Well, alright then*, I thought and paced in front of the door.

"You might as well sit," Rex said. "Babies can take a while."

"I just thought—"

"What?" he asked.

I bit my tongue. "Nothing. I'm fine." I sat and studied my hands. Finally, after what seemed an eternity, the nurse and the midwife left the room and headed down the hall. I jumped up and entered to find Jenn dressed and putting on her jacket. "Is everything okay?" I asked.

"I haven't had a contraction in almost thirty minutes," Jenn said and wound a scarf around her neck. "The midwife and the nurse think it's a false labor and I'll be more comfortable at home."

I glanced at Hannah and then Shane. "And you are okay with it?"

"We all talked it over and this is the best plan of action," Shane said. "Plus, I now have both the nurse and the midwife on speed dial."

"And Hannah?" I asked Jenn.

"It's okay for her to go back with Rex," Jenn said. "Oh, and I might have made her an appointment to see a lawyer before the hearing tomorrow morning. Because I'm pretty sure you're going to solve this thing."

"Right," I said, and watched Shane hold the door for Jenn and step out into the hall. I turned to Hannah. "Is there anything else you need before you go back to the jail cell?" I winced at the sound of those words. "I mean it's going to be a long and uncomfortable night."

Hannah shook her head. "No, thanks. I guess I'm pretty used to long uncomfortable nights." She stopped and grabbed the box of tissues. "I'm pretty sure I'm going to need these, though. I just can't stop crying whenever I think about the fact that Matthew is dead and he's never coming back."

I hugged her, and Rex pushed the door open. "You ladies ready to go?" he asked.

"Yes," I said.

Hannah nodded and held out her wrists. I watched as Rex cuffed her and my heart sank.

What if I couldn't prove it wasn't her? Ugh. You can't prove a negative. The only way is to prove it was somebody else.

"Can Allie walk with us back to the police station?" Hannah asked.

"If she's okay with it," Rex replied.

"Yeah . . . yes!" I said and sent her a smile. "I'd be happy to walk with you."

After Hannah was safely returned to her jail cell, I headed home. It was a cool night and the stars twinkled brightly. Any other time, I'd say it was beautiful, but now I had other things on my mind. A glance at the time and I saw it was nearly eleven. I still needed to walk Mal before I could go to bed. It was going to be a very short sleeping night.

I hurried up the back steps to the apartment and unlocked my door. Mal greeted me with a bark, and I grabbed a leash and harness off of the hooks I had near the door. "Come on, baby," I said. "I know it's late. Let's take you out for your late-night walk." I snapped her in and straightened, only to be startled by my mother's appearance on the other side of the breakfast bar. "Oh, Mom, you scared the dickens out of me!" I held my hand over my heart, willing it to slow down. "How did you get into my apartment?"

"It's the owner's apartment," Mom said briskly. "Your father and I have keys, remember?"

"Oh, right." Mal pulled me toward the door and jumped on it, begging me to go out now. "I've got to take Mal out for her last walk. I'll be right back."

"I'll come with you." Mom grabbed her jacket and put it on as she rounded the breakfast bar and into the kitchen.

"Great," I mumbled and opened the door. Mal and I hurried down the stairs and over to the patch of grass across the alley. I looked up and saw Mom locking the door and heading down the stairs. Mella watched us from the window. "Here we go," I whispered to Mal.

"You're home for the night now? How's Jenn?" Mom asked.

"It turns out the labor stopped, and they sent her home," I said. "I came home right after they went home."

"I see," Mom said as we walked down the alley. "Why did they need you so much that you couldn't have dinner with your mother and an old friend you haven't seen in years?"

"Jenn needs her doula, and I was the only one who could get her," I explained. "She's my best friend, Mom, and if she needs me when she's having a baby, then I will be there for her."

"What about the father?" Mom asked crisply.

"He was there," I said.

"And Jenn's mother?"

"No, she wasn't there," I said.

"Whyever not? Trust me, when you have children, I will be there," my mom said.

"I don't know." I paused. "I guess that's a question for Jenn, and I'm not having kids until a few years after I get married."

Mom was silent for a moment, and we turned down the side street to walk the long block around the McMurphy. "Are you seeing anyone besides that police officer?"

I sighed. "You mean Rex, Mom? You know that I'm seriously dating him."

"Darling, that boy has been married twice before. I think that says a lot about his track record in serious relationships." Mom shook her head. "I hope you realize that police officers are public servants and that means they work long hours for very little pay."

"What does that have to do with anything?" I asked as we turned down Main Street. At this time of night only the bars were open, and the sidewalks were eerily empty.

"I thought I raised you to think about these things." She frowned at me. "If you marry a public servant, you will have to work your entire life. Your children will have to be raised in day cares, God forbid, and will be lucky if you can afford the cost of college. Unlike Brett, who can more than afford to take care of you and your children."

I chewed on the inside of my cheek in an attempt to not say anything. It didn't work. "I thought he wants to be the governor. Isn't that a public servant?"

"You know that's completely different. If only you hadn't broken up with that nice Trent Jessop." She sighed. "You aren't getting any younger, dear, and neither am I. You'll see, when you get to be my age, the only thing that makes any difference is to bring good children into the world. And when you do, you need to be in the best financial situation you can to help them make a difference in the world."

I was silent for a long time. As an only child, I must have severely disappointed her when I became determined to run the McMurphy. "I'm in love with Rex."

"You think that now," she said. "But in twenty years when you are still struggling to give your kids what they need, you'll realize I'm right."

She stopped me and looked me in the eye just as we approached the McMurphy. "Honey, I know your Papa Liam put this romantic notion in your head that living and working on the island full-time is the only thing you were born to do. But I'm telling you, it's not. There's a whole big world out there. If you continue down this path, your children will leave you just like your father left his parents."

"Mom, I—"

"It's late, dear." She covered her mouth with her hand in a fake yawn. "I have already told Brett you would be delighted to have lunch with him at the yacht club tomorrow. Please, dear, do something with your hair and wear a nice dress." She straightened the collar of my plaid jacket. "Remind him why he proposed to you the first time. Mark my words, the future of your children depends on it." Then she used her key card to let herself into the McMurphy through the lobby door.

I stared at her retreating back for a few long moments, letting emotions wash over me. "Come on, Mal," I said, not sure if I was angry, sad, or resigned at my mom's actions. We walked the entire block and turned up the side street.

That's when I came face-to-face with Rex's Second Ex-wife, Melanie. "Oh," I said, startled to find anyone on the street this late at night.

"Hello, Allie," she said, and stopped.

Mal sniffed her suspiciously.

"Melanie," I said. "I thought you found a good job in Grand Rapids. What brings you back to the island?"

"Oh, Rex didn't tell you?" she asked with false sweetness as she bent down and scratched Mal behind the ears.

"Tell me what?"

"I'm this season's manager of the Old Tyme Photo Shop." She straightened. "I'm also staying in the apartment above the shop. It looks like we're neighbors now."

"Oh." I plastered a smile on my face. Could this day get any worse? "Good for you. I didn't know you were into photography."

"There's a lot you don't know about me." She studied my face, then sent me a small flash of a smile. "Anyway, see you around. You, too, Mal." Then she stuck her hands into her jacket pockets and walked away.

I looked at Mal and she looked at me. "This is going to be a very interesting season, isn't it?"

Ruff!

Chapter 12

Chocolate Lemon Bonbons

This recipe is perfect for spring!

Ingredients:
16 oz. cream cheese, softened
1 to 2 lemons, zested for 2 tablespoons of
    zest, juiced for 3 tablespoons
1 teaspoon lemon extract
1 cup powdered sugar
2 cups dark chocolate chips (melted)
Yellow sprinkles or accent topping of
    choice

Directions:
In a large bowl beat the cream cheese, lemon zest and juice, and lemon extract. Slowly add powdered sugar and combine thoroughly. Cover and freeze for 2 hours. Line baking

sheet with parchment or waxed paper. Use a small melon scoop or ice cream scoop to make 1-inch balls and place them on the baking sheet. Carefully dip balls one at a time into melted chocolate until coated, allowing excess to drip off. Roll dipped balls into topping of choice and place back onto parchment and let stand until set. Store in refrigerator. Remove just before serving. Makes 3–4 dozen. Enjoy!

I got maybe two hours of sleep. My thoughts whirled round and round about Jenn, about Hannah and Matthew, then there was the situation with my mom and Brett, and now Melanie. I got up early and made the usual fudges. Boxed and packed the online orders for shipping, and scrubbed the shop clean, all before Frances arrived just before eight.

"What's got you in a tizzy?" she asked, popping her head in to say good morning.

"Nothing," I said, and rinsed the cleaning cloth and draped it on the shiny stainless-steel sink. "Everything."

"I see," Frances said. "Want to get some coffee?"

I glanced at the lobby, which was filled with guests grabbing coffee, tea, juice, and the continental breakfast I provided, consisting of pastries and sweet rolls along with bananas and apples.

"No, thanks," I said. "I checked the Ungers out early this morning and the Fentails said they would be checking out at eight."

Frances glanced at her watch. "I'll catch them.

Why don't you go upstairs until your ten o'clock demonstration, then? I can handle things here."

"Thanks, Frances," I said, and took off my chef's hat and walked out of the shop with her. I did need a break. Then I ran into my mom on the way up to my apartment.

"Oh, good, you're free," she said. "Do you want to go get breakfast somewhere?" Mom always looked put together. Today she wore a beautiful pair of wool slacks with a satin blouse in a pleasant, jewel-tone green. It highlighted her green eyes and champagne-blond hair.

"Good morning, Mom," I said. "Did you sleep well?"

"I did," she replied as we stood on the third-floor landing of the stairs. "My goodness, you smell of sugar and chocolate."

"I've been working," I said, resisting the urge to straighten my chef's coat. "Listen, I have some more work to do and a demonstration at ten. How about I make you breakfast in the apartment? If I remember right, you like a soft-boiled egg and a half a grapefruit."

"That's right, dear." She smiled at me. "Do you have grapefruit?"

"No," I replied. "But I can make a soft-boiled egg and a nice cup of coffee. If you want, there are fresh croissants in the lobby. I can go down and snag a couple."

"Oh, no, sweetheart." She gave a short laugh. "It's difficult to keep your figure at my age. I haven't eaten anything with bread or sugar in years. You'll see one day." She couldn't help herself and adjusted the shoulders of my coat. "But I will take you up on the coffee and the egg."

"Wonderful." We walked up into the apartment. Mal rushed up the stairs to run headlong into the apartment first, forsaking the possibility of a tasty snack from the guests eating breakfast in the lobby.

"You need to teach that dog some manners," Mom said with a frown.

"Sorry, Mom, she's a little excited. I don't get visitors very often."

"Probably because you don't invite people to come visit." Mom stepped into my apartment.

"I guess I'm busy working." I unbuttoned my chef's coat and hung it and the hat on the hooks by the door.

"Yes, I remember how your grandfather didn't have any time for his family, either. Always working, always storytelling in the fudge shop." She shook her head.

"He loved it." I walked into the kitchen and made coffee while she took a chair at the two-person table that sat on the other side of the breakfast bar under the window to the alley.

"I remember this set," Mom said absently, running her hand over the oak finish of the tabletop. "Very Americana. It was a style in the seventies."

"It's one of the few things I was able to save from Grammy and Papa's," I said. "It was a bit battered when the roof fell in, but I sent it out to a furniture restorer, and he was able to do wonders."

"It does look well done." She noted the smooth finish.

"I found a local guy who is a wonder." I poured

us fresh coffee. Hers black, of course. Mine had a touch of cream in it.

"Thank you, dear." She watched me bustle about the tiny kitchen, soft-boiling two eggs. "I wish I understood your fascination with this place. I mean, it's so much work. Frankly, I'm proud of you for sticking it out and getting your culinary degree and your hotel management degree."

"That's not what it sounded like last night." I placed both eggs into egg cups and put one in front of her along with appropriate silverware and a cheery napkin. Then I took a seat and cracked into my own egg.

"It's just so . . ."

"What?" I asked and took a bite of a perfectly cooked egg.

"Rustic," she said. and cracked into her egg. "With your talent and achievements, not to mention your drive, you could really go far. I was telling Brett all about it last night. Although, I'm beside myself as to why you would want to help the police find killers. If you ask me, the rash of murders on this island should be enough to bring you back safely home."

"Mom, this is my home." I put down my spoon and got up when my two slices of toast popped in the toaster. I buttered them with real butter. Cut them diagonally and placed them on a plate and brought them back to the table.

"Bread will put weight on you fast," Mom said, pointing her spoon at the toast.

I picked up a slice, and looked right at her as I dunked it in the creamy yolk and took a bite. "Rex likes the way I look."

"Let's change the subject, shall we?" She took a sip of coffee. "Brett said he will be here one more night. The Realtor wanted to show him a bed-and-breakfast that could use an investor or two. After that we're both going home."

"Alright," I said. "I really wish you had let me know you were coming. I could have prepared to entertain you . . . both. But I don't have an assistant right now in the fudge shop, and that means that I can only take off a couple hours a day."

"I did worry about that." She sipped her coffee. "But I had hoped seeing Brett again would encourage you to make time for a visit."

I sighed. "Mom, yes, Brett's handsome and clearly has money, but the whole reason I didn't marry him is because he wants a wife who hosts parties and helps entertain clients." I gestured at my pulled-back wavy hair, pink and white striped polo, and black slacks. "That's not me."

"Oh, honey"—she touched my hand—"I can help you with that. I know a great etiquette coach. And clearly you can cook elegant meals, with your degree."

I withdrew my hand and stood, silently taking my mug and dishes to the sink.

"What did I say wrong this time?" she asked as she sat at the table.

I turned and leaned against the sink, clenching my hands into the cold stainless, trying to control myself. "You don't know me at all, do you?" I asked slowly, carefully. I wasn't sixteen anymore, but it was pretty clear she still thought so.

"Of course, I know you, darling." She stood and brought her dishes toward the sink. "I'm your mother. I gave birth to you and poured my heart and soul into your care for twenty-three years. Longer if you include your master's in hotel management."

I swallowed the rant that threatened to burst from my chest. Luckily, my phone rang. I grabbed my cell and saw it was Carol Tunisian. "Hello, Carol," I said. "What can I do for you?"

"Oh, my, someone got up on the wrong side of the bed today," Carol said. "Am I interrupting?"

I glanced at my mom, who poured herself another cup of coffee. "No, you're fine," I said.

"I might have more information for you about Hannah and Matthew."

"Oh?" I glanced at my mom, who now watched me like a hawk.

"Can you meet me and the girls for coffee? We're at the Coffee Bean."

"Sure," I said. "I'll be right there." I ended the call and grabbed Mal's leash and harness and geared her up. Then took my jacket from the hook near the door. "I'm sorry, Mom, I have to go out. It's urgent."

"But we haven't finished—"

I closed the door on her and rushed down the stairs with Mal and down the alley before anyone else could stop us. It was always an adventure with my mother. You never knew what ideas she had, and there was no way to convince her otherwise. Mal seemed to understand, not stopping at her usual spot. Instead, she walked as quickly as I did down the alley, up the side street to Market Street, and over to the coffee shop.

The ladies were inside, I picked Mal up and

stepped in. The bells on the door jingled and the warmth of the shop carried the smell of coffee and sweets.

"Allie!" Carol waved. "Over here."

I walked over and the ladies grabbed a chair for me. I sat with Mal on my lap.

"You look upset," Irene said. "What's going on?"

"Do you need coffee?" Carol asked. "Or tea to calm you?"

"I'm sorry," I said. "My mother is visiting."

Helen laughed "Oh, honey, that's enough to make any woman upset."

"What is she up to this time?" Carol asked and they all leaned toward the table. "She surprised me with my old boyfriend. Then she tells me a girl can love a rich man as easy as a poor man." The ladies laughed and I joined in. It really was classic, wasn't it?

"That advice has stood the test of time," Carol said and patted my shoulder.

"What she really wants is for me to give up the McMurphy, pop out grandbabies, and help Brett become the next governor. She thinks I'd make an excellent State of Michigan first lady. This morning she went so far as to offer to get me etiquette lessons."

The ladies became quiet.

Then Betty piped up. "Look on the bright side, the governor does have a summer home on the island."

Tears filled my eyes, so I looked up at the ceiling to stop them. It was a trick I'd learned in high school.

"Betty, really!" Carol scolded her.

"What did I say?" Betty asked.

"Never mind that, dear," Carol told me. "You go on doing what you love. You're passionate about the island and fudge. Why, you're a true islander. Only a fudgie would leave for money or politics."

"If I were just looking for a husband, I'd have left for Chicago with Trent." I dashed the tears away and changed the subject. "What information do you ladies have for me?"

"Well," Carol began, and they all leaned in, "we learned that Matthew's old girlfriend Angel is pregnant."

"How did you hear that?" I asked.

"The rumor mill, of course," Betty said.

"I mean, how does the rumor mill know this? And is it confirmed?" I looked from one to the other.

"I suspect Angel started that rumor herself," Carol said.

"That's certainly something she would do," Helen added, and the ladies all nodded.

"But that's not the only thing," Carol went on to say.

"We heard that her pregnancy corresponds with the night everyone saw her with Matthew, having dinner," Irene added.

"Okay," I said. "Do you think the prosecutor is going to use this against Hannah?"

"Most likely," Carol said. "But Angel was seeing someone else before and after the date."

I tried to follow. "Right, her boyfriend. Do you know who that is?"

"Vincent," Helen said.

"Vincent?" I asked. Mal and I looked from one lady to the next.

"Vincent Trowski," Carol said.

"Vincent Trowski," I repeated. Why did that name sound familiar? A glance at my phone told me I had twenty minutes until my demonstration. I stood. "Thanks for the update, ladies."

Mal and I hurried home, I debated simply going in the front door and not returning to my apartment, in case my mother was still there. But then I remembered I'd hung my chef's hat and coat in the apartment. I did have others, but I knew I had to take back my home sometime. "Put your big-girl panties on," I told myself. I marched up the stairs with Mal in hot pursuit. What's the worst that could happen?

Chapter 13

It was eleven thirty. With my demonstration over, I had changed into a crisp sundress. My hair was combed and hung free around my face. As a nod to my mother, I'd slapped on some mascara and colored lip gloss. Like a dutiful daughter, I sat at a small table for two inside the yacht club. Brett had not shown up yet. I twirled my water glass by the stem and regretted promising my mom I'd have lunch with Brett.

I only had two hours between demonstrations, and I could have used those two hours to get more information about Vincent Trowski, who I considered my number-one suspect. After all, it must have been terrible to see his girlfriend go out to dinner with her old boyfriend.

Glancing around, I reassured myself I was not doing the same thing. I hadn't asked Brett; my mom had. Besides, Rex didn't know he was my old boyfriend. Guilt inched up my spine. Fine, I'd tell him everything after I figured out who really killed Matthew.

I'd been texting Jenn back and forth all morning. She hadn't been having any further contractions, but Shane had her on bed rest and drove her crazy, hovering. As much as I wanted her to have her baby, I was kind of glad I had a little bit more time to figure out who really killed Matthew. Especially if Hannah couldn't make bail. In the meant time all I could do was hope the judge was lenient.

Ugh. My mom and dad are on their way here for the foreseeable future, Jenn texted.

That's a good thing, right? I texted back. **Most girls want their mother there when they give birth. I know my mom will be there whether I want her to or not.** I texted a horrified emoji.

My mother is terrible at emergencies, Jenn texted. **It's why I took first aid in seventh grade. My mother just freezes up and stares at the sight of blood. I wanted to know what to do when my twin brothers came in bleeding from whatever escapade they had been through.**

Aren't they ten years younger than you? I texted.

Well, by seventh grade I'd started babysitting my cousins, all boys, I might add. And when Mom gave birth to the twins, I knew someone had to know what to do around boys.

I laughed. **It's going to be fine. Your mother actually approves of Shane.** I texted back.

"Allie?"

I looked up to see Harry Winston standing in front of me. "Oh, hello, Harry," I said and got up to give him a hug. Harry was a dear friend, rich, and handsome in that blond-surfer way. He had purchased a bed-and-breakfast on the island and was doing a great job as its host.

"What brings you here during the week?" Harry asked. "Aren't you usually busy with the fudge shop and the McMurphy?"

"Hello, there," Brett said. "Sorry I'm late." He eyed Harry.

I sent him a small smile. "Harry Winston, this is my old friend Brett Summers. Brett, Harry. He owns a—"

"Bed-and-breakfast on the island," Brett said and shook Harry's hand confidently. "Nice to finally meet you, Harry. I'm with Hanover and Schmidt. We handled a few of your father's properties."

"Right," Harry said. "And you're old friends with Allie? What a small world."

"Actually, we dated all through high school and college. Allie was my first love." Brett looked at me with his golden eyes. "A man never forgets his first love, does he, Harry?"

"There's a lot of truth to that," Harry said thoughtfully.

"Brett is on the island to look at a few properties. My mother ran into him down south. When he mentioned he was coming up for a business, she asked him for a ride up to surprise me," I explained quickly. "Isn't that nice?" I put on my best brave and happy face. But I doubted it was fooling anyone.

"Very nice," Harry said. He turned to me. "Is your mother joining you for lunch as well?"

"Oh, no," I said. "She had to visit some old friends."

We all stood in awkward silence for a long moment.

"Well," Harry said, "I've got to meet my friend Owen. Have a good lunch, Allie. Would love to get coffee soon."

"Of course," I said. "We should catch up."

"Summers, nice to meet you. Any friend of Allie's is a friend of mine." We both stood there and watched him walk away.

Then Brett stepped closer and gave me a hug. "Sorry I'm late."

"It's okay," I said, and stepped back. He pulled out my chair for me. "Thanks." I sat, putting the napkin on my lap.

He sat and glanced over in Harry's direction. "I didn't know you knew Harry Winston."

"We met last year when he took over what was the old Billings place," I said.

"Hmm," Brett replied.

The waiter walked up and handed us our menus and recited the specials for the day as the busboy refilled my water glass.

"Thank you," Brett said. "Could you bring a bottle of your best crisp white wine."

"Oh, no, thanks," I said.

"Oh, come now," Brett said. "I happen to know you love a cold white wine for lunch." He glanced at the waiter. "Please."

"Yes, sir," the waiter said.

"I really can't," I explained. "I have another demonstration at two and relaxing wine and hot sugar do not mix."

"Don't you have an assistant for that?" he asked as he eyed the menu.

"I hire assistants for the season. The rest of the

time, it's just me," I said, and put my menu to the side.

"Hmm," he said. "And the season starts?"

"Officially the first weekend in June. But our May weekends are quite popular as well. By May almost all of the staff needed for the island proprietors has been hired." I purposely put my elbows on the table and rested my chin in my folded hands. I knew my mother would have a fit if she saw me. "Tell me, Brett, how are you doing?"

He set his menu aside and smiled that charming smile at me. "I'm good. Things are very good. I'm progressing nicely toward my long-term goals."

"Is there a Mrs. Summers yet?" I asked, purposefully going there.

"No," he said. I think my direct questions made him a little nervous as he straightened his silverware. "It took me a long time to get over you, and then I got busy with work."

The waiter appeared, took our orders and the menus. Then the sommelier arrived, offered a bottle to Brett. He nodded. I watched as a tasting portion was poured into Brett's wineglass, and he swirled it, sniffed it, and then tasted it. Finally, he gave a nod of approval.

"Very good, sir," the Somm said and bent to pour wine in my glass.

I placed my hand over the top of my glass. "No, thank you."

"Certainly, miss," he said, and poured more into Brett's glass and then left the bottle.

Brett lifted his glass. "Are you sure? It's very good."

"I'm sure it is," I said. "But I'm sure."

"Well then, cheers." He lifted his glass toward me.

I lifted my water glass and touched his. "Cheers." I took a sip and set it down. The gesture brought back a lot memories. It was a thing we used to always do from the time we first started dating. It started with colas, then progressed into wine and cocktails as we came of age.

"I missed you," he said softly, gazing into my eyes. "To be honest, I ran into your mother on purpose, hoping she would tell me what you were up to these days. I was ecstatic to hear you are managing the McMurphy and making—what did your mom call it?—world-class fudge."

His words surprised me. "You were?"

"Of course," he said. "I know all of that was your dream and you've achieved it."

"Yes, I have, haven't I?" I said. "And your dream of running for governor?"

"Still working on the right connections." He shrugged. "It takes a lot of time to make proper connections. But I think I'll be set to try my hand at running for state senate next year."

"Wow, congratulations," I said.

"Thanks." He sat back, looking very pleased. "Once I'm in the state government, it will be easier to make the move to governor. Then who knows?" He waggled his eyebrows. Something I've seen him do a million times and it still made me smile. "The White House."

I laughed and lifted my water glass again. "Brett Summers for president."

He picked up his glass and touched mine.

"Brett Summers for president." He sipped and I sipped. It was a forgotten ritual but now brought back all the times we'd done it for good luck—and, more times than not, whatever we toasted came true.

The waiter came over with our lunches, and we dived in, talking about this and that. My questions became less pointed, and he regaled me with stories about his business endeavors. How he found the perfect house for him, and then why he decided to get a vacation home.

"Are you really here to look at properties for work?" I asked.

"Yes," he said with a nod. "I have some investors interested in Mackinac. They want to build a new resort complete with state-of-the-art rooms, a full-service spa, an incredible gym, a retreat center, golf course, and luxury pools. Nothing but the best in food, service, and hospitality."

"Hmm," I said.

"What?" he asked.

"Tourists come here for our authentic Victorian feel," I pointed out. "Especially families. They like the sense of nostalgia, our wholesome fun, state parks, and real forts."

"Yes but think back to why Mackinac Island became a tourist destination." He put down his fork. "The very wealthy came here to enjoy the fresh air, the sunshine, and the quiet. My investors want to bring a portion of the island back to that sensibility."

I tried a new tack. "Do you have the zoning for that?"

He shrugged. "The properties are already zoned for hotel. There are three Victorian bed-and-breakfasts there now. There's no reason we can't purchase them and put our luxury hotel there. Trust me, we plan to hire an architect to give the façade a Victorian-era look, but the interior will be as modern, digital, and smart as possible."

"Smart?"

"Oh, yes," he said. "It will be wired to connect to your devices as soon as you enter the building. No need for reception lines. You will be guided by a voice of your choosing toward your room. Your door will open by facial recognition and all your favorite things will be waiting for you in your room. Is your favorite color purple? The LED wall will change the room color to match your preferences. Like fine art? We can simulate that as well. The beds will be smart beds set to your precise liking and the linens all will be crafted from the finest Egyptian cotton—in white, of course," he said.

"Of course," I muttered.

"That way they won't clash with whatever color or colors you prefer in your room. And each room will have an interactive exercise coach in a full-length mirror, but if you prefer to exercise with others, we'll have that fully decked-out gym along with steam saunas, infrared saunas, Nordic saunas, plus a Himalayan salt room as well as an ice room. No expense will be spared."

I sipped my water, trying to keep my expression neutral. "It sounds like you've been working on this idea for quite some time."

"I've wanted to do this for years now, but I could

never find the right location. You know, a location that says *Pure Michigan!*" He emphasized the state slogan with his hands as if he were putting up a marquee.

I sat back. "I didn't realize we had three bed-and-breakfasts for sale on the island."

"Oh, they're not up for sale yet, but after I make the owners a very lucrative offer, the deal is a slam dunk. Trust me, I've done this more than a couple of times." He looked proud.

I tried to imagine his proposal going to the island council. There wasn't a single person on the island that would agree to the monstrosity. We liked our quaint authentic Victorian-era island. Why, it took the New Grander hotel five years to get approved and they had to use reclaimed wood, fixtures, flooring, doors, etc. The only thing new about the New Grander Hotel was the wiring and plumbing—well, maybe the insulation. Nothing beyond the guts.

"It's an interesting idea," I said, and twirled the stem of my water glass.

"It's a brilliant idea." He reached out to touch my hand. "I think you are the perfect person to get the proposal approved. I've done my research, Allie; not only are you well-liked and respected, but you've been able to make real changes in policies on the island."

I nearly snorted at how ridiculous that was. Instead, I schooled my face, withdrew my hand and said softly, "I'm going to have to pass." Then I glanced at my phone. "And look at that, it's nearly time for my last fudge demonstration." I stood and walked around the table and put my hand on his shoulder. "Thanks for lunch. It really was nice to catch up."

Then I held my head high and walked calmly but firmly out of the yacht club. The last thing I needed was to be part of that fiasco. I had a hotel to run, fudge to make, and a murder to solve.

Chapter 14

I finished the demonstration, drawing a crowd of twenty, which was great for this time of year. I'd even managed to sell nearly all of the fudge I'd made this morning. But my mind wasn't far from Hannah's arraignment.

When I'd gotten home to change for the demonstration, Jenn had texted me that the judge had set Hannah's bail at five hundred thousand dollars. The poor doula didn't have any idea how she would raise that much money and was currently stuck in jail. Even though Hannah had used my friend William Barrett as her attorney, the prosecutor was passionate about her guilt. He charged her with murder in the first degree and told her she was lucky the bail was as low as it was.

Jenn was upset, not to mention her parents were expected to arrive at any minute. I kind of understood that dilemma. My mother had spent the afternoon watching my every move. As I packed a box of fudge for the last remaining customer, a guy walking past the shop window caught my eye. It was the same guy who nearly mowed Jenn down the morning of the shooting. "Thanks for coming in and have a great day," I said with a smile and handed the customer their bag.

"I just love coming here and enjoying the nostalgia of Mackinac," she said. "And your fudge is my favorite. I knew it the minute I saw you on that candy show last year."

"Thanks," I said and watched her leave. As expected, she turned and gave me a wave as she went out the door. That was the kind of response I loved to hear. When I turned to do a final cleaning of the shop, my thoughts were a mile away. What was the name of that guy? Darn it, was I getting old? I finally gave up and figured I'd just call Monica and ask her again.

The fudge shop doors opened, and I looked up to see my mom standing at the counter looking over the fudges.

"Hi, Mom," I said. "Is there a flavor you'd like to try? I have penuche, I know that's Dad's favorite."

"No, no, I don't need candy, but I will take a pound of that for your father. I also thought it might be fun to offer some of your fudges to the girls at the club."

I packed up a box for my dad and a sample box for her ladies at the club. My mother was oddly quiet. Finally, when I handed her the last box, she spoke. "How was lunch with Brett?"

I shrugged. "It was okay. He spent a lot of time telling me about his planned development for the island."

"Oh, exciting," Mom said. "I know his company

only creates very high-end, exclusive properties. It would be exciting to have one of those on Mackinac Island."

I shook my head. "I can't imagine anyone agreeing to zoning for that."

"Whyever not?" Mom asked as we stepped out of the fudge shop. I unbuttoned my chef's coat as we walked.

"It's counter to everything that Mackinac stands for." I could feel my emotions rising. "We are a nostalgic trip back in time for families; good old-fashioned fun with our natural state parks and our beaches. An exclusive 'smart' resort is counter to all of that."

"Well, it may be time to bring Mackinac Island into the twenty-first century," Mom declared.

I bit my tongue. I've found that sometimes it's best to stop trying to change someone's mind if they are bent on being correct. The fact that my mom didn't truly understand what the island was and what it stood for just reinforced the fact that she would never understand me. To be fair, I gave up trying to share who I am with her years ago.

"Well," Mom said when we hit the stairs. "Did he talk about future plans he might have with you?"

"Like what, Mom?" I headed up the stairs and left her trailing behind me.

"Like getting back together," she said. "I'm sure he could even help you with the McMurphy. With his money, you could really spruce up the place and hire fudge makers and you could even move back home, while still keeping the family tradition."

I was silent the rest of the way up the stairs.

When we hit the office level, I sighed and turned to face her. "Mom, the McMurphy is fine as it is now. I just rebuilt and remodeled it. And I love being a fudge maker."

"Darling." She stopped beside me, breathing a bit heavy from walking up four flights of stairs at my speed. Then she brushed a wayward hair behind my ear. "I wasn't trying to insult you. I was thinking it would be nice for you not to have to work so hard. Maybe you could think about other, more important things if you hired help in your fudge shop."

"Important things?" I tilted my head a little.

"Like getting married and having a family," she said. "You're not getting any younger, and I had hoped I'd have grandchildren by now."

"Frankly, Mom, Brett was only interested in using me to get his development through local zoning laws."

"Well, that's disappointing," Mom said.

I turned and unlocked my apartment door. Mal, who had followed us up the stairs, rushed inside to torment Mella, who was curled up on the couch.

"What did you tell him?" she asked as we both entered the apartment, and I closed the door behind us.

"If you must know, I said no. Then I left to go back to work."

"And that's it?" she asked. "Didn't he at least make you an offer, if you did it?"

"It doesn't matter if he made me an offer or not." I walked straight to my bedroom to change. "I would always say no."

"Why?" Mom asked.

"I've got to shower," I answered, then closed the door in her face and stripped out of my sugary clothes and into a bathrobe.

When I opened the door, she stood there waiting for me to answer her. I took a deep breath. "Why would I always say no?" I repeated her question to try to convince her how ridiculous that question was, but she simply looked at me like how could I not help Brett? "I like Mackinac Island just the way it is. Now excuse me, Mom. I've got to go shower. Jenn wants me to come over and keep her company." I pushed past her and went into the bathroom.

"I thought she had a husband for that," Mom said behind me.

I closed the door on her, locked it, and turned on the shower. Actually, my hope was that Brett got what he needed, and he and Mom would leave tonight. I couldn't say that though. Just like I couldn't tell her that I had a murder to solve, and the clock was ticking.

Chapter 15

Mal and I did not head toward Jenn's house. Instead, we made a detour to Mrs. Tunisian's. I admired the lovely first-of-spring flowers that grew with lush abandon along her walkway. She planted hardy varieties because it often snowed in April. A quick knock and Carol opened the door.

"Oh, good, you're here." She waved me inside. "Take off your coat and shoes and stay awhile. The rest of the book club is here, and we have a murder board all set up." She closed the door behind me, and she took my jacket and waited for me to take off my shoes and leave them in the foyer along with everyone else's. "There's a small towel to wipe Mal's feet," she said as she hung up my jacket in the coat closet near the door.

"Thanks," I said, and Mal waited patiently while I dutifully wiped her feet.

"Allie, get in here," Irma said.

"Yes," Betty said. "Maybe you can help us solve an argument."

I let Mal off of her leash and placed it beside my

shoes and she ran in to say hi to the ladies and see if she could get one of them to give her a cookie.

"Ladies, please," Carol said. "Let Allie get some tea first."

I followed her into the kitchen where she dug out a mug for me. "I didn't realize you had the book club over." Carol's book club had decided sometime last year that it was much more interesting to help me solve crimes than to simply read about them.

"Yes, well, don't mind them." Carol opened a box of assorted tea. I picked out a nice oolong. "I just heard today that Rex's ex-wife, Melanie, got a job as the manager of the Old Tyme Photo Shop. She's going to be right next door to you, day and night."

"Yeah." I leaned against the counter and crossed my arms. "That's not at all uncomfortable."

Carol laughed. "Ah, sarcasm, my favorite kind of response." She handed me my mug of tea. "Let it steep for a couple of minutes."

"Carol!" Irma shouted from the other room. "Stop hogging her."

"Guess we'd better get out there," Carol said. "But I'm not done with this conversation."

"No, I didn't figure you were," I said and followed her out. I took the last place on the couch and settled in to sip my tea. "What's the argument?"

"Are you into true crime?" Betty asked. "Because the argument is whether it's better to cooperate with the police fully or to get a lawyer before you say a word."

I tilted my head. "What? Why? Is someone here in trouble?"

"No one's in trouble," Carol replied.

"If you watch enough true crime," Irma said, "you start to see that more often than not the police trip people up in the interview process."

"And that's bad because?" I asked, trying to understand their train of thought so that I could help. Not that I had time to watch television, let alone true crime shows.

"Because" Betty replied, "police often need to solve the crime quickly and formulate a theory of who did it. Then they do their best to fit the suspect to the crime."

"Not that they always do that." Carol patted my knee.

"This means innocent people go to jail at least a third of the time, while the real culprit gets away," Irma said. "All because the police tend to spend all their time trying to prove their theory rather than find the real killer."

"Some of us think you should always cooperate with the police," Betty said. "There shouldn't be a need for a lawyer if you are innocent."

"While some of us—" Irma gave Betty the side eye. "Some of us believe, for your own good, if you are ever asked a question after your rights are read to you, you should say *I would like a lawyer, please.* No matter how small the offense."

"Asking for a lawyer first means you're guilty," Barbara Vissor declared. Her round face held a resolute expression.

"Not true," Mary O'Malley disagreed. "It's a basic right to have a lawyer. My brother-in-law is a lawyer, and he says to always ask for one right away. Even if they are simply questioning you."

"That's because he wants to get paid," Barbara said, and the ladies laughed.

"Allie, what do you think?" Betty asked.

"First of all, you must keep in mind that I don't watch true crime shows," I said, carefully choosing my words. "Secondly, I think that Rex keeps an open mind when he investigates."

"You have to say that because you're dating the man," Barbara said with a confident nod. "If you weren't dating Rex, what would you do? Be honest."

"I'd cooperate," I said. "Historically that's what I did."

"Aha!" Betty said.

"That being said," I continued, "if you are still being questioned or detained after an hour, I would recommend you get a lawyer."

"See!" Irma said.

"She just agreed with both of you," Judith Schmidt pointed out.

"Can you have it both ways?" Carol asked.

"It really makes the most sense." I sipped my tea. "I mean the moment you feel uncomfortable, ask for a lawyer."

"Did Hannah do that?" Irma asked.

"She did," I said.

"And yet she was still arraigned," Carol said. "Which is why we're all here. Allie and I don't believe for one second Hannah killed Matthew. She loved him."

"That doesn't mean anything," Judith said. "It could have been a crime of passion."

"That's certainly what the prosecutor wants everyone to believe," I said. "But Hannah said that she and Matthew told each other everything."

"I heard they were seen arguing and it got heated," Irma said and bit into a butter cookie.

"That's the thing," I said. "Hannah said they didn't fight, but Monica Grazer swears she heard them fighting, and she'll testify about it."

"Did anyone else hear this fight?" Carol asked.

"I don't think there was another witness brought up," I said. "No one's told me if there was, anyway."

"Then it's she said/she said," Carol murmured. "That's suspicious."

"But why would Monica lie about something like that?" I mused out loud.

"That's the question, now, isn't it?" Irma asked.

"Maybe it's Hannah who's lying," Betty said and received several dirty looks for saying it out loud.

"Maybe we should ask Monica if she simply mis-remembered," Carol said.

"I tried that already," I said. "She was certain that she heard the fight, and I don't think she was lying."

"Then why would Hannah lie?" Betty asked. "I mean, it would only make her seem even more guilty if she lied."

"I don't think she's lying either," I said.

"How can that be?" Judith asked.

"I don't know yet," I said. "But I intend to find out."

Chapter 16

After I finished my tea, Mal and I left the book club and headed straight to Jenn's house. I felt a little guilty over not spending my usual amount of time at the McMurphy, but I was pretty sure Frances would cover things there. She knew my mother well, having worked for Papa Liam for years. She would know how to handle my mother's outrageous behavior better than I would.

To be honest, I secretly hoped that she would send me a text letting me know that Brett and Mom had checked out and were on their way to the airport. But so far, that hope had not come true. I bucked up. With everything going on, my mother and Brett were the least of my worries. I mean Jenn was practically in labor and I had yet to help her doula go free.

"Hello, the house," I said as Mal and I entered Jenn's back door. I took my shoes off and headed toward the living room.

"I'm in the bedroom," Jenn called.

The house was a classic bungalow that she and Shane had spent her entire pregnancy remodeling. Although, the last month, Shane wouldn't let her help. They had a small mudroom, where I left my shoes, which opened onto a kitchen that opened to the dining room and the living room. Off the living room was a bedroom. But left of the kitchen was the master bedroom, a full bath, and the baby's nursery. I switched directions and headed to the master bedroom and stopped in the doorway.

Jenn was propped up on the bed, a peach throw blanket tucked around her belly and legs. Her phone was nearby, and she worked on her laptop. Mal took the opportunity to jump up on the bed with her and snuggle.

"Do you want me to grab you anything to eat or drink?" I asked.

She glanced up. "There's some seltzer water in the fridge," she said. "Help yourself to some as well."

"Will do," I said and went back into the kitchen to take out two orange-flavored waters, opened the tops and took both bottles to her room. I handed her one and sat in the rocking chair by her bed. "How are you doing? Any more contractions?"

She put her laptop to the side, took a swig of the drink. "One or two, but they are more than an hour apart. I heard that Hannah couldn't make bail."

"I think her lawyer is working on that." I tried to sound hopeful.

"How's the investigation going? Have you gotten any more clues yet?"

"Nothing," I said. "I'm still trying to figure out what fight Monica overheard. Hannah swears it wasn't her. Monica swears it was."

"Did Monica see them fighting or did she just hear them fighting?" Jenn asked. "If she just heard the fight—"

"She might have assumed it was Hannah." I finished the thought for Jenn.

"Exactly," Jenn said. "If it wasn't Hannah, then we need to find out who it was."

"And it all hinges on what Monica remembers," I said. "If it wasn't Hannah, he did fight with a woman. I highly doubt that Monica would mistake a man for Hannah."

"Our killer is a woman," Jenn concluded.

"Not necessarily." I started to rock the chair back and forth in thought. "It could still be a guy and have nothing to do with the fight Monica heard."

"Hmph." Jenn set her drink on a coaster on the white-painted nightstand. She had decorated her bedroom in peach and white. A touch shabby chic and a touch farmhouse, although she had told me she knew neither design was currently in fashion. It seems like home décor styles change every six months now. I was glad that Victorian was the style expected on the island.

Jenn had picked the peach because not only was it calming, but it helped make her skin look better. And, she had added, the place you really want your skin to look good is the bedroom.

"I do have a question that I'm hoping you know the answer to because for the life of me, I can't remember," I said.

"I have pregnancy brain," she warned. "I'm not sure my memory is all that good right now, either."

"Do you remember the name of the guy who nearly plowed you down the day we found Hannah and Matthew in the alley?"

She closed one eye in thought. "I think Monica said his name was Vincent Trowski. Why?"

"We didn't get very far down that alley before we saw Matthew on the ground and Hannah on the stairs." I took another sip of the orange-flavored drink.

"Ooooh, you think Vincent killed Matthew?" Jenn's expression perked up.

"Maybe, I don't have a motive yet," I said. "I need to go speak to him. Do you or Shane know where he lives?"

"You can't ask Rex?"

"I could, but then it gets complicated," I said and twirled my bottle absently. "Look, Rex told me there's a new county prosecutor who wants to make a name for himself, and he's all for starting with a slam dunk." I took a sip. "Rex said to let it go."

"No, no, no," Jenn said. "You can't let it go. I need her. You saw what last night was like." Tears welled up in her eyes. "You know how much I need her to advocate for me and help Shane."

"I know, I know." I made a hand gesture to try and get her to calm down. "It's okay. I'm still going to help. I just can't go to Rex for information. I have Carol and the book club helping. If you can't help that's okay. I'll figure out a different way to talk to Vincent."

"Okay." She grabbed a tissue, dabbed her eyes,

and blew her nose. Then she stopped for a minute, held her stomach, and started breathing in short breaths like she was doing when she was in labor last night.

I grabbed her hand and sat on the bed with her until she blew out one long breath.

She looked at the clock on the table beside her. "That one was early."

"Oh, boy," I said. "Do you need me to stay? Where's Shane? Do you need me to get him?"

"No." She shook her head. "Don't get him. He's in the lab with his new assistant, and he is on a baby monitor." She pointed to the white monitor.

"He's listening to everything?" I asked, slightly concerned.

"They are listening," Jenn corrected me. "It's okay. They're busy. Plus, Shane knows you are trying to help."

"But won't they get upset because I'm messing around with their case? I mean, I'm pretty certain they are working up the forensics for this, right?"

"Shane knows you're trying to help keep me calm." She patted my hand. "I'm going to be alright for the time being, but please, please figure out this murder fast. I don't think this baby is going to give us much more time."

Chapter 17

I glanced at my phone. It was already after five and Frances hadn't contacted me to tell me my mother and Brett had checked out. I sighed and knew I had to get home before six and go to dinner with my mother. I was still upset with her, but she was my mother, and I only saw her every few months. Maybe if I stopped at Doud's and got some ingredients she would let me make her dinner.

But first, I needed to call Carol and find out if she knew anything about Vincent Trowski. I stopped at the corner and got Carol's number from my contacts list and rang her.

"Hello?" Carol answered.

"Hi, Carol, it's Allie."

"Oh, hi, Allie." Her tone brightened. "What have you discovered about the murder?"

"I'm still pulling on a thread," I said. "Listen, what do you know about Vincent Trowski?"

"Hmm, I knew his grandmother, Terry Mondale," Carol said. "Unfortunately, she passed about six years ago. Why?"

"I need to talk to him," I said. "Do you happen to know where he works?"

"Hmm."

I waited patiently.

"No, sorry, but one of the other ladies might," Carol said. "How about I text you when I find out."

"Thanks," I said. "Maybe his home address might help as well. I really need to talk to him."

"He's part of your investigation," she surmised.

"I'm sorry, I need to pick up some things for dinner from Doud's. My mom is still here, and I hope to fix her something." I started walking.

"I thought you were angry with her," Carol said.

"I am, but I'm hoping she's going home soon, and I thought I'd make her a farewell dinner."

Carol laughed in my ear. "Oh, honey, she isn't going home until she's good and ready."

I sighed. "Yeah, I was afraid of that."

"I'll text soon," Carol said. "Have you told your mom how important this investigation is to Jenn?"

"I told her, but she seems to think that Jenn has plenty of help, and Jenn's parents will be here on the last ferry," I said and looked at my phone. "Which is going to be here soon."

"Your mother has a point," Carol said. "She does seem to have a lot of help."

I rolled my eyes. "Please text me if you find out anything."

"I will," Carol said.

"Thanks," I said, ended the call, and hurried to Doud's. I had no idea what I could cook, but I'd figure it out when I got there. "Come on, Mal, let's go let Mary Emry glower at us." Mary didn't like it when I brought Mal into Doud's with me, but I think she was slowly coming around.

"You've been gone a long time." Mom sounded slightly accusatory as she petted Mella. Mal jumped up onto the couch to steal attention from Mella.

My hands were full of paper grocery sacks filled with ingredients. "I thought I'd make you dinner." Setting the sacks on the counter, I closed the door behind me and hung my keys on the hook near the door.

"Brett has invited us to dinner at the Grander," Mom said and stood. "He's not going to be here much longer and you, missy, are screwing up a chance of a lifetime. I mean, you already turned him down once. If you don't take a second shot, you'll be stuck here making fudge and being single the rest of your life."

I put the grocery bags on the counter and set out the ingredients.

Mom watched silently for a few minutes, letting her silence gather like a storm cloud, and I could feel her getting more and more upset with me.

Finally, I broke the tension. "I was hoping to have you to myself tonight and make your favorite ham and scalloped potatoes, since I had lunch with Brett." Then I turned to her. "But if you would prefer we not be alone together, then I'll change into more appropriate clothes for dinner at the Grander."

She studied me for a minute, aware that I had verbally outmaneuvered her. Either she would have to say she would rather not spend time with me alone and we should go to the Grander, or she would give up this relentless matchmaking and let me cook her dinner.

She let out a long sigh. "Fine, we can have dinner together. I'll let Brett know."

"Wonderful." I grabbed the bag of potatoes and started the washing and peeling process. I listened to her tell Brett that we weren't going to make it. He seemed fine with it from the look on her face after she ended the call.

"He said that he would be sad to miss us, but that he was about to call us and let us know his sellers had invited him to dinner." Mom sat down on one of the stools under the breakfast bar.

"Great." I peeled the potatoes and cut them into thin slices. "See? He took away the burden of having to ask for a rain check."

Mom frowned.

"Let me get you an iced tea," I said. "It's green tea and lavender. You'll like it." I reached for two glasses, added ice from the freezer, then opened the fridge to remove a glass pitcher of tea. I poured us both glasses and pushed hers toward her. "I know you don't like sweet tea. This doesn't have any sugar in it but it has a nice floral taste. I do have honey if you'd like a bit more sweetness." I lifted my glass. "Cheers."

She lifted hers and touched my glass with it. "Cheers," she said and took a sip. "This is quite good."

"Thanks, Jenn got me hooked on it last fall." I went back to preparing the potatoes. To speed up the process, which often took an hour or two, I washed the potatoes slices and put them in a pan of clean water with a dash of salt and set them on the back burner to parboil. Once soft, it would be easy to layer them with cheese and white sauce and bake them for twenty minutes. "Mom, I really wanted to talk about you and me," I said.

"What about us?" she asked, putting her tea down.

I turned to face her. "I feel like you aren't understanding who I am and what I want."

"Hmm," was her reply and she twirled her cup, not looking at me.

"Mom." I stepped closer until we only had the breakfast bar between us. I waited for her to look up. "I know you only want the best for me."

"That's right," she said. "I love you, and I don't want you to feel stuck here simply because your grandfather had some romantic idea about this hotel staying in the family." She reached out and took my hand. "I want you to understand you have choices. I know that this place reminds you of your grandparents and happy times growing up, but you are talented and beautiful. I hate to see you stuck here with some guy who has failed at marriage twice already. It's a big world out there and you never took the time to see it."

I took in her words. In a way, she was right. Papa Liam has been grooming me to take over the McMurphy since I opened my eyes. I had never considered anything else. I'd always known this is where I should be. Was it because of Papa? Where would I be if he had sold the McMurphy?

"I'd never thought about it that way." I squeezed her hand. "But Brett is not the answer. He is not in love with me, and he never was. Marrying his high school sweetheart looks good for his political ambitions. You see, Brett has made it clear to me that his ambition is his mistress. I would always be second fiddle to that. You don't want that for me, either. Do you?"

Mom sighed. "No, I don't. I just want to see you happy and fulfilled."

"Plus, you want grandchildren," I teased as I tested the potatoes then drained them.

"I'm not unusual for wanting that." She took a sip of tea.

I made dinner and we talked about Dad and her garden and what they were up to for the summer. Finally, we settled on a week for her and Dad to come visit in September when the tourist season had calmed a little and before the snow started.

Mom left to go to her room around seven and I texted Jenn to see how she was.

My parents came in at six, she texted back. **Someone needs to save me from my mom. Now she's hovering and I can't even catch a breath without her asking me if it's a contraction.**

I sent her a laughing emoji. **I'd help**, I texted back. **But I need to figure out who killed Matthew first. Right?**

Yes, she texted and sent me a GIF of a clock and time ticking quickly. I suddenly felt guilty that I had let my mother and Brett distract me from my investigation, and Jenn might be the one who suffered.

Chapter 18

Simple Cookies and Cream Fudge

Ingredients:
   14 oz. sweetened condensed milk
   3 cups white chocolate chips
   Dash of salt
   1 teaspoon vanilla
   25 chocolate cookies or chocolate sandwich cookies. Gently crumbled.

Directions:
   Line an 8 x 8 baking pan with parchment. In a medium saucepan, mix sweetened condensed milk, white chocolate chips and salt. Melt over medium heat until smooth. Remove from heat and add vanilla. Reserve ⅓ cup of cookie crumbles, add remaining cookie crumbles to the fudge, and gently stir. Pour into baking pan and smooth. Top with re-

maining crumbles. Chill until firm. Cut into squares. Makes 20. Enjoy!

I grabbed my jacket, hooked Mal up to her halter and leash, and took off down the back steps. Thank goodness the book club had texted me Vincent Trowski's address. My first item of business was to visit him and see if he saw anything the day he nearly ran us over exiting the alley.

It was dark and cool outside. "This way," I said, going to the right, not the normal left. Vincent lived on the far side of Harrisonville, so I chose to go up past Market Street. The roads were uphill, and I needed the exercise anyway. Mal didn't miss a beat, her little legs working quickly but efficiently. I was the one out of breath when we got to the top. She waited patiently for me to catch my breath, sniffing the grass along the road.

My phone rang and I answered it. "Hi!"

"Hi, beautiful." Rex's rich voice vibrated through the phone, warming my heart. "It's been a while since I've heard from you."

"Well, you have a case." I continued my considerably slower walk to Vincent's home. "And my mother is in town."

"The case is in the hands of the DA's office now," Rex said. "How's your mother?"

"She was pushing Brett on me, so I made her dinner tonight and had a heart-to-heart with her," I said.

"How'd that go?" he asked.

"As well as can be expected," I replied. "She's concerned that I'm only here because Papa Liam brainwashed me." I shrugged but knew he couldn't see me. "She asked me to think about what I want to do, not what Papa wanted me to do."

"I see," he said.

"I've never realized that she might be right," I said, wondering how those words felt in my mouth. "I grew up certain I would be a fudge maker and a hotel keeper, just like Papa. Mackinac Island was always the goal. But Mom asked me what I would be doing if Papa Liam had sold the McMurphy."

"And?"

"And I've never thought about it before," I replied. Mal and I walked down Caddot Avenue. Mal sniffed the ground as we walked, reminding me of Scooby-Doo.

"I see," he said, his tone thoughtful. "Maybe that's something you should spend some time with."

"I suppose," I said. "But I want to be careful that I'm not letting my mother influence me, either."

As we walked, a late-night carriage clip-clopped past us.

"Are you outside?" Rex asked.

"Yes, I wanted to take Mal for a walk. Yesterday I didn't have time to walk her because I was busy with Jenn and her labor. I thought I'd let her have a nice long one tonight." It wasn't exactly a lie, I told myself.

"Hmm," he said, and I realized he knew me well after two years.

"What are you doing tonight?" I asked, cheerily changing the subject.

"It's been quite the week," he said. "I've got

forty-eight hours off and tonight I'm sitting on my couch with my feet up and a nice beer in my hand. Want to come over?"

I loved the sound of his voice when he asked me that question. A glance at my phone told me it was already seven thirty. How would I explain being late to his home? "I would love to, but Mal and I have been hiking and it might take us a while to get there."

"Hiking in the dark?" He sounded suspicious. "That is not safe."

"Well, not exactly hiking," I said, knowing I'd gotten caught.

"You're still investigating."

"I just need to talk with someone," I said. "I'll be safe."

There was silence on the other end of the line. I felt his judgment. "Look," I said. "I've put up with my mom, and with Brett, telling me what they think I should do or how I should act. I've had my fill, and I really don't want another lecture from you, Okay? I'm a grown woman and not a single one of you owns me. Just . . . stop telling me what I should do." I ended the phone call and marched down the street about a half mile before I could get ahold of myself. I stopped and took a deep breath and let it out slow. Mal jumped up on me to ensure I was doing okay. "It's okay, Mal. I'm okay." I scratched behind her ears. "It's been a crazy few days."

I bent down and gave her pets, then straightened and realized I was in front of Vincent's home. Walking up the sidewalk, I stepped up onto the concrete porch and knocked. At first there was no response. I rang the bell and knocked again. Mal sat and looked from me to the door and back.

A glance in the window told me that the TV was on. Someone should be home. Reaching up to knock one more time, I paused when the porch light came on and the curtain moved. The door opened suddenly, and the smell of fish and cigarettes wafted out. "Yeah, what do you want?"

I swallowed hard. "Vincent Trowski?" I asked, even though I was certain this was the same guy who nearly ran Jenn down that day.

"Who wants to know?" He leaned against the door frame, crossing his arms defensively.

"Hi, I'm Allie McMurphy," I said, and boldly stuck my hand out for him to shake.

He ignored my hand until I pulled it back. "Why are you knocking at my door this late at night? You selling something? Need a donation? What? Can't you read?" He pointed to the NO SOLICITING sign next to his bell.

I swallowed again. "No, no," I said. "I'm not selling anything. I don't want your money."

"Then what?"

"You hurried out of the alley the day that Matthew Jones was killed," I said. "You nearly bowled my pregnant friend Jenn down; you were in such a hurry."

"What of it?" He was belligerent.

"I was wondering if you saw anything. The murder couldn't have happened much before you left the alley."

"What do you care?" he asked, not budging.

"I don't believe that Hannah Riversbend killed

Matthew," I said. "All the DA has on her is that she was holding the gun."

"Sounds open-and-shut to me."

"Are you sure that you didn't see or hear anything?" I pushed.

"Like what? Matthew's girlfriend gunning him down?"

"Did you see that?" I pressed.

"Look, I already talked to the cops. They got their killer, end of story." He grabbed the door. "Don't bother me again." He went to close the door, but I stuck my foot out and stopped him.

"Did you see Hannah pull the trigger?"

"What if I did?"

I sighed. "Is that what you told the police?"

"Look, lady, leave me alone," he said. "And get your foot out of my door or I'll call that cop boyfriend of yours."

"How did you . . ."

"Small island, idiot. Now move your foot."

I did as he asked, and he slammed the door in my face. I heard the lock engage, and the light went out, leaving Mal and me in total darkness. "Well, that was interesting, wasn't it, Mal?" I turned toward the road and stepped off the porch.

"*Woof.*"

Chapter 19

When we arrived at the stairs to my back door, Rex sat there waiting for us. I let Mal go when I saw him, and she ran to him, her little stump tail wagging. She jumped in his lap and gave him kisses. He laughed and the sound went straight to my heart. I bit my bottom lip. I had every right to be upset. I shouldn't have to apologize. Why did I feel like I should?

"Hi." He stood, holding Mal.

"Hi." I studied him. He looked good in the back porch light. With us both being busy the last couple of days, we hadn't seen much of each other, and I missed him.

"Listen, I wanted to apologize." He petted Mal. "I know you are smart and careful. I also know you don't take any more risks than you need to in order to help solve a murder."

"Thank you." I fought the urge to pull him into my arms.

"I wanted to tell you that I see you. You're really good at figuring out who's a killer and who's not. I know that often things are vastly different than our working police theory, and you always seem to be on the right track."

"Thank you," I said again, and he placed Mal in my arms. "Do you want to come up? My mom went to her room at seven."

"Okay." He followed me up the stairs. The light was on over the landing. I unlocked the door and put Mal down. She went running into the darkness in search of Mella. And I said a little prayer that they wouldn't fight. Mal loved Mella and kept trying to get her to play. Mella, on the other hand, had different ideas.

I turned on the kitchen light and he walked in behind me, closed the door, and engulfed me in a loving embrace. I leaned into it, and we kissed.

"Forgive me?" he asked.

"Yes," I said. "Of course. I'm afraid one too many people tried to address my behavior, and I kind of took it all out on you."

"Even your old boyfriend, Brett?" he asked.

I stepped out of his arms and got down two glasses and filled them with ice and iced tea. "Brett wants to buy up several properties, demolish the old bed-and-breakfasts, and build an exclusive smart resort with all the latest bells and whistles." I handed him his tea, walked to the couch, turned on the light and sat. Mal and Mella both joined us on the couch. I shouldn't say "us." It was more like they both wanted Rex's attention as much as I did.

"A smart resort?" he asked as Mella curled around his shoulders and Mal sat in his lap to be petted.

"He says it would have facial recognition to get you in and out of your room and other places, like the spa. He also wants the rooms to have one or two LED walls so that you could program your favorite color room."

"Right, he'll never get a permit for that," Rex said as he indulged both of my pets with scritches.

"Yeah, well, he had a plan for that," I said, took a sip of tea, then settled sideways on the couch and faced him. "He thought he could wine and dine me, and then I would do him a favor and convince the council it was a great idea."

"What did you say?" Rex asked.

"I said no, of course." I put my tea down on the end table and pulled my cat into my lap, where she curled up and purred under my attention. "Then when I told my mom what he wanted, she thought it was a great idea." I shook my head. "She thinks I should give up my life here and marry Brett and help him become governor. That was always a goal of his and it still is. My mom said that my children would be much better off than if I should stay on Mackinac Island and marry a local."

He sat silent for a moment, petting Mal. "She wouldn't be wrong."

I snorted. "Please, if I was looking for a rich husband, I would have married Trent and gone and lived in Chicago. That's not what I wanted . . . that's not who I wanted."

"I take it your mom doesn't approve of me," he said, taking his gaze from Mal to me.

"I don't care what my mother thinks," I said. "I'm a grown woman and I'll choose my own path in life."

"Hmm," was his answer. He put Mal down and reached for me. We kissed and I leaned against him, listening to his heartbeat. "Earlier you said you needed to think about whether all this"—he waved his right hand—"is what you really want or merely what your grandfather drilled into you from birth."

"No," I said, and ran my thumb across his palm. "I said, I needed to think about that concept. I mean, it never occurred to me what I might have done had Papa Liam sold the McMurphy when Grammy died."

"Mackinac Island is the life *I* chose," he said. "From the throngs of fudgies during the season to the frozen semi-isolated winters. I'm here because I love it. But my first two wives . . . didn't."

"Which reminds me." I sat up and looked him in the eyes. "I ran into Melanie. She's back on the island and managing the Old Tyme Photo Shop next door for the season."

"I know," he said.

"I imagine she was quick to let you know she was back," I said, and tried not to be too worried.

"I told you, Allie, I'm done with her. I don't care how long she stays on the island. I'm in love with you." His blue gaze studied me. "Even if you were to give up and leave the island, I wouldn't go back to her."

"That's what I love about you," I said. "You are loyal to what you love."

"Who I love," he said. "Marry me."

I settled back into his arms, my ear against his heart, and studied our intertwined fingers. I started to answer him when my phone chimed. Sitting up quickly, I pulled it out of my pocket. "It's Jenn. Her mom is taking her back to the clinic."

I texted her back. **I'm on my way.**

"Jenn's mother's here, too?" Rex asked as we both got up from the couch.

"Both her mother and her father. In fact, I'm surprised Shane's parents aren't visiting as well. This is the first grandbaby on both sides."

"Oh, they're here," Rex said as we both pulled on our shoes and headed toward the door.

"They are? Jenn hasn't said anything." I grabbed my jacket and kissed my pets before heading out the door.

"Shane says they're staying in a nearby bed-and-breakfast. They want to be available for the big moment. Shane's supposed to text them when the midwife confirms the baby's on the way."

"That might be sooner than we think." I locked the door behind us. We hurried down the stairs and out into the alley on the way to the clinic. "I really wish you could let Hannah out. You saw Jenn. She was lost without Hannah last night."

He shoved his hands in his jacket pockets and kept pace with me. "Politically, it's out of my hands now."

"I know," I replied. "That's why I've been investigating."

"And?" he asked as we hurried toward Market Street.

"And I'm still trying to figure out why Monica says she heard Hannah and Matthew fighting when Hannah said they didn't. Then there's Vincent Trowski."

"What about Trowski?" Rex asked as we turned left down Market toward the clinic.

"I told you he came hurrying out of the alley

when we got to the mouth of it. In fact, he nearly mowed Jenn down. Didn't you get his statement?"

"I did," Rex said, not at all affected by my tone. "He said he was visiting a friend and was late to work when he rushed out. He never heard anything. Didn't even know anything happened."

"And you believed him?" I asked.

"There wasn't any evidence to counter him. He was late to work and barely clocked in on time," Rex said. We stopped outside of the clinic.

"Unless I can prove otherwise, Vincent is a dead end."

"You prove Trowski is the killer—without getting near him and I'll help you nail the bastard," Rex said.

I reached up and kissed his cheek. "I need a little time."

"If you're trying to help Jenn, you may be running out of time."

Chapter 20

"**O**h, thank goodness you're here," Jenn said when I entered the room. She reached out and took my hand.

"What's going on? Is the baby coming?" I asked. Rex had spotted Shane in the hallway, so we split up.

"I'll tell you what's going on," Jenn said. "My mother is driving me crazy."

"You're not in labor?" I asked.

"I told them I was." She pointed to the monitors that tracked her heart rate and any contractions. "Then I got Sarah alone and told her I needed a night in peace. She told me she'd see that I got one. I think she told them all I needed was to spend the night for observation, and she'd let them all know should my labor progress." She used air quotes around the word *progress*.

I sat down on the edge of the bed, not letting go of her hand. "Why did you text me?" I asked, a bit confused.

"Well, for starters I needed them to believe I was

having trouble with the baby," Jenn said. "They all know you would come running should I text. I didn't get you out of bed, did I?"

"No, I was hanging out with Rex," I said.

"Oh? How's that going?" she asked.

"He asked me to marry him again tonight," I replied. "But it was right after I told him my mother wanted me to marry Brett. I didn't answer. Then you texted."

"You didn't!" She sounded aghast. "Allie, that's just mean."

"I wasn't trying to be mean," I said. "I was complaining about my day. Oh, did I tell you I ran into Melanie; did I tell you?"

"Oh, no, now what?" she asked.

"Melanie is back on the island and managing the Old Tyme Photo Shop for the season," I said. Like I needed yet another thing to worry about.

"Yikes, that's—"

I finished her sentence. "Right next door to the McMurphy."

"Which means—"

"That she's also living in the apartment next door," I said. "Yeah."

"What's Rex got to say about that?" Jenn asked. "Did he know?"

"Oh, he knew," I said, and tried not to let my emotions show. "But he said he would never be interested in her, ever again."

"I tend to believe him," Jenn said and then inhaled sharply while her tummy monitor went off.

"Breathe," I said, copying what I had heard Hannah say when she was here. "Hee, hee, hee, haw."

We breathed through it. Thankfully, the contraction didn't last that long.

"Are you sure you're not in labor?" I asked suspiciously.

"I'm fine," she said. "I've been having these off and on for a week now. False labor, remember? Now please tell me you're still investigating Matthew's murder."

"I am," I said.

"How's it going?" she pressed.

"I went to see Vincent Trowski," I said. "He was belligerent and told me that he already talked to the police. He didn't have to talk to me."

"Did you ask Rex about him?"

"I did," I said. "Apparently Vincent was visiting a friend at the end of the alley and was late for his shift. That's why he nearly pushed you down. According to Rex, Vincent claimed he didn't hear anything or see anything."

"And Rex believed him?" Jenn's eyes grew wide with incredulity.

"There was no evidence that he was lying," I said.

"Did they at least test his hands for gunshot residue?" Jenn asked.

"I didn't ask that," I said thoughtfully. "Shane would know the answer to that, right?"

"I would know the answer to what?" Shane entered the room alone.

"Did you test Vincent Trowski's hands for gunshot residue?" Jenn replied.

"I think my work is the last thing you should be thinking about right now," Shane said, and took her hand from mine.

I got up and let him take my place. My hands went into my pockets as I watched his look of concern grow.

"You know I need Hannah," Jenn said, her eyes welling up with tears. "Allie is working hard to get her here."

"Honey, we've been over this. She has been arrested and bond set. She can't post the bond, which means she'll be in jail until her trial."

"And when will that be?" Jenn asked.

"It could be months," Shane said.

"Then I'll just hold our baby in until she is acquitted," she said, tears rolling down her cheeks.

"You know you can't do that, sweetheart." He handed her a tissue. Then he turned to me. "The answer to your question is no, we didn't check Vincent for gunshot residue. He gave his statement, and the DA didn't think it needed to go any further."

"But you tested me," I said, confused.

"That was before the DA got involved," Shane said.

"Can you test him now?" Jenn asked and then blew her nose.

"No." Shane shook his head. "Even if we did and found traces of gunshot residue on his hands, we have no proof it's even connected to Matthew's murder."

"It doesn't seem right," Jenn said.

"My boss says he's satisfied he has the killer, and other cases need work." Shane looked into her eyes. "Besides, you are my highest priority right now."

"You heard her," Jenn said softly. "Midwife says I need rest. Did my parents go home?"

"I sent them back to the house," Shane said. "But I promised I'd call should anything change."

"Good." Jenn seemed to visibly relax, then she glanced at me. "Allie, you know what I need, right?"

"I'll do my best," I promised. It was after ten at night and that meant all I could do was go home, get some sleep. "Please, keep me posted on your progress."

"I will," Jenn and Shane said at the same time, then smiled lovingly at each other.

"Allie, you'll do the same, right?" Jenn said as I leaned in to give her a quick hug and kiss good-bye.

"I will," I promised, then left the room to find Rex waiting for me in the hall. He took my hand, and we walked out of the clinic.

"How is she really?" Rex asked. "Shane's worried."

"She's okay," I told him. "She's having a few real contractions, but mostly she needed her mom not to be hovering over her night and day. I kind of feel the same right now."

He squeezed my hand. "Listen, when I'm officially off the clock, like now, I can help you with your investigation."

I looked up at him, confused.

"I know," he said. "It sounds like I'm doing a 180-degree pivot on this one, but I'm not convinced Hannah is the shooter. The DA hamstrung us when he decided this was going to be the case to start his career off right. You know, I don't like injustice."

"I know," I said.

He glanced at me as we turned off of Market

Street toward the alley behind my apartment. "I wasn't even close to finishing my investigation when he arrested her. Now the trial is set for less than a month from now. I protested but was told by the mayor to let him do his job, especially if I wanted to be police chief someday."

"I didn't know you wanted to be police chief," I said thoughtfully. "I thought maybe a detective. You are really good at detecting, you know."

"I know," he said. "Even when you do your darndest to undermine my investigations."

"I'm not undermining them," I protested, and he laughed.

"I see you don't like to be teased."

I smacked him lightly on his bicep. "How was I to know you were teasing?" We turned down the alley and walked in silence for a bit. "Seriously though," I said. "I never mean to undermine you. Mostly, I'm simply helping friends, and as a civilian, I don't need to follow the same rules and procedures you do."

"Honey, those rules are there to keep us safe, and to ensure a conviction sticks," he said. "That's why I worry about you when you go all maverick on me and investigate. My biggest fear is that something very bad is going to happen to you, and you have to admit that you have had more than your fair share of near scrapes."

"Yeah," I admitted as we approached my stairs. "I think they want to name a room at the clinic after me because I'm such a frequent flyer."

He stopped and faced me in the lamplight of my back porch. Then he took both of my hands. "When you put yourself in danger, you put my heart in danger."

"You know I'm not looking for danger," I replied. "I try to be as safe as possible."

"It's not really you that I don't trust. It's the murderer you're after," he stated.

I felt his sincerity in my heart and gave an ironic chuckle. "As the girlfriend of a cop, I'm the one who is supposed to be worried every day you are on shift that it might be your last day."

"Do you?" he asked.

"Do I what?" I tilted my head, trying to understand what he was looking for.

"Do you worry every time I'm on shift?" he asked, searching my expression.

"Yes, of course," I replied. "But I also trust in your instincts, training, and mostly your intelligence to keep you safe."

He lifted the right corner of his mouth in a half smile. "Unlike you. I really want you to stop getting involved over and over in these things. You should leave it to those of us with criminal justice degrees and police training."

"Wow," I said, and dropped his hands, then headed up the stairs. "We keep having the same fight over and over. It boils down to the fact that you don't trust me to take care of myself. I'm not some princess in a tower waiting for a man to come save me."

"Allie—" He took a step toward me.

"Maybe we should take a break."

"Why?" he asked, following behind me.

I hit the landing and unlocked the door.

"Why, Allie?" he asked gently, and I turned to see him standing on the edge of the landing, his arms crossed over his chest. "I told you I want to help you with this investigation but only because my hands are tied, and I don't like someone being railroaded. I asked you to marry me. What about that means we need to break up? Is It because your mom doesn't approve of me?"

"I feel like we've been fighting a lot since we said *I love you*," Tears sprang into my eyes. "Don't want to live like this, always fighting. It's like you never really listen to me." I paused. "Sometimes I wonder if I hadn't said *I love you* out loud, would you and I still be fighting this much?"

"Okay," he said. "That's not fair at all. Look, I've been here before. What I know is that it can be difficult when two strong people miscommunicate on a regular basis. I don't really want to control you, and I know you don't really want to control me. What we're doing is working through our communication styles to come to a better understanding of our own feelings of vulnerability."

"Now, you sound like a therapist," I said.

"Just think about what I said."

"I can't do this right now," I told him.

"Is it someone else?" he asked.

"Really? Really, that's what you think of me?" I was incredulous. "Is that why you ask me to marry you whenever I speak to my friends? Go home." I turned, opened the door, slammed it shut behind me and locked it. Then I ran to the bedroom and cried myself to sleep.

Chapter 21

I didn't sleep. When I wasn't tossing and turning, I dreamt about Matthew's killer and babies coming too soon. Needless to say, I got up at four a.m., made coffee, and got to work on the day's fudge. By seven the fudge counter was filled, the fudge shop cleaned and prepped for the ten o'clock demonstration. Coffee, hot water, and continental breakfast set out. I called Carol. I knew she was usually up by six and done with her workout by now.

"Hello, Allie," Carol said. "How's Jenn? Any baby news yet?"

"No, so far, they're simply trying to get her well rested. Her parents are in town and staying with her and Shane," I said.

"I hope she has a good relationship with her mom and is happy they are staying," Carol said.

"Yes, I really do think she loves her mom, and they get along well," I said. "But I think she's stressed because her doula, Hannah, is still in jail."

"How's the investigation going?"

"Not well. The only sort of clue I have is the thing about Vincent Trowski we talked about. Like I said, the DA had already pinned it on Hannah because she was holding the murder weapon."

"The book club and I have been going over your eye-witness report and creating a timeline based on what we know. The real question about Vincent is, does he have the means and the motive to kill Matthew?"

"Great question. I've been up most of the night trying to figure out next steps." I drummed my fingers on my chin. "Where did the gun come from? And was there any bad blood between Vincent and Matthew?"

"Remember the island rumor mill says that Matthew's old girlfriend, Angel, got pregnant," Carol reminded me. "Did you know that Angel and Vincent have been having an affair, even before she broke up with Matthew?"

"Vincent is the boyfriend she wanted to make jealous. That gives him motive to kill Matthew," I said. "Then why did Monica say she heard Matthew and Hannah fighting?"

"I heard that the DA thinks that Hannah found out about Angel and confronted Matthew. When he didn't deny it, she picked up the gun and shot him out of sheer anger," Carol said.

"I don't know Hannah that well," I said. "But I do trust Jenn, and she says that Hannah would never get that angry. I mean, think about it, have you ever gotten so mad at a man you love that you instantly grabbed a gun and killed him?"

"No," Carol said, then laughed. "I might have wished him dead a time or two, but I couldn't hurt a living soul. It's hard enough knowing other people do that, let alone do that myself."

"Yes, I don't see myself ever doing that," I said. "What if we're looking at this all wrong? What if instead of an act of passion, it was an act of opportunity?"

"What do you mean?" Carol asked.

"What if the killer had already thought of the how they were going to kill Matthew, but they hadn't yet figured out the perfect *when*."

"Then, when Hannah and Matthew were overheard fighting," Carol deduced, "the killer, who was nearby and prepared, gunned Matthew down maybe as he was leaving the apartment, wiped the gun, and hid."

"Waiting for Hannah to find him, and the fact that she picked up the gun was pure luck," I mused.

"Vincent is our killer," Carol said, her tone certain and excited. "We simply need to put that gun in his hands."

"Thanks for the direction," I said. "I think I know how to find out who owned the gun."

"I'm looking forward to hearing who owned it and how the killer got his hands on it," Carol said.

"I'll let you know when I know," I promised. Then said goodbye and ended the call. I went upstairs and washed and changed clothes. I had a little over two hours until I had to be dressed in a clean uniform and demonstrate fudge making. "Come on, Mal, let's go for a walk."

Mal went straight to the back door, her tail wagging. I put on her halter and snapped her leash to it, then grabbed my jacket, and we headed out the door. Mella slipped out with us and curled up on the landing.

We were nearly to the mouth of the alley when we ran into Mr. Beecher. He looked dapper in his slacks, waistcoat, dress shirt and tweed jacket. He tipped his hat. "Good morning, ladies."

Mal raced straight to him and sat pretty. Mr. Beecher always had dog treats in his pockets for his morning and evening walks. Mal thought he was the best person ever to see on a walk. He took out a small dog biscuit and gave it to her, then patted her on the head while she ate.

"Good morning," I said. "We haven't seen much of you lately. Are you doing, okay?"

He smiled at me and straightened. "I'm fine. I've changed my walk times. If I get the morning walk in earlier, then it's cooler and less crowded."

"And I'm usually working until after eight when Frances gets in to mind the guests," I surmised.

"But you're early today," he pointed out. "Did Frances come in early?"

"No," I said. "I was awake, so I got up early and when everything was done, I left the reception desk with the night shift sign thanking the guests for staying and giving step-by-step instructions on check-out. We have some fishermen who stay, and they are all out of their rooms about five a.m. Instead of hiring someone to come in ridiculously early, we decided this was a good solution."

"I thought you were up and working early," he said.

I smiled. "It's hard to be working with hot sugar and be distracted by checking people out."

"Ah," he said. "That makes sense. I hope whatever kept you from sleeping isn't an unsolvable problem."

"Thanks," I said. "Have a great day."

"You, too," he said and headed in the opposite direction.

"Come on, Mal," I said, and we hurried down the road. Rex's house was behind the police department. I knew his twelve-hour shift started at noon today, which meant he should be home. I bit my bottom lip. At least I hoped he was home. I suppose I should have called first.

As soon as we turned down Rex's street, Mal knew where we were going and started running. I let her go and ran with her. That way I didn't think about it too much and chicken out. We arrived on the steps to the front porch of his bungalow, and I stopped to catch my breath. Mal was already at the door scratching it as her way of knocking.

I stepped up and lifted my hand to knock when the door opened. Rex had clearly been working out. He wore long shorts and nothing else. His defined chest glistened with sweat, and he wiped his face with a small white towel.

My mouth went dry, my heart rate sped up, and all I could do was stare. Meanwhile Mal jumped up on his leg, her stump tail wagging hard.

"Well, hello, Mal," he said, and bent down to pick her up and greet her face-to-face, the way she liked. After a moment or two of mutual admiration, he looked at me. "Hello."

"Hi," I said, thankful that he greeted Mal first because it gave me a moment to focus on why I was there. "Sorry to interrupt your workout."

"Come on in," he said and held Mal with one hand and the door with the other.

"Thanks." I entered his house. It smelled of

fresh coffee. "I won't keep you. I wonder if you can help me with a question about the investigation."

He closed the door, looked at me for a moment, then put Mal down and headed toward his galley kitchen. "Sure, like I said, I'll do what I can. Want a coffee?"

"No, thanks." I followed him into the kitchen, where he poured himself a cup of coffee. He drank his black while I like half-and-half in mine. "I was wondering if you knew where the gun came from that killed Matthew."

He faced me, leaning his hips on the counter, and sipped his coffee. "That's a good question. It belonged to Matthew's dad, but his dad reported it stolen last month. It was the strangest case that I've worked on so far this year. Someone got into the house, presumably through the unlocked back door, and the only thing missing was the gun."

"Okay." I blew out my breath and frowned. "How's that connected to Hannah?"

"The prosecution is saying she had access to the gun because she was over at his house with Matthew nearly every week."

"So, what? Are they now saying that she stole the gun and planned the murder? I thought they were saying it was a crime of passion, which would imply it wasn't preplanned."

"Hannah says she picked up the gun in the alley, right?" he asked.

"Right," I replied.

He sipped his coffee and thought for a moment. "I didn't find any evidence that she had the gun previously or that she was the one who took it. I'm thinking the prosecution will simply offer the premeditated story to the jury but won't rely on it for the case. Hannah's lawyer will argue there is no evidence that she stole the gun or stored the gun. Which means they'll gamble that since the prosecution can't prove she stole the gun, and no one witnessed Matthew's murder, that the jury will have to acquit."

"And will they?" I asked. He knew I was asking for his opinion.

"Hard to say." He shrugged. "It depends on who is on the jury and how well the arguments go in court. Without an eyewitness or confession, the jury tends to believe the most convincing argument."

"Do you think Vincent could have stolen the gun?"

He studied me over the top of his mug, then put the coffee down on the countertop and straightened. "You think Trowski is good for this murder?"

"He had a motive," I explained. "He was having an affair with Angel before Angel and Matthew broke up. Matthew's coworkers said his crazy ex-girlfriend, Angel, was trying to get back with Matthew now that he was engaged."

"I see." He crossed his arms over his bare chest.

I went on to explain, "Matthew said no, of course. But Angel talked him into a very public dinner to make her boyfriend jealous and get him to make their relationship permanent."

"I hate that kind of manipulation," Rex said.

"Yeah, me, too," I agreed. "Half the island saw them having dinner and leaving together. Then Angel discovers she is pregnant and now the rumor mill is saying that the baby is Matthew's."

"Yes." He nodded. "It's what the prosecution is using for Hannah's motive."

"But Hannah isn't the only one who would be angry enough to kill," I suggested. "Vincent could have just as easily been angry and killed in the heat of the moment. That's why he was in such a rush that he nearly knocked Jenn down."

"Hmm."

From his reaction I could see he was considering the idea. "His prints weren't on the gun, and he wasn't tested for gunshot residue."

I thought about that and picked Mal up absently. It was something she loved, and I did it now more out of habit than anything. "He wasn't wearing gloves when he ran into us. I would have noticed that. In fact, he only had a hoodie on over a T-shirt and jeans, even though it was chilly out."

"If I were still on the case, we might be able to get a warrant and test the clothes he wore that day," Rex said.

"But wouldn't that be like testing him for gunshot residue now? I mean, who's to say he didn't go to the shooting range that afternoon? Wouldn't it be better to somehow prove he was the one who stole the gun?"

"While this speculation could help Hannah's defense, it won't get her out of jail in time for Jenn's baby," he said.

"Darn," I muttered, then I looked up at him. "What we really need is to find someone who'll post Hannah's bail."

"Good luck with that," he said wryly. "Most of our residents don't have that kind of money, and those who do would most likely side with the DA."

"Right," I said, my thoughts whirling through who I knew. There was the Jessops, but I hadn't talked to any of them in over a year and calling to ask for money was the last thing I wanted to do. Trent had always been on the lookout for people who tried to get close to him simply for his money, and I didn't want that label. Then a thought came to me. "I've got an idea." I turned and Mal and I hurried through his house toward the front door.

"Allie? What are you going to do?" he asked as he quickly followed me and opened the door.

"Sell my soul to the devil," I replied.

Chapter 22

"Have you seen my mother or Brett?" I asked Frances when Mal and I came through the back door of the McMurphy. I took off my dog's leash and halter, and she ran to greet Frances, who was hard at work checking guests out.

"Coffee bar," Frances replied with a tip of her head in that direction. Mal greeted the guests, and I turned to see my mother having coffee and chatting up one of the guests.

"Good morning, Mom," I said, interrupting her as I gave her a peck on the cheek "Do you have a minute to talk?"

"Yes, of course," she said and excused herself from the conversation.

"Do you mind if we talk in my apartment?" I asked.

"No, not at all," she said, and followed me up the stairs. "Why aren't you dressed for your demonstration?"

I blew out my breath. "I was out with Mal. I'm

going to change now, and I thought we could talk while I did that."

"I see," she said as we hit the fourth-floor landing and walked down the hall to my apartment, where I unlocked the door and let us both in.

"You can make coffee if you need more." I pointed toward the kitchen as I hurried to my room. "The pot is all set up. All you have to do is hit the *on* button."

"Thank you, dear," she replied, closing the apartment door and following me. "But I've had quite enough already. Your coffee/breakfast bar is a wonderful addition to the McMurphy."

"Thanks," I replied and pulled off my jeans and top and grabbed black pants and a pink striped polo shirt out of my drawer. "I was wondering if you and Brett are going to be around all day today."

"Oh, yes," she said, and sat on my bed as I dressed. "We're set to leave tomorrow morning. Brett had a last-minute meeting with a bed-and-breakfast owner."

"Great," I said. "I was hoping I could have one more lunch with him."

"Well, I'll text and ask him." She seemed brighter and happier. "I'm glad you changed your mind about making up with him."

"We'll see," was all I replied.

Mom texted while I threw my hair up in a top-knot and put on work shoes and a chef's jacket. "He says he'd love to go to lunch with you and has asked us both to dinner tonight."

"That's nice," I said absently. I couldn't think about dinner right now or even what I was going to do at lunch with Brett. I had to be focused on my demonstration and Jenn. Which reminded me, I needed to text Jenn and see how she was doing. "What time can he meet?"

"He says he can meet you at the Nag's Head for a quick lunch at one." Mom beamed as she studied her phone screen. "I texted back that you would meet him then." She looked up. "I heard you broke up with that police officer."

"His name is Rex."

"That's not important now. I knew if I let you sleep on it, you would see that I am only looking out for your welfare."

"Thanks, Mom." I gave her a peck on the cheek before leaving the bedroom to go down to the fudge shop.

"I'll make us all a dinner reservation at that new Grander Hotel's restaurant," she called after me. "I heard they have the most divine French menu."

I closed the door behind me and hurried down the stairs, leaving Mal with my mom. I was doing the right thing, I told myself. I would make a deal with the devil himself to help Jenn. I just hoped everyone would understand.

After the demonstration, I sold almost half of my fudge inventory, making it a successful morning. A quick glance at my phone told me that Jenn had texted me back.

They are keeping me here, she texted along with a frowny-face emoji. **The midwife said that my contractions are getting closer together and because this is my first baby, she feels safer keeping me here. Can you get Hannah here?**

I texted back. **I'm working on it, promise.** Then I let Frances know I was going out to lunch and asked her to watch Mal for me. She was happy to do so. I debated changing clothes again, but with a second demonstration coming at two it was probably better if I wore my uniform, or most of it. I hung up my chef's jacket, put away my hairnet, slapped on fresh lipstick, grabbed my purse, slung it over my shoulder, and went out the front door.

The Nag's Head was three blocks down and across the street from the McMurphy. I arrived five minutes early and snagged a table, letting them know I was waiting for a friend. I texted Jenn again to see what else I could do for her.

She texted back. **The contractions are 45 minutes apart. I need Hannah.**

I'll know within the next hour if I will be able to get Hannah out of jail, I texted back.

Hurry, was her only reply.

"Oh, hello." I looked up to see Brett grinning at me. He wore aviator sunglasses, a pale blue polo shirt and casual slacks. He looked like something straight out of *GQ*, and it hit me suddenly why we had dated so long. I'd always been attracted to him.

"Hi." I put my phone down. "Thanks for having lunch with me."

He pulled out a wooden chair and sat down across from me at the tiny table. The décor in the Nag's Head was based on old English pubs, but with less of a cool original vibe and more of a touristy knockoff feel.

"Of course," he said with that charming smile. It was a charm trick to get people to relax and agree with him. "I figured you would want to see me again."

I tried not to roll my eyes at his arrogance.

He picked up the menu. "What's good here?" he asked as he perused the listed sandwiches and salads.

"The Reuben is good," I said. "I know you like rye and sauerkraut."

"That sounds perfect." He put down the vinyl-covered menu. "How's your day?"

The waiter came over and I ordered water and a turkey sandwich, then he ordered a Diet Coke and a Reuben.

"My day was busy," I said, and thanked the waiter for the water and Brett's pop. "The preseason is heating up."

"Yes, I've reviewed the numbers, and the tourist trade is improving here year over year. Are you finding that with your hotel?"

"I am," I said. "I was hoping it was due to my marketing and online campaigns along with being on the fudge-baking show."

"Now I'm sorry I missed that." His eyes seemed to twinkle at me. "That was filmed on the island, right?"

"Yes," I said.

"I bet that helped drive more people here, and once they come, they always want to come back. That was a great publicity stunt." Then he toasted me with his glass. "You are good for the island."

"Thanks." I didn't believe a word he said. Years of dating taught me that. The waiter came with our orders.

"This Reuben looks great." He took a bite. "It's

perfect. I always trusted your innate ability to pick out the best food in a place."

"Part self-taught," I said, not touching my sandwich. "Part honed by culinary school." Frankly, I couldn't eat. I had to get to the reason I asked him to lunch. "I've given your proposal a lot of thought."

"And?"

"And I'll do it, I'll champion you through the permitting process, but there is something I need you to do for me."

"What's that, darling?" He waggled his eyebrows as if he thought I was going to beg him to take me back. I tried not to gag.

"I need fifty thousand dollars," I said plainly.

That seemed to catch him unaware. "That's a very specific amount." He leaned closer. "Are you in trouble?"

"It's not for me," I said and meant it. "And I need it in the next hour. Can you do it?"

He sat back and put his sandwich down. "A business deal, then." He picked up his phone and texted someone. "I'll have my lawyer write up an agreement. Once you sign it, you'll have the money put straight into your account. It shouldn't take much more than an hour or two. Will that work?"

"Yes," I said and sat back. "The sooner the better. Thank you."

"No, thank you." He picked his sandwich back up. "For a few minutes there, I thought you were going to ask me for a lifetime commitment. Don't get me wrong, I'm not opposed to that at all. I once asked you to marry me, and I can easily do it again. You'd make a great governor's wife with your connections to both Detroit and Mackinac. Hell, I'd even let you have a couple of kids and send them to the best schools. I'd make sure they started their lives off right. I know that's what your mother wants."

It sounded cold when he said it. It made me look at him again and go over our entire relationship. All he cared about was how I looked on his arm. He probably proposed because he liked the idea of marrying a childhood sweetheart. It would certainly go over well in the polls.

I sighed and glanced at my phone. "Listen, I have to run. I have another fudge demonstration coming up. I'll be at the McMurphy until three. If you can't deliver by then, then I'm sorry, the deal is off."

"Got it." He saluted me as I stood. "Nice doing business with you, Allie."

I turned on my heel and left the restaurant. I needed fresh air, a lot of fresh air. Whatever was my mother thinking when she saw Brett?

Chapter 23

The demonstration went well. I made the crowd chuckle with one of Papa's favorite island stories. Then nearly sold out of fudge. It was closing in on three o'clock, and I'd heard nothing more from Brett. It was almost a relief. I don't know what I was thinking asking for that kind of money anyway. Well, it was simply that I knew a bail bondsman would take 10 percent of the bail in cash and Hannah could be free.

That sum was fifty thousand dollars.

At the bare minimum it would give me more time to put the gun in Vincent's hands. Maybe I could find the gloves and turn them in as evidence. They would surely have gunshot residue on the outside, and Vincent's DNA on the inside. That kind of evidence would change everything.

I finished cleaning up the shop and stepped out to take off my chef's coat and hat. The doorbells jangled as someone came in, and I looked up to see Brett. He grinned like the Cheshire cat and stepped toward me.

"Did you get it?" I asked.

"I've got it," he said. "You sign the agreement and I'll push a button that immediately transfers the amount into your account."

"Great," I said. "Where's the agreement?"

"It's on my phone," he said and brought up a legal document. "You can sign it like you do a credit card at a store."

I glanced at my phone. It was 3:05 p.m. I knew that even if I paid the bail by three thirty it might be an hour or two before Hannah was released. I took his phone and quickly glanced through the agreement. In it, I agreed to champion his new development through the permit process for a single fee of fifty thousand dollars. I knew I had to do it, even if it ruined my reputation and pissed off most of the island residents. I would do whatever I had to in order for Jenn to get what she needed for a safe and happy birth experience.

Without much thought, I scrolled to the bottom of the document and signed it with my finger. I showed it to him, and his grin widened. "Perfect. Now my turn." He pressed a button and my bank app dinged.

I pulled out my phone and saw a deposit of fifty thousand dollars, as promised. "Thank you," I said, and gave him a kiss on the cheek. Then I hurried out the door. I didn't have much time to pay a bail bondsman; luckily, Hannah's attorney, William, had put me in touch with a guy he knew. I'd emailed him and gotten fee details. He would wait for me until four. Then he would simply close his shop for the day.

I practically ran to his place, just a few blocks

east of the police department. The sign over the door said BAIL TODAY FOR A BETTER TOMORROW. I rolled my eyes and went straight in. There was a woman at a desk.

"Hello," I said. "Chet is waiting for me."

"He's in his office." She nodded toward the open door. I hurried inside.

"Chet? I have the fifty thousand dollars for the bond for Hannah Riversbend." I showed him my bank account balance.

He used reading glasses to check the numbers. "Alright then, transfer it to me and I'll get everything over to the courthouse and have them release her tonight."

I quickly transferred the money to the account he gave me. Once his phone dinged telling him of the deposit, he reached out and shook my hand. "Be at the jail at five and I will guarantee you can walk out with her," he said. "Just know that if she doesn't show up for her court dates, then not only will you forfeit all the money, but I will send out skip bonds to track her down and bring her back to jail."

"Deal," I said, and pumped his hand. Then I left, feeling like I finally had something useful to tell Jenn. I arrived at the clinic to find nurses running everywhere. And the sound of the midwife talking Jenn through breathing, along what seemed like a crowd of people breathing with her.

I poked my head in the room just as the contraction wound down. Jenn's room was indeed crowded. Shane was there, of course, but so were both sets of parents and the midwife and two nurses who had just run in. It was chaos.

I decided to not go in and simply text Jenn my news. I stood in the hall and texted her that I had made Hannah's bond, and she was to be let out by five p.m.

She responded with a delighted, **Oh, thank goodness. Only Hannah can handle these parents and give me some room to breathe without breathing in everyone else's air.**

I laughed.

"Allie?" I heard Jenn call from inside the room.

I poked my head in. "Yeah, I'm just outside. There's a lot of action in here and I didn't want to add to that."

"You are a doll," she said. "Could you show my father and my father-in-law where the break room is and help them to get drinks and snacks?"

I knew Jenn well and knew this was a cry for help, I smiled bright. "Certainly. Gentlemen, come with me, please." I herded the two older men out and introduced myself. "I'm Allie McMurphy. Jenn and I met in college, and she works out of my hotel and fudge shop."

"Of course. I'm Bob Christenson," the tall man with Jenn's eyes said as he held out his hand. I gave it a shake. "Jenn has told us all about you."

"Ralph Carpenter," the tall skinny man wearing thick round glasses said. "Shane has told us a lot about you as well. It seems you're a bit of a celebrity in the forensic circles."

I blushed. "I'm a fudge maker and hotel keeper," I explained as we walked to the far end of the hall, and I waved them into the last room on the left.

Bob made a beeline for the refrigerator and opened it to find it stocked with waters of all types, from plain to flavored seltzer. There were protein packs that included cheeses and a boiled egg along with apple slices and crackers. He grabbed one for him and one for his wife.

"I feel guilty eating when Jenn can't," Ralph said.

"Well, she can't in case they have to do an emergency C-section," I explained. Anyway, it's what I assumed. I didn't know anything about having a baby.

"Besides, Ralph, you and Diane needs to keep up your strength," Bob replied, loaded down with drinks and snacks. "Jenn doesn't need us fainting or getting cranky out of solidarity."

I had to hide my chuckle after he said that. Ralph caved and got water and a protein pack for him and his wife. "Maybe you and your wives should go sit in the hall and take a break while you eat," I suggested.

"Great idea," Ralph said.

I watched both men go down the hall and ask their wives to step out of the room, before I texted Jenn. **Mission accomplished. I'm off to get Hannah.**

Thank you, Jenn texted back.

I walked out the door and down the few blocks to wait for Hannah at the police station. When I entered, I waved at the desk officer, Smith. As I went to sit in the reception area, he stood. "Are you waiting for Officer Manning?"

"Oh, no," I said, and shook my head. "I'm here to get Hannah Riversbend when she gets out. Jenn Carpenter needs her."

"Is Jenn in labor?" he asked. "Shane called work and took the day off."

"She is," I said. "But it's going slow. You might want to let everyone know it may be a few days before Shane comes back."

"More like months," Smith said. "The department offers eight weeks of paternity leave."

"Oh, how wonderful," I said and meant it. Paternity leave meant both Jenn and Shane had a few months to bond with the baby. Not all families were that lucky.

Just then Rex walked in, removing his cap as soon as he entered. He saw me sitting and came over. "Hi, Allie, are you looking for me?"

I stood and knew he didn't like any sign of affection while he was in uniform, so I didn't touch him, but I did give him my best smile. "Hi, no, I'm waiting for them to release Hannah so that I can take her to the clinic. Jenn's in labor."

"I heard you posted a bond for her," he said low and gentle. "Where did you get the money?"

"I made a deal with the devil," I replied.

"What does that mean? You didn't say at the house this morning."

"I wasn't sure it would work," I said. "But it did."

"What did?"

"I signed a deal with Brett," I admitted. "He paid me the fifty thousand dollars, and I promised to champion his hotel deal through the permitting process."

Rex looked taken aback. Then he whispered, "Are you sure you want to risk your reputation for money?"

I put my hands on my hips. "I will do whatever it takes to help Jenn, and since the investigation isn't going fast enough, this was the next best thing.

What's a reputation anyway? Some people on the island were just waiting to criticize me."

"You didn't need to give them the fuel to hurt you," he replied gently.

"I did it for Jenn." I raised my chin up. "I'd do it for you. Whatever it takes."

He took a step closer and leaned to whisper in my ear. "You are the best kind of friend, Allie McMurphy, and I'm proud to say I am in love with you." Then he turned on his heel and left, going straight through the door to his desk.

I glanced at my phone. It was nearly five. So, I hurried to the reception desk. "I was told Hannah would be out by now. Do you know where she is in the process?"

"Let me check." Officer Smith picked up the phone. I waited patiently while he spoke to someone in the jail area. Finally, he hung up and turned back to me. "She'll be right out. They're returning her property to her now."

"Thanks." I stepped back to lean against the wall and wait.

Just as Jenn texted **Contractions now 15 minutes apart. Where is Hannah?** Hannah walked out into the reception area.

"Hi, Hannah," I said and moved toward her.

"Allie, hi," Hannah said. "Was it you who posted bail?"

"Yes," I said. "Jenn's in real labor. The contractions are fifteen minutes apart. She needs you desperately. Her and Shane's parents are trying to be helpful but are just in the way."

"Got it," she said, and we walked out the door and hurried toward the clinic. At the door to the clinic, she stopped and gave me a hug. "Thanks for everything you're doing to help me. No one else believes me. I'm grateful to have you."

I hugged her back. "I'm going to keep trying to find the real killer. Just please don't jump bail. I'll lose the money and our bail bondsman will send out a couple of bouncer-looking guys to find you."

"Got it." She opened the door. "I promise to show up to all of my court dates."

"I knew you would," I said. "Just one more thing. Please text me when Jenn starts pushing. I want to be there for her, but I won't add to the crowd of family in her room."

"I will," she promised and then disappeared inside the clinic.

I stood there for a moment and let myself feel a little accomplished for having provided Hannah as I promised. Then I stepped off the small porch and walked back toward the McMurphy.

What I needed now was a moment to regroup and figure out how I was going to connect Vincent with the theft of the gun and Matthew's murder.

Chapter 24

"Did you try talking to Vincent?" Frances asked. She was putting on her coat to go home for the day.

"I did, but he told me he'd already told the cops all he knows, and then he shut the door in my face. Well, he tried that anyway." I leaned on the reception desk.

"Then I would go see his father, Raymond Trowski," she said as she buttoned her coat over her white blouse and flowing mid-calf skirt.

"Do you think he can help?" I asked and straightened away from her desk.

"It couldn't hurt," Frances said. "Raymond is an upstanding guy. I trust he'll do whatever he can to help you. Even if it means discovering the truth about his son."

"Good suggestion, then," I said, and took out my phone to figure out where Raymond Trowski lived.

"Oh, all the rooms are full," she said. "We don't have any checkouts scheduled for tomorrow. And the coffee supply is getting low. It will definitely need to be replenished tomorrow."

"Got it," I said and made a mental note to order coffee once I was home for the night. My mapping app told me that Raymond owned a home near the airport. I went to the back and took Mal's harness off the hook. She came running from the dog bed beside the reception desk at the sound of her harness jingling. "Good girl," I said as I harnessed her and hooked on her leash. I grabbed my jacket. It was cool out now, but the temperature would drop as soon as the sun went down, and I didn't want to be caught without a coat when that happened.

We stepped out into the alley; the McMurphy's back door locked as it shut behind us. Then we headed toward the Trowski house. It was about a quarter of a mile from Vincent's place. Close enough to keep in touch but far enough that unless Vincent was visiting his father, he would not know I was talking to him.

It was just after six when I knocked on Raymond Trowski's door. Mal sat beside me, curious why we were at a stranger's house. When I knocked a second time, the door opened to a man who looked remarkably like Papa Liam. They were the same height and build, but this man was bald and wore a goatee. He also had brown eyes while Papa Liam's eyes were blue.

"Hello? Who do we have here?" he asked as Mal jumped on his leg to beg to be picked up.

"Hi, sorry, she likes to be face-to-face with people," I said and grabbed Mal and held her like a small child so that she could be face-to-face as we talked. "This is Mal and I'm Allie McMurphy. Do you mind if I come in?"

"Hello, Allie," he said and opened his door. "Your reputation precedes you."

His words were an arrow to my heart. Very soon my reputation wouldn't be worth anything on the island. I swallowed hard. He closed the door behind us when I was hit with a wave of warm air.

"Cold out there," he commented. "Come in, come in. Can I get you a cup of tea or anything else to drink?"

"No, thanks," I said and sat. "Please sit, I have some questions that I think you may be able to help with."

"Well, then"—he sat down in the recliner across from me—"by all means, ask your questions."

"Your son, Vincent, he was running from the alley right before Jenn and I entered it and discovered Matthew's body."

"Yeah, he told me," he said.

"What did he tell you?"

"He told me that he was at his girlfriend, Angel's, apartment at the mouth of the alley. He lost track of time and had to run to get to work on time."

"Okay," I said. "That's what he told the police. Did he say if either he or Angel heard the shot?"

"As far as I know, they didn't hear anything," he said.

"Okay, I'm doing everything I can to help a friend. Would you say that Vincent is the same way?"

"That boy would do anything for the people he loves," Raymond said.

"Even lie about the sound of gunshots?" I pressed.

"I suppose if he needed to for some reason," he said.

I decided to pull back a bit and take another tack before he suspected I was trying to blame his son. "Did Vincent know Matthew well?"

"They were friends," he said. "Vincent and Matthew went to school together and often picked up summer work in the same places."

"When you say they were friendly, did he ever visit with Matthew's parents?"

"Oh, sure, he liked them since he met them. He would come home and tell me that they would have various things that needed doing around their house. But they were in poor health, and Vincent didn't know how to do anything to help. I suggested he offer to do things around the Joneses' house for a slight fee. They called me, of course, and I told them it was my idea to offer to have Vincent work for them, but that it was Vincent's idea to help them."

"So, they hired him? A kid the same age as their son?" I asked. I must have sounded upset because Mal started licking my face, concerned about me.

"Matthew wanted to do it for free, but they wouldn't hear of it so they hired him," Raymond said. "Vincent shared his knowledge with Matthew and the two boys took care of things. Thank goodness I taught my son to do things around the house to prevent issues or to fix things that were broken. He and Matthew even checked out books from the library to figure out how to fix things. You see, I hadn't had time to show them."

He sounded so proud. It warmed my heart. "Does he still go over there and help sometimes?" I asked.

"No." He shook his head. "Not after he and Matthew had a falling-out about Angel."

"When I talked to Vincent, he swore to me that Angel had told him she dumped Matthew way before they started seeing each other. He was shocked to hear Angel had dinner with Matthew and they went back to his apartment because Hannah was away." I tilted my head and watched his face. "But Hannah had another story. She said that it was Angel who asked Matthew out and he discussed it with her. They both decided what was the harm of having dinner in a public place with an old friend. At the end Matthew hugged her and they went their separate ways."

Raymond shook his head. "Vincent didn't even know about the dinner until Angel told him that she was pregnant and it might be Matthew's. Well, Vincent exploded with anger and asked her how, and Angel told him about the dinner that night. When Vincent checked, people told him that they did see Matthew and Angel having dinner in front of everyone that night as if it were nothing. That's when things got ugly, and I don't blame my son."

I nodded my understanding. It was easy to see how Angel had played the two men. I stood. "The thing is, Raymond, no cameras caught Matthew and Angel together after they hugged that night. Including the next-door neighbors, who have a camera on their door that can see not only their porch, but Matthew's and the Kozickis' next door. Angel lied to Vincent, hoping he would get jealous, and Vincent didn't disappoint her."

"Why?" Raymand asked. "Vincent was in love with her."

"Some women crave drama." I shrugged. "Or

maybe she wanted Vincent to marry her and give her the little house in the UP they'd been talking about for years. This would give him the incentive to act quickly to get her away from the same alley that Matthew lived on." I moved to the door, "Thank you for clarifying what Vincent went through. I'm pretty certain the baby is Vincent's, and at the very least I know it's not Matthew's." I put my hand on the doorknob, stopped, and turned. "Can I ask you one more thing?"

He looked stunned and upset. "Whatever." He waved his hand as if it were a white flag.

"Does Vincent still have a key to the Joneses' house?"

He looked up at me suspiciously. "Why?"

"Someone stole Mr. Jones's handgun a few weeks back."

This time he stood, his face red with anger, and strode toward me. The door was open so others could see. I raised my eyebrows and lifted my chin, letting my posture dare him to touch me.

He stopped a few feet away and said through his teeth, "You better not be blaming that on my son!"

"I'm not," I said casually and honestly. "I simply wondered if he still had a key. And if so, did he lose it? Or did he give it back to the Joneses? For all I know, they lost it."

That seemed to calm him a bit as he practically pushed me out by putting his hand on the top of the open door. "He hasn't been over there in years. For all I know, he gave it to Matthew."

"Thank you," I said. "For everything. I didn't mean to be intrusive."

"But you were," he said, and slammed the door in my face.

Well, that had gone better than I thought. No wonder the men had a falling out. Vincent's girl said his baby might be someone else's. There was only one disappointment– I still had no idea who had the key.

I put Mal down and we headed toward home. It was indeed dark now and chillier. Mal seemed to know we were going home and pulled me along, retracing our steps. For a moment I thought I heard someone running behind us. I turned to look, but no one was there, and Mal was fully focused on going home. I shrugged and kept up with her.

I had to hope that no one had followed me from Raymond's house. We got safely to the apartment, and Mella waited by the door for us. We went inside and I fed and watered my pets. Then I heard my phone ding. I grabbed it because I was worried that it would be from Hannah or Jenn. It wasn't. It was my mother.

Chapter 25

I'm coming up, she texted.

I sighed and there was a knock on the door. My mom had a key, but she didn't use it tonight. I opened the door and let her in. "Hi, Mom," I said and gave her a quick kiss.

"Well, dear, you are still in your work clothes. For goodness' sake, get dressed. We're supposed to meet Brett for dinner."

"I thought because he and I went to lunch together, and then I saw him again around three, that I didn't need to attend dinner."

Mom took my hand and patted it. "Honey, you certainly don't know the tiniest bit about social cues, do you? I definitely should have put you in etiquette classes. As the governor's wife, you'll need to get better at understanding the subtlety of the social set."

"I love you too," I said, and let her lead me to my bedroom. I stripped while she picked out my outfit. By this time, I had given up. They were leaving in the morning. It didn't matter if I had dinner with them. I might as well acknowledge the devil I worked for.

"There, dear, don't you look tempting." Mom clapped her hands as I stood in front of the mirror. Somehow, she had found an old bodycon cocktail dress I had purchased for a friend's wedding and stuck in the back of my closet. It was a spring turquoise blue and made my wavy hair and hazel eyes pop. She had insisted I do my hair and wear my only pair of heels, which were beige with two-inch heels. The woman even brought her makeup kit and now I looked nothing like myself.

But I met Mom's approval.

"I thought we were only going to the Nag's Head," I said. "I'm way overdressed for that."

"Oh no, dear, remember he made reservations at the Grander Hotel." She grabbed my clutch purse and put her arm through mine. "Let's go, we're already fashionably late."

Ugh. I felt like a teenager whose mom insisted I be a debutant. Somehow, I had barely squeaked by having to do that when I turned sixteen. With my dad's help, I was on a "school field trip" the week of the deb ball and couldn't go.

We walked down the stairs to the third-floor guest hall and took the elevator down to the lobby. There was no way I could manage these heels down any more stairs.

"I have a horse-drawn taxi waiting to take us," she said. "I didn't want to take the chance of you getting disheveled before we got there. You know how quickly you can undo your hair and makeup."

"Gee, Mom, you think of everything," I said sarcastically.

"Of course, dear." She patted my hand and waved

to the taxi driver, who got out and opened the door for us. He wore a black suit and tie, and white gloves. He opened the carriage door and helped us into the carriage before climbing up in the driver's seat and getting the horses started.

"Wow, I've never seen a taxi driver dressed up," I said.

"It's a special white-glove service that's starting up to take people to important dinners, parties, and weddings," Mom said proudly. "It's a wonderful idea, if you ask me."

"Hmm," I said, wondering whose idea it was and who sponsored the permits from the council. As a soon-to-be advocate for permits, it might not hurt to understand this program and how the new Grander Hotel got through the zoning and permit process and how to schmooze the city council. Not that a taxi service needed anything but permits. The Grander was probably the best thing to study.

"You are quiet, dear," Mom said.

"It's a quick ride," I pointed out as we stopped in front of the hotel. The driver got down and opened the carriage door for us, then helped us down. "Thank you."

"I imagine we'll be done in two-to-three hours," Mother told him as she slipped him a tip.

"You can simply tap the app on your phone when you are ready to leave and I'll be waiting outside," he said, then bowed to us and climbed back up into the cab.

"How nice," Mom said.

I shivered. The air was quite brisk coming off the lake. Mom had thought of everything but coats. "I'm freezing. Can we go inside?"

"Certainly." She took my arm, and we hurried up the walk onto the porch, where a valet opened the door for us and ushered us in. Mom explained to the hostess who we were supposed to meet.

"Ah, yes," she said. "He's already seated. Please, follow me." It was Emily Hoyt. I knew her from my time with Trent. She was a beautiful woman with long brown hair and alabaster skin. Having the height and slender build of a model, she dressed in a black wrap dress.

We followed behind her and I was glad she was so pretty. It took away from the eyes that surely stared at me. It made me uncomfortable, and I pulled at the hem of my dress as we walked.

"Allie?" It was Harry. He stood at the sight of me. Harry was such a good-looking man. He looked like he should play Thor in a movie.

"Hi, Harry." I stopped as he gave me a hug and brushed a kiss on my cheek. Then he held me at arm's length.

"You look . . ."

"Weird," I offered and tried not to pull the bodice of the dress up and the hem down. I heard my mother in my head, saying, "Don't fidget. Let a man admire you."

"I was going to say, stunning," he replied and winked at me. Then he turned to my mother. "And who is this lovely friend?"

"Oh, Harry, this is my mom," I said. "Mom, this is my dear friend Harry Winston. He just bought a bed-and-breakfast on the island and is doing very well with it."

"Mrs. McMurphy, it's a pleasure to meet you." He held out his hand.

I'd never seen my mother blush before. But blush she did, and even stammered a little as she took his hand.

"How very nice to meet you," she stammered, and I swear she almost curtsied. It was funny, really. Suddenly I had a glimpse into where I might have gotten my awkwardness. It's just that my mother had so much control over herself. I've never suspected it might be because her mother had been constantly harping about propriety and self-control.

The insight made me feel bad for her, and more compassionate.

"Allie, you didn't mention how handsome Harry is," Mom scolded me.

"She also didn't mention how young and beautiful her mother is," Harry said, causing my mom's blush to deepen.

We must have stopped for too long. I realized that Emily had gone back to her station and Brett was approaching us.

"Ladies," he said, interrupting. "Winston." He gave Harry a strong handshake and patted him on the back like they were old friends.

"Oh, dear." Mother giggled. "How rude we are, keeping Harry from his dinner, and Brett waiting. Please forgive us."

Harry chuckled. "Forgive me, ladies, I believe I encouraged it. I'll let you get back to your dinner date." He kissed me again on the cheek. "Let's talk soon."

"Sure," I said. Then saw that Brett had taken my mother's arm and started walking to the table. I followed behind, tugging at the hem of the dress.

He pulled out a chair next to his for my mom,

then helped push it back in. A waiter rushed up and pulled out my chair.

"Thanks," I said, and sat as the waiter pushed my chair toward the table.

"Of course," the waiter said. He took my napkin and placed it in my lap, then did the same for my mom. The napkins were black. My mother had once told me that black napkins were a sign of respect. It seemed white napkins tended to leave white lint on customers' clothes while black showed less.

"You look wonderful tonight, Mrs. M," Brett said.

"Thank you, dear," my mom said.

Brett turned his gaze on me, his eyes twinkling. "Allie, you look . . . good."

"Thanks," I replied, and picked up my menu to cover my chest from his gaze. We both knew our current relationship was far from romantic, after I asked for money. Only my mom thought otherwise. Which made the dress, hair, and makeup rather awkward. "Mom liked this look."

My mom twittered at my comment. "Oh, dear, don't let her kid you," my mother assured him. "Allie loves a chance to dress up."

"Well, it's a huge improvement over lunch," he said as he perused his menu.

I felt a blush rushing up my cheeks and I struggled not to defend my work uniform at lunch. I had to remember that I didn't care what he thought. He would be gone tomorrow, plus ours was now a working relationship. I put down my menu, grabbed my water glass, and gulped down water until I no longer felt the need to comment. I was sure if I had, Mom would have been very upset.

She put down her menu. "Brett, dear, I trust you to pick out something yummy for all of us."

I opened my mouth to protest when she sent me a withering look. I grabbed my water glass and took a couple more swigs.

"Wonderful," Brett said.

The waiter must have been watching because the moment Brett's menu touched the table, he was right there. "Ready to order?"

"Yes," Brett said. Then he went on to order a five-course meal that included a bottle of wine for every course. It was highly extravagant, and I opened my mouth to protest, when my mom sent me a warning look.

"Very good, sir," the waiter said. Then with a snap of his fingers a busboy came over, placed appropriate wineglasses in front of us, then refilled my water.

The sommelier arrived soon after, opened the white wine, poured a bit into Brett's glass, and waited patiently while Brett swirled it, sniffed it, and took a sip.

"Perfect," he said. The Somm nodded poured wine into mom's and my glasses. Then put the wine bottle in a chill container and stepped away. Brett raised his glass in a toast. "To seeing old friends."

My mother raised her glass and so did I. "Here, here," she said, and we all touched glasses before taking a sip. The dinner seemed to go on and on as Mom prattled and Brett soaked up the attention. Every now and then she would kick me under the table and glare because I wasn't fawning over Brett, too.

Luckily, after the third course, my cell phone rang. Mother sent me a glare. But I didn't care. "Excuse me," I said, and got up to answer my phone as I walked to the lobby. "Hi, Hannah," I said as I walked out.

"It's time for you to come to the clinic," Hannah said. "Jenn's calling for you."

Chapter 26

French Silk Fudge

Ingredients:
⅔ cup evaporated milk
3 cups sugar
¾ cup butter
7 oz marshmallow crème
2 teaspoons vanilla
6 oz. milk chocolate chips
6 oz. semisweet chocolate chips

Directions:
Line an 8 x 8-inch pan with parchment paper. In a large saucepan combine milk, sugar, and butter. Bring to a rolling boil, stirring constantly until candy thermometer reaches 234 degrees F. Remove from heat and add marshmallow crème, vanilla, and chocolate chips. Stir until well combined. Pour into

pan and refrigerate until cool and set. Cut into squares. Makes 20–24. Enjoy!

"I'll be right there," I said, hit end, and walked back to the table to grab my clutch. "I'm sorry, but that was Jenn's doula. She's close to giving birth to her first child and is calling for me. Thank you for the dinner, Brett."

Brett stood. "Should I call you a taxi?"

"Thank you, but I'm fine with the walk," I said. "If I don't see you in the morning, have a safe trip back."

"Certainly," he said. "I'll be calling you soon."

I brushed a kiss on my mother's cheek, well aware of the simmering astonishment and anger beneath her perfectly set expression.

Then I hurried out of the hotel as if the hounds of hell were nipping at my feet. Despite the high heels, I ran all the way to the clinic and arrived in ten minutes. A quick glance at myself in the window reflection and I sighed. My hair was windblown and looked like I never brushed it. My lipstick was nearly gone, making my eye makeup look oddly out of place, as if I only did half my face. Also, my face was very red from the wind, and the run.

It didn't matter. I was here for Jenn. I tugged my bodice up and my hem down and opened the clinic door, then scurried to Jenn's room. The parents sat out in the hall on chairs that hadn't been there before.

"Good luck getting in," Bob said. "The darn

doula kicked us out. She said the room was too small for us all."

"Got it," I said. "I'll just step in to let Jenn know I'm here." I pushed the door open, stepped in and let it close behind me. Hannah looked up as she, Sarah, and Shane all helped Jenn breathe through a contraction.

"Come in." Hannah waved me over as the contraction wore down. Jenn looked exhausted.

"Jenn, I'm here," I said.

She patted the side of the bed opposite of Shane. "Please come and hold my hand."

I walked over, but before I could take her hand, Hannah had a blue gown for me to put on over my clothes. I slipped my arms in and took Jenn's hand while Hannah tied up the gown in the back.

"She wouldn't push unless you were here," Sarah said. "Okay, Jenn, Allie's here now. With your next contraction, I want you to push."

Jenn squeezed my hand. As the machine showed the contraction beginning, she bore down, pushing as best she could.

"You're doing great," Sarah said. "The baby is crowning."

Within twenty minutes it was all over. "You have a beautiful, healthy baby boy." Sarah placed the baby on Jenn's chest.

Jenn let go of my hand and stared at her son in wonder. Shane looked relieved and happy, while Sarah worked with the final contractions to ensure everything was good with Jenn.

"He's beautiful, simply beautiful." Even I had tears in my eyes. "Do you know what his name is?"

Jenn looked at Shane, whose eyes shone with pride. "We're naming him Benjamin Andrew Carpenter," Shane replied.

"After my grandfather, Ben, and Shane's grandfather, Andrew" Jenn said.

"All good family names," Ralph said as Hannah ushered the parents in for their first look at the baby after Sarah finished her ministrations.

I got up and stepped away as the grandparents huddled around the bed, vying for the best view of the baby.

"He has a head full of hair," Diane exclaimed.

"He should enjoy it while he has it," Robert said, running a hand over his bald spot and looking at Ralph's bald spot.

"Not fair," Diane said. "Shane hasn't lost his hair yet. And my father hasn't lost his."

"Hopefully it runs through the mother's side, like they claim," Ralph said as he stroked the baby's head.

I went to Hannah. "Thanks for letting me be here," I said low so as not to interrupt the family. "Please let Jenn know I'll come visit her tomorrow."

"You're welcome," Hannah whispered back. "But I was simply doing my job. She should be checking out of the clinic tomorrow afternoon. Sarah likes to keep an eye on the mother and baby for the first twenty-four hours. Then I'll help them get home and stay with them for a few weeks to advise and guide them on feeding, changing, and bonding."

I nodded and gracefully left the room. In the hall I tugged the tie loose on the back of my paper gown and pulled it off, folding it carefully, and took it to the nurse's station.

"All done?" Esha asked.

"It went very well," I replied, "and Jenn has a beautiful, healthy baby boy."

"Thanks for letting me know. I know it's a bit crowded in there, but I'll sneak in and take the baby, clean him up, and do the second Apgar test on him and a few other newborn things. Then I'll call the doc to come do a quick check on them both."

"I'll be back tomorrow." I headed for the door and ran into Rex. Seriously ran right into him. He steadied me with his hands on my arms.

"You look amazing," he said with a surprised tone.

"Are you surprised because I got dressed up or because I never wear makeup?" I asked, taken aback by his reaction. I mean, come on, I'd just run nearly a mile and helped Jenn. I never expected him to be surprised by how I looked. Or was he kidding? It didn't look like he was kidding.

"Oh, sweetheart, I didn't expect you to be dressed up at the clinic, that's all," he said.

"Oh," I said. He was commenting on my dress. I tugged on the hem. "My mom dressed me, and I feel weird in this dress. I'd forgotten it was in the back of my closet. I'm a tad bit self-conscious." I tugged on the bodice.

"How's Jenn?" he asked, taking the spotlight off of me.

"She's great, she and Shane had a beautiful baby boy, Benjamin, but go on in and see for yourself."

"I will," he said, but didn't move. "It's really cold out here, and dark. Let me walk you home first."

"No, I'm fine," I said, not wanting him to fuss. "You go on in."

"At the very least take my jacket," he said as he peeled off his police jacket and put it around my bare shoulders. I had to admit it felt warm.

"Thanks," I said and stuffed my arms into the sleeves, then zipped it up. The coat was much bigger than I, and I was happy it covered my hands.

"Please text me when you get home so that I know you are safe," he said.

"Okay," I agreed and headed down the sidewalk. My feet were killing me. I wasn't used to the heels and after running in them, my feet were swollen, and the blisters had formed and broken. I hadn't even noticed when I was with Jenn. It wasn't until I started walking home that I realized just how badly my feet were hurt.

But I kept walking like nothing was wrong until I turned out of sight of the clinic. Then I stopped and took my shoes off and carried them. The sidewalk was cold and not exactly free from the occasional piece of gravel. I limped along, kind of mad at myself for having to take a long time to get home. I decided to go in through the front door since the alley was made up of mostly gravel. I used my master key card to unlock the front door and pulled the door closed behind me. Michelle Kwan, my part-time night clerk, greeted me as I stopped to text Rex that I was home safe.

"Hi, Allie," she said.

"Hi, how's the night going?" I asked as I texted Rex, hit send, and limped across the lobby to the reception desk. Michelle worked from five until ten on my busy days: Friday, Saturday, and Sunday. She was a senior in high school and liked the work because she could study. The doors locked up at nine and only people with keys could get in.

The reception desk was open until ten for any guests that arrived after Frances left for the day. I let her work until ten to answer any guests' questions. "The night has been quiet," she said. "Your mom came in about a half hour ago. She said she left a message on your phone but if I see you, I'm supposed to tell you to stop by her room when you get back."

"Thanks." I went to my apartment first to wash my face, brush out my hair, then change into lounge-wear and fluffy slippers. After all, who wants to hurry to what would surely be a scolding from their mother after a long, hard day?

Chapter 27

"Oh, good, you're back," Mom said and opened her door. "Come in, come in."

I brought Mal with me as, hopefully, a distraction, and maybe mom would soften her scolding if she had a dog on her lap. Mal ran right into Mom's room and jumped up on the bed. I sat on the edge of the bed and ran my hand over Mal's soft curly hair. "What time are you leaving in the morning?" I asked, then added, "I want to get a kiss and hug goodbye."

"Of course, dear," she said and sat down on the nearby overstuffed chair. "Brett wants to leave by eight and has already ordered a taxi for me."

"That white-glove taxi was amazing," I said. "What a wonderful thing to start here."

"Yes, and don't think I didn't hear Brett when he said he would call soon," Mom said. She scooched up on the edge of her chair. "But, honey, I did a little background check on your handsome Harry Winston. Do you know he has millions?"

I tilted my head, trying to figure out what angle she was taking now. "Yeah," I said and nodded. "I know. I think he made a lot of money investing in tech companies that took off. Unicorn status, I think he said."

Mom leaned forward and put her hand on my knee. "Honey, he's the handsomest man I've ever met, and polite and kind."

"Yes," I repeated. "He's a really nice person and a great friend."

"Darling." Mom was using her excited voice. In fact, she was so excited her hand trembled. "Forget about Brett. You need to marry Harry. I saw the way he looked at you. Don't let this opportunity slip through your fingers."

I couldn't help it. I laughed. "Mom, what is it with you? Why are you concerned about my love life?"

"Honey"—Mom sat back—"we've had this conversation. I thought you understood. All I want for you, and more importantly my grandchildren, is to have a better life than I did. Now, don't get me wrong, I love your father. I know we've had a difficult time of things lately, but I do love him. While he's a wonderful and well-respected architect, he doesn't make nearly the money my parents did. Why, I have to budget everything just to keep us in a good lifestyle. I don't want that for you."

"I love you," was my only reply. I knew from my friends at school and at college that I had a privileged childhood. I had had to really study in my accounting classes to understand budgets because my parents had paid for everything, including my car, my college, my room and board, and my culinary supplies, which were quite expensive. I had even inherited the McMurphy with no financial outlay.

"I'm glad you understand," Mom said. "Now, how is Jenn? I assume she's alright since you're home relatively early."

I glanced at my phone; it was nearly eleven, well past my bedtime. "Yes, she's doing great. I got to be there when she gave birth to a beautiful baby boy. They named him Benjamin."

"Oh, that's nice. Benjamin is a good strong name."

"Yes, it is," I said, then yawned. Mal looked up at me. "I'm sorry, Mom, but it's past my bedtime and I have to make fudge in the morning."

Mom stood. "You work way too hard, dear. Do you ever take a day off?"

"No." I shook my head. "I'm trying to boost the fudge shop's reputation."

"What's it been? Two years now? And you only took off once to come see your dad and me at the Christmas holidays. We missed you this year."

I gave her a quick hug and a kiss. "I was lucky enough to have a lot of last-minute orders to send out."

"Well, I think you should think about taking at least one, if not two days off a week. Frances only works five days."

"She's not the owner," I replied.

"It's not good for you to live your whole life for this old place. Please consider what I've said. You don't want to get burned out."

I opened her door and Mal ran out. "I will, Mom. Good night."

"Good night, dear," she said. "Don't forget to give that nice Harry a call."

I saluted her and went back to my apartment. Mal was already at the door waiting for me. "Well," I said to Mal as I unlocked and opened my door, "I guess now Harry is a front-runner for my future spouse." I laughed and shook my head. Locking my door behind me, I put my key in the container on a little table next to the door. I glanced at Rex's jacket that hung on a hook above the keys. Then I leaned in and took a deep sniff. It had a slight scent of Rex's aftershave and my heart squeezed.

I loved the guy. I mean, really loved the guy. Yet, I'd asked him to take a break in our relationship. All because he was one too many people trying to tell me how to live my life. The worst part was, he was simply worried about my safety.

Sighing, I let go of the coat and turned off the lights on the way to bed. When I got to the room, both Mella and Mal had curled up on the bed. Mom was right. What I really needed was a day off. In order to do that I needed to hire more than an assistant. I needed to hire a second fudge maker and give up my control of Papa Liam's stories.

Sighing, I took off my fuzzy slippers, rubbed my swollen and blistered feet, then climbed into bed. Maybe in the morning, after a night's rest and Mom and Brett were gone, I could have time to ponder how to hire a second fudge maker and what to do about Hannah's arrest. But mostly, I could try to understand how I was going to maintain my reputation, while promoting Brett's awful resort idea.

The next morning, after finishing the fudge making around seven and stocking the breakfast and coffee bar, I said goodbye to my mother and helped her take her suitcases out to the taxi. While the ferry docks were a mere block or two from the McMurphy, the airport was another story.

I waved goodbye and went inside to text Jenn. **How are you?** I texted. **How's Benjamin and Shane?**

Shane stayed the night at the clinic with me, and we took turns caring for Benji, Jenn texted back. **I'm afraid we only got two hours of sleep at a time. Hannah warned us it would be this way for a while and to nap whenever the baby napped.**

Sounds like good advice, I texted back.

Frances came in to start her shift, followed by a young woman who proudly showed off a small belly bump with a cropped top that said BABY ON BOARD, with an arrow pointing down.

"Allie McMurphy," she said in an angry tone. "I have something to say to you!"

"Um, how can I help you?" I asked. She already wore a complete face of makeup that included contouring, large false eyelashes, micro-bladed eyebrows, and red lips.

"You went to my soon-to-be father-in-law and were asking questions about my Vincent. I'm here to tell you that you should mind your own beeswax!"

"Uh, Angel Monroe?" I asked.

"Yes, and I'm going to give you a piece of my mind!"

"Why don't you come up to my office," I said and started up the stairs. She berated me the entire way up. I opened my office and waved her in. Mostly I listened and replied in the appropriate pauses with "I see," a lot. I wasn't surprised at her anger. It was rare for me to get people riled up. But then I knew it was a hazard of sleuthing. "Please have a seat. Can I get you some water? A flavored seltzer or a caffeine-free pop?"

She seemed to have calmed down a bit after her long rant. "I could use a seltzer water. What flavors do you have?"

I opened my office mini fridge and rattled off a bunch of different flavors.

"The raspberry lemonade will do."

I grabbed a can for her and a can for me. "Would you like a glass and some ice?"

"Just a glass," she replied. "Sipping from a can causes mouth wrinkles."

Well, that was a new one. I got us both glasses and opened her can and pushed it and the glass toward her. Then I opened mine and began to pour. "I'm sure you've heard that I'm looking into everyone who was in that alley that day," I said gently. "I truly believe Hannah didn't do it. When I found out the murder weapon was a handgun stolen from Matthew's father's house two weeks before, I simply wanted to figure out who might have been in the alley who had previous access to the Jones home."

"I can't believe you were trying to make my

Vincent out to be a killer. He would never!" She sipped her water, eyes narrowed. I could tell she was getting worked up again, I did my best to keep my demeanor and my voice calm.

"Can you think of anyone at all who might have access to the Jones home? I'm told the thief didn't have to break in and took only the gun."

"Most of the town could have done that. I mean, I've been there multiple times with Vincent, and even my mom was there in the last month. The Joneses, being housebound, love to entertain. I bet half the island has been through that house for one reason or another in the last month."

"Huh." I leaned my elbows on my desk and rested on my folded hands. "I hadn't heard any of that," I said. "Thanks for letting me know. I understand you were close to Matthew."

"Yeah." She took another gulp and put her glass down. "We dated a few years," she said proudly. "He wanted to marry me."

"What happened there? If you don't mind sharing," I qualified.

I figured that most people like to talk about themselves, and Angel seemed no different.

"Well, I liked Matthew and all, but after a year, it got kind of boring. I mean, he was always working, and when he wasn't we went to bars or for hikes. After a while all that gets old, you know? I mean, Mackinac is a pretty small island." She sat back and took another swig. "Then I met Vincent. He was hot and interesting. Boring is the last thing I thought about when I thought about Vincent. It's been a couple of years now, and I'm still not bored, and I'm having his baby." She hugged her barely-there bump. "We're getting married in a couple of months. That's why you have to believe me when I say my Vincent had nothing to do with what happened to Matthew. Besides, he was with me. We were having breakfast and kissing and such when he realized it had gotten late. He had to rush out to try to clock in to work on time."

"And neither of you heard the gunshot?" I pressed.

"No." She shook her head and her mouth turned down in a frown. "Strange, isn't it?"

"The killer must have used something to silence the gun," I said. "Only Hannah heard the shot, and she said it was just enough to make her look out her window."

"That girl did it, plain and simple," Angel said. "I don't know what Matthew saw in her."

"I heard that you and Vincent were having a hard time, and you asked Matthew to take you to dinner so that you could make Vincent jealous. Is that true?"

She laughed. "I don't know where you got that idea. It's the other way around. Matthew wanted to get back with me. I went to dinner to turn him down, gently of course."

"I see." I watched her gaze, which shifted left a few times, then right. It was as if she couldn't look at me straight on when she lied. Everyone had a tell. This must be hers.

"When I explained to Vincent what happened," she said, "—I had to because you know how people talk—Vincent was upset. We went together to confront Matthew."

"Vincent wasn't upset enough to harm Matthew?" I pressed.

"Oh, no," she assured me. "Vincent told Matthew to never darken my door again. Matthew got it and never even said hello to me again." She looked proud of that.

"When was that?" I asked, this being the first time I had that tidbit of information.

"A few weeks before the murder." She sipped more water. I studied her in silence, and she put down her glass. "But Vincent didn't kill Matthew. I know this because not only was he with me, but he himself told me that he understood my kindness in having dinner with Matthew. Vincent told me he trusts me completely. I'm glad he understood."

"I see," I said. "Thanks for being honest with me." I stood when I noticed her glass was nearly empty, then walked to the office door. "Is there anything else you want to tell me?"

She stood, leaving her glass and the can behind. "I'm glad you got the real story," she said and walked toward me. When we got nose to nose, she leaned it, her eyes flashing. "You stay away from my Vincent. He's innocent."

I raised both hands. "I will."

"You better." She walked down the stairs with her nose in the air. I waited for her to be out of sight, then I recycled both cans, and took the glasses to my apartment where I could wash them out later.

My mind whirled. Was Angel telling me the truth? Or did she come here to insert her story into my investigation? Maybe Carol and her book club could discover more. For me, I planned to take her threat seriously. I didn't want to be the next murder victim.

That left only one other person near that alley that day. Monica Grazer. Angel just said she had access to the Joneses' home. Could she have stolen the gun and then coldheartedly killed Matthew? If so, what was her motive?

Chapter 28

After I gave my ten o'clock demonstration, I sat down next to Frances. "I blistered my feet pretty badly yesterday."

"How'd you do that?" Frances asked.

"Mom dressed me for dinner with Brett." I frowned and rubbed my now bandaged feet. "She made me wear my one pair of heels, which was fine because she had ordered us a taxi."

"But?"

I sighed. "But then Hannah called, telling me to come quickly to the clinic. I ran all the way from the Grander Hotel. I didn't even realize how bad my feet were until I walked home."

"Why didn't you get a taxi to the clinic?" Frances frowned at me.

"That would have been the smart thing, wouldn't it?" I asked. "I never even thought of that."

"Poor dear." She patted me on the shoulder. "Why don't you go upstairs and soak your feet. It will help. Douglas and I will look after the place."

I sent her a wry smile. "Mom says I need to take at least a day a week off."

"She's not wrong," Frances said. "Douglas and I have been worried that you might start to burn out."

"The idea of burnout never occurred to me until Mom said the same thing last night." I sighed. "Days off means either less business or I have to get a part-time fudge maker. Someone who will be faithful with Papa's recipes."

"I'm sure you can find someone from the school you went to in Chicago who is looking for experience and willing to work part-time. Maybe three days a week. One day together and two on their own."

"Hmmm," I said. "I'll definitely consider that while I'm soaking my feet. Come on, Mal." I called my dog, and she ran up the stairs ahead of me. "Call me if you need me, Frances."

"I'm sure we'll be just fine for a few hours."

"Thanks." I hobbled up the four flights of stairs to my apartment. Mal ran straight in to look for Mella. Once she found her and bothered her a bit, she went to the water bowl and drank it dry.

I carefully walked over and filled her bowl with fresh water, then put on the tea kettle. As it started steaming and before a full boil, I poured myself a hot footbath and added essential oils and Epsom salts. I figured it might hurt, but it was good for the swollen areas. I carried the bucket to the couch area and sat down with a towel to catch any spillover and slowly put my feet in. It stung hard, but then it felt much better. I sat back against the couch and closed my eyes.

I went over what Angel had told me this morning. I had to wonder if it was the truth and I should be looking at Monica instead of Vincent. She made a compelling argument why it couldn't have been Vincent. But it was also harder to believe that a nice woman like Monica could shoot a man in cold blood. She didn't even look winded when we ran into her walking down the sidewalk.

Also, there wasn't any blood on her clothing. She barely looked wrinkled. Plus, what would be her motive to steal a gun and kill Matthew?

Maybe that was another good question for Carol and the crew. They knew her better than I did.

Chapter 29

"Jenn and her baby went home," Judy Walton, the traveling nurse on duty, said when I stopped in the clinic. Judy allowed Esha a day or two off every week.

"Thanks," I replied and turned around, pushing the clinic door back open and stepping into the sunshine. Next was to text Jenn. I figured she was too busy with the baby to even think to text me that she was home. **Hey, Jenn**, I texted. **How are you doing? Let me know if and when you want me to stop by.** I figured she was probably exhausted and trying to settle into her home again.

When I walked toward the coffee shop, I saw Carol and her group at their usual table by the window When I walked in, Carol greeted me and waved me over to the table. "We heard about baby Benjamin," she said. "How wonderful for Jenn and Shane. We're going to send some food over. They may be too busy to eat healthy."

"That's a great idea," I said. "I know they will appreciate it."

"How's the investigation going?" Carol asked.

"Pull up a seat and join us," Irma said, pointing to an empty chair nearby.

"Ladies," Betty said. "Let the girl get her coffee first."

"Good idea." I took my place in line while the ladies made room for me at the table. I got a skinny latte and went back and sat down in the empty chair they had pulled over.

"So?" Carol asked.

"I had a visit from a very angry Angel Monroe this morning," I started.

"Oh, no," Betty said.

"Why was she angry?" Irma asked.

I gave them a wry smile. "Because I went to see Mr. Trowski, Vincent's dad," I replied.

"Did you?" Irma said. "That was brave and forthright."

"Thanks," I said. "I asked him about Vincent and Matthew's relationship. I figured they had one since they both went to school on the island."

"And?" Carol asked.

I took a sip of my warm latte. "And it turns out the boys were best friends for a long while. The Jones family hired Vincent when he was in high school to help them with handiwork around the house. Matthew wanted to learn about the work Vincent did, and the two boys became inseparable. Matthew doing most of the work while Vincent trained him, and whatever they both didn't know they went to the library to check out books that showed them what to do."

"Oh yes, I remember seeing them always running around together," Betty said.

"What happened to that?" Irma asked.

"It was that girl," Carol said. "That Angel was always trouble. I never saw what Matthew saw in her. But she wasn't faithful and started to have an affair with Vincent while dating Matthew."

"Huh," Betty said. "Is that the girl that had dinner with Matthew recently and then turned up pregnant?"

"The very one," Irma said. "Those two were still fighting over her?"

"No," I said. "Matthew was devoted to Hannah. According to Matthew's coworkers, Angel kept coming by Matthew's work and bugging him. She told him that she wanted to show Vincent she was still able to see other people. She begged and begged Matthew to take her to dinner. To stop the harassment, with Hannah's full knowledge, Matthew took Angel out to dinner as a last friendly gesture."

"Then the girl came up pregnant the next month," Carol said. "She wanted everyone, especially Vincent, to think it was Matthew's baby. Vincent would beat Matthew up and then ask her to marry him. What a nasty trick."

"Why would she want Vincent to beat Matthew up?" I asked confused. "Didn't they break up two years ago?"

"Because Matthew had the nerve to find another woman and ask her to marry him," Betty said. "In all the time they dated, Matthew never even considered marriage with her, and they went out longer."

"Revenge is best served cold," Irene said, her chin high.

"Are we certain Angel didn't kill him?" Carol asked.

"Hmm," Irma said. "Her apartment does open up to the mouth of that alley. She could have shot Matthew, tossed the gun next to him, and gotten back into her apartment before Hannah came out."

"Right," I agreed. "And Vincent was also with Angel. They are each other's alibi and there's no way to prove otherwise. But here's a clue I'm trying to figure out. It turns out the gun that shot and killed Matthew was Mr. Jones's handgun that had been stolen the week before."

"Huh," Carol said." I wondered where the gun came from."

"It's why I went to Mr. Trowski in the first place," I told the other ladies. "I wondered if Vincent had been in the Joneses' home in the last two weeks. You see, there was no sign of a break-in, which means the thief was someone who'd been invited into the home."

"And you were trying to place Vincent at the Joneses' home, where he could have taken the gun," Irma said.

"Exactly," I said, and tapped my fingers against my chin as I remembered what exactly Mr. Trowski had said.

"And was he?" Betty asked.

"According to Mr. Trowski, Vincent did have a key to the Joneses' house because he did so much handiwork for them until the falling-out. But he also said he didn't believe his son would steal a gun or murder anyone."

"Vincent had an opportunity to steal the gun," Carol said. "And everyone knows he's angry at Matthew for having dinner with his girlfriend."

"Now fiancée," I said. "But when Angel came storming in to give me what for, I offered her a drink and just listened. When someone is that angry, they tend to spill information they otherwise wouldn't."

"Maybe you were getting too close to the truth," Carol surmised.

"I do find it interesting that Vincent had access to the gun, and it went missing, suggesting the murder was premeditated." I took a sip of my coffee.

"What information did you learn from Angel's rant?" Irma asked.

"She said that the Joneses held a lot of parties, and anyone could have stolen the gun, even someone like her mother, or her." I took another sip and watched Carol and Irma digest that information.

"We have more suspects," Irma said.

"And no way to tie them to anything," I said softly.

"We have to find out who stole that gun," Carol said.

"According to Rex, there were no fingerprints taken at the scene of the theft, and their investigation turned cold."

"I do remember the Joneses holding a big Welcome Spring party a few weeks back," Carol said.

"Yes," Irma agreed. "It was a very chilly backyard barbecue put on by the church at the Jones home and all the locals were invited. I was there, and so were Carol, Betty, Irma, and most everyone from the senior center. The kids came and went once the food was served."

"They built a big bonfire," Betty said dreamily. "And had those heat lamps scattered around. There wasn't any snow, but it was still chilly."

"Huh," I said. "Welcome Spring, was that on the spring equinox?"

"Oh, yes," Carol said. "March twenty-first or twenty-second. Allie, I don't remember seeing you there."

"I had quarterly taxes to take care of," I said. "I was either making fudge for my online orders, or up in my office doing paperwork. But I do remember Frances and Douglas left early that day to attend."

"If that's the party Angel is referencing," Carol said,

"Which means, the gun mostly likely wasn't stolen then, or Matthew's dad would have discovered it missing sooner. I know he was religious about locking up his handgun," Irma said. "And he usually kept it in a gun safe when they had company over, for the safety of the children."

"Why didn't he leave it in the gun safe all the time?" I asked.

"Oh, the days he felt well enough to go out, he loved it when his buddies took him to the shooting range in Mackinaw City, and he always told us seniors that he kept it in a drawer in case anyone were to break in," Carol said.

"I remember that," Irma said. "Especially since that first murder."

"Most all of the seniors have some sort of protection now. Especially since my abduction," Carol said. "And the break-in and beating of my neighbor last fall."

"Wait." I sat up straight. "All of you have guns?"

"I didn't say we all had guns," Carol said. "Most of the men do have hunting rifles that they keep close by, only one or two have handguns."

"We can't all afford a fancy security system like Carol," Irma informed me.

"Oh, I understand." I had resorted to all kinds of security measures, including new key cards whose codes could be changed often and cameras on every stairwell and in the elevator. I rarely looked at the recordings, but that didn't mean I don't keep them.

"Which brings us back to our three suspects," Carol said.

"I want to know how well you know Monica," I said. "Do you think she's capable of stealing a gun for Angel or Vincent?"

"Monica Grazer?" Betty asked. "I highly doubt it. She's always welcoming, and even volunteers at the senior center in her free time."

"Yes," Irma agreed. "But I've also heard she spoils Angel, since she is Monica's only child. In fact, she gave up a very high-powered job to come to the island because Angel loved it."

"She might have stolen the gun," Carol said. "But of the three suspects, I think she's the least likely. How would she have access to the gun to steal it? I don't remember her coming to the party."

"Yeah," Irma agreed. "I don't even think she

knows the Joneses, only Matthew because he dated Angel."

"Which leaves two," I said.

Carol looked at Irma. "We'll take over looking into Angel, if you want to continue looking into Vincent."

"Deal," I said.

Chapter 30

I got a text from Jenn shortly after my two o'clock demonstration. **I'm tired, but happier than I imagined. Benjamin is a perfect baby.**

That text warmed my heart. **Then I doubt you are up for visitors.**

All the parents are still here and will remain until Sunday, she texted and sent a frowny-face emoji. **Hannah is helping us wrangle them and helping me with breastfeeding tips. It's harder than I imagined.**

Hugs! I texted back. **Let me know when you need a friend, and I'll be there as soon as I can.**

Thanks. How is the investigation going?

I've got a couple of interesting clues that we're working on, I replied, my thumbs flying quickly over the phone's keyboard.

You are the best, she texted back. **Please keep me up-to-date.**

Will do. Get some rest.

I went upstairs to shower and change into jeans and a T-shirt. It was time for me to ask the Joneses about Vincent.

* * *

Twenty minutes later, Mal and I arrived at the Joneses' house, and I knocked.

"Hello?" Mrs. Jones said as she opened the door.

"Hi," I said. "I'm—"

"Allie McMurphy," Mrs. Jones said. "I'm Roxanne, do come in." She opened the door wider and waved me in with her forearm crutch

I stepped inside and kicked my shoes off, placing them carefully by the door. When I straightened, I discovered that Mal had jumped up on the arm of a nearby overstuffed chair and Mrs. Jones petted her warmly.

"Your puppy is wonderful," Roxanne said. "I had a bichon a few years ago. She was my favorite dog ever. After she died of old age, I couldn't bring myself to get another dog, and my husband wanted to be able to travel before we got too old."

"Mal is my first dog," I said, and scratched under Mal's chin. "My mother didn't want animals in her house, and I couldn't bring myself to keep a dog outside."

"That's something we both have in common." She waved toward the living room. "Please have a seat."

She followed me in and signaled for Mal to get down. My pup gathered up her leash and jumped up in my lap, where she did one circle and settled in.

"Can I take your jacket?" Roxanne asked.

"Oh, no," I said. "I don't want to be any trouble. I have a few questions to ask you and your husband about Matthew and his friends."

"Larry will be happy to help." Roxanne looked excited by the prospect. "I'll go get him. Can we get you something to drink?"

"Oh, no, don't make a fuss over me."

"Are you worried about these?" she lifted one crutch off the ground. "Don't worry, Larry will bring in the beverages."

"Whatever you have would be nice, thank you."

"Of course." She hurried off toward the kitchen in the back of the house.

I looked around at the pleasant living room. It was decorated minimally for a small Victorian home. The wall colors were cream, and the floors were covered in plush wall-to-wall carpeting.

Finally, she came back. Larry trailed behind carrying a tray with iced teas, a plate of homemade cookies, and a dog treat. I stood. "That looks great!" Then as she placed the tray on the coffee table, I put out my hand to shake. "Hi, I'm Allie."

"Hi, Allie." The tall man with hair the same dark brown as Matthew's, only with gray at the temples, shook my hand. "Don."

"Please sit, everyone," Roxanne said. And, having spotted the dog treat, Mal moved to beside her chair and sat. She lifted her paw for a shake. "Oh, my goodness, aren't you the prettiest thing!" Roxanne picked up the dog treat and gave it to Mal, who ate it quickly and then jumped up in her lap, her stump tail wagging.

Don chuckled at his wife's delight. "Looks like we might need to get another dog."

"I know some people who would love to dog sit when you have an appointment or want a quick vacation," I said, falling short of actually volunteering. Oh, I wanted to volunteer, but with the fudge shop it was probably not a good idea.

"Don?" Roxanne looked at him as she hugged Mal.

"We'll talk later," he said.

"I heard that Mackinac County has a lot of wonderful dogs at the animal shelter," I suggested. "You may be able to adopt an already house-trained puppy."

"An already potty-trained dog would be less work," he said. Then he turned to me. "I understand you have questions. Why? Didn't they get Matthew's killer?"

"I suspect the DA was too fast to charge," I explained. "I don't think a proper investigation was done."

"I see," Don said and glanced at Roxanne. "We never believed Hannah did it. She's really in love with Matthew and she has a big heart. I mean she's a doula, which doesn't pay much but helps new mothers."

"That was one of my questions." I leaned forward, putting my elbows on my knees, resting my chin on my hands. "Usually the family is certain they know who did it and why."

"Oh, we have a suspect in mind," Roxanne said as she continued to pet Mal.

"Really? Who and why?" I asked.

"We suspect that horrible Angel," Roxanne declared. "I never liked her. She was sneaky and all about herself. Just awful, and I don't usually feel that way about the girls Matthew dates."

"We were happy when he finally saw her true colors and broke up with her," Don said. He coughed a deep ugly sound that rattled his chest.

"Are you okay?" I asked, looking at him with concern as he continued coughing.

"It's okay, dear," Roxanne said and patted my knee. "It's COPD. He has an inhaler nearby." She shrugged. Some days are better than others." She motioned at her husband to take a dose from his inhaler. "Today is a good day."

"I breathed a sigh of relief," Roxanne continued. "I know he was devastated, but then after a year he met Hannah, and when he brought her home, I knew she was the right one."

"My wife has a strong intuition when it comes to people," Don gave her a smile filled with pride.

"And you suspect Angel," I said. "Do you know what the murder weapon was?"

Don sighed and ran a hand over his face. Then glanced at me with a tortured gaze. "We do, and I wish I had never bought that gun."

"Or at least kept it in his gun safe," Roxanne said and hugged Mal until she squeaked.

"You put in a police report that it was stolen?" I asked.

"Yes, the minute I realized it was gone," Don said.

"But no one broke in," I stated.

"That's right," Don said. "There was no evidence of a break-in." He coughed again. This time it didn't last as long.

"Do you keep your doors unlocked?" I asked and raised my hand in a stop sign. "I'm not blaming you at all. I'm trying to figure out who might have stolen it and how the killer got it."

Roxanne sighed. "I don't remember. I know we've been locking our door more since that first murder."

"But sometimes when we're home, we forget," Don said. "The police think it was someone who just walked in, knew where we kept the gun, took it and walked out."

"Who would know when your door was unlocked and where the gun was kept?" I asked. "I
understand you keep it in a gun safe when you
have a party."

"We've been racking our brains ever since it was
taken," Don said.

"Angel came to me this morning and said that
anyone could have taken it because you have parties all the time and just let people in," I said.

"I told you that Angel was no good!" Roxanne
looked at Don while she said that. "Can you imagine? Saying it's our fault the gun was stolen."

Don shook his head. "Our last party was on the
spring equinox," he said. "I know the gun was still
here afterward because I left it in the gun safe
until the Sunday it was taken. I took it out then because I had a friend ask me to go to the gun range
with him. I went, and when I got home, I cleaned
the gun and put it in the drawer with a half-
opened box of ammo. My friend and I had been
talking about going back the next day. I would
never leave a loaded gun lying around."

Roxanne looked from him to me. "Don told me
when he left it, so that it wouldn't surprise me
when I dusted and cleaned. I saw it there that
Monday when I dusted, and Tuesday when I needed
a pen for a crossword; you see, our pens are kept
in the same drawer."

"It was here on Tuesday but gone by Thursday?"

"Yes." Don sighed. "I went to get it and put it
back in the gun safe. It was gone along with some
of the ammo. The box was still there, but a handful of bullets were missing. When I asked Roxanne, and then Matthew, if they took the gun, they

both said no. I called the police immediately to alert them that it was gone."

"Okay," I said. "I had a chance to see the police report. It says you thought maybe someone wanted it to get rid of the squirrels in their yard?"

"It was a lame idea I had," Don said. His cough came back again, shorter still. "There isn't a lot of poaching on the island, and I figured whoever took it was just borrowing it."

"But you reported it?"

"Yes," he said. "In case the thief had nefarious ideas for the gun."

"There have been so many school shootings that we became concerned," Roxanne said. "There hasn't been any trouble on the island, but you can't assume anything these days."

"Ah." I picked up my tea glass and took a sip. "This is great! It has lemon?"

"Yes." She smiled. "I cut up a lemon and steep the tea with the lemon, then strain it and cool it."

"I never would have thought of that," I said.

"My mother used to make it that way and I loved it, so I make it that way." She put Mal down. "You should try a cookie, they're my favorite."

"Roxanne is amazing in the kitchen." Don patted his wife's knee. "She's even considered selling her baked goods online."

I picked up a cookie and took a bite. It had a beautiful delicate crumb and flavors of almond and honey. "Amazing," I said. "This is better than some of the cookies from the chefs who graduated from the Culinary Institute where I got one of my degrees."

Roxanne blushed. "Now that is high praise. Thank you!"

I tilted my head and an idea popped into my tired brain. "Do you ever make candy?"

"Oh, her candy is even better than her baked goods," Don said.

"Really?" I looked at her. "I'm looking for a fudge maker who can allow me to have two days off a week and help out a couple of hours a third day."

"Oh, doing demonstrations like you do?" Roxanne said. "I'm fifty, are you sure you want to train me?"

"You aren't going to leave Mackinac Island anytime soon, right?" I asked.

"No, Don wants to retire here," she said. "We will be traveling a bit, though."

"How often?"

"A week every other month," he said. "I get unlimited paid time off at work."

"He works remotely," she said with a smile. "He's a VP of operations for a startup. Everyone there works remotely."

"That would be fine with me," I said. "Talk it over and come visit me in a few days to give it a trial run."

Roxanne blushed. "Oh, that would be exciting!"

"I'm excited, too." I picked up Mal. "But before I go, do you think Angel stole your gun?"

"I never saw her near the house," Don said. "But that doesn't mean she didn't pay someone to steal it for her."

"Vincent still has an old key to your home," I said. "His father told me. Has Vincent been around lately?"

Don sat back, surprised by this news. "I thought he'd given that back."

"He could have had it copied first," Roxanne said. "You could ask Zak at the hardware store."

"Did you see Vincent that week?" I asked.

"Come to think of it, he was in the neighborhood that week," Don said. "He does some handiwork for the Samsons across the street. They had had a water leak."

"And why do you suspect Angel and not Vincent?" I asked.

"That girl is trouble," Roxanne said. "The Vincent we know wouldn't steal or kill."

"That's what his dad said," I stated.

"But if Vincent has a key to our home," Don stated, "that means Angel does, too. He might have texted her that I was out washing my car, and then she could have gone in through the back gate, let herself in, taken the gun and ammo and left, locking the door behind her."

"How would she know where the gun was?" I asked, leaning forward.

"Her uncle Ted Monroe is the guy who I went shooting with," Don said. "I might have told him where I keep the gun when it's not in the gun safe."

Chapter 31

Easy Cappuccino Fudge

Love the taste of coffee? This fudge is right for you.

Ingredients:
  2 tablespoons dark brewed coffee or
    espresso, cooled
  4 tablespoons butter, divided into two
    2-tablespoon portions
  2 cups dark chocolate chips
  1 16 oz. can of dark chocolate frosting
  2 cups white chocolate chips
  1 16 oz. can of vanilla frosting

Directions:
  Line an 8 x 8 inch pan with parchment paper. In a microwave-safe bowl, place chocolate chips and 2 tablespoons of butter. Microwave in 30-second intervals, stirring between,

until melted. Microwave the chocolate frosting until melted. Pour melted frosting into melted chocolate chips and stir until creamy. Pour into pan and set aside. Microwave vanilla frosting until melted. Pour in the coffee and stir until well combined. In a microwave-safe bowl, melt white chocolate chips and remaining butter in 30 second intervals, stirring in between until melted and smooth. Stir the coffee mixture into the melted white chocolate chip mixture and stir until smooth and creamy. Slowly pour over the top of the chocolate fudge. Let set until firm. Cut into squares. Store in an airtight container. Enjoy!

Armed with this interesting news, what I needed was to put Angel in the Joneses' neighborhood the day the gun was stolen. For that I needed to know more about Angel, but Carol and the crew were investigating her. Not that they were any better at sleuthing; whenever Carol looked into a murder there was always a bit of mischief involved.

I took Mal home and fed her and Mella. It was nearly seven p.m. I grabbed a microwave steamer meal and got on my computer to research how much I should pay a part-time fudge maker. Me, I worked for maybe fifty cents an hour, but it added to the value of the McMurphy, and the profits were better every year, just like Brett suggested. Soon I would have the second mortgage paid off and could save for more repairs and updates to the old girl.

That's when I got a call from Brett. I debated not answering, but in the end, I had to come face-to-face with the fact that I had signed a contract. I hoped I could solve this mystery and get the bond money back minus the bondman's fee, which was 20 percent of the bond. Thankfully, he felt sorry for me and agreed he would only ask 20 percent of the $50,000 I gave him if I could solve the mystery before the trial.

Twenty percent would be ten thousand dollars—the amount I would have to come up with if I wanted to buy back my contract. But all the recent updates to the McMurphy meant I needed a seventy-thousand-dollar mortgage. I hoped that as soon as I solved the case, I could go see the banker and convince him to add the ten grand onto my current mortgage, which was now down to fifteen thousand.

My phone continued to ring, until I finally hit the green button. "Hello, Brett."

"Ah, Allie." His phone voice sounded dark and rich, just as I remembered it. Funny thing about it though, it didn't make me shiver with delight like it did all those years ago. "I was afraid you would be in bed already. I'm glad you're not."

I glanced at the clock; it was after eight. "I'm usually heading that way about now. But I had to catch up on some work this evening."

"Great, I'll make myself a note to always call you before eight. How's that?" he asked.

"That would be ideal," I replied. "How can I help you?"

"I said I would call, and I did," he said. "I'll be emailing you the slide deck that explains in detail what we're proposing, along with the estimated number of jobs it would add and the estimated increase in tourists coming to the island."

"Okay," I said. "But the locals call the guests 'fudgies' because Mackinac is the fudge capital of the world."

"Got it," he said, and I could hear him taking notes. "I'll add that to the deck. I'd like you to take a close look at the deck, maybe run it by a friend or two and then tell me what works and what doesn't."

I had to bite the inside of my lip to prevent myself from saying the whole idea wasn't going to work. But I had signed a contract. "Okay."

"We're looking at presenting next week. We'll close on the three properties we chose, one week after the presentation. It's of the utmost importance that you rush this successfully through the permitting process."

"I'll do my best," I said with my fingers crossed.

"Good," he said. "I've talked to my business partners, and they have agreed to give you a second fifty thousand dollars as an extra incentive to be successful. But you'll not get a bonus if the deal doesn't pass zoning and permits."

"Alright," I said, knowing I would never see that bonus.

"Good." He sounded pleased with himself it made me slightly nauseous. "Well, I won't keep you. Look for that email tomorrow."

"Good night." I ended the call and stared at my phone for a minute. The idea of the bonus was tempting. There was a lot I could do with an extra fifty thousand dollars, including paying off the mortgage and giving Frances and Douglas a raise. But I knew the only thing that would happen when I presented the proposal to the committee was my reputation would be in shreds. I would be seen as an outsider for the rest of my life for presenting plans for a resort that flew in the face of everything Mackinac Island stood for.

Even the new Grander Hotel had to meet the historical committee's demands. There was no way any of the committee members would agree to a modern "smart" hotel.

Then I got a text. It was Harry. **Hi beautiful. Still up? How are you doing?**

I texted back. **Okay, I guess**, along with a shrugging emoji. **How are you?**

Great now that I'm talking to you. It was nice to meet your mother.

My mother is a handful, I wrote and added a horror emoji face.

He sent back a laughing face. **She seems nice, but I did just meet her. Tell me about your friend Brett. I saw you with him twice now.**

It's a long story, I texted. **I didn't see you at the Grander Hotel.**

He went silent for a moment, then my phone rang. It was Harry. "Hi."

"Hi," I said, and sat back on my couch with Mal in my lap and Mella beside me.

"I eat there because I know the chef and I hate to cook." His voice was filled with warmth. "Tell me the long story."

I sighed. "You really don't want to hear it."

"Yes," he insisted. "Yes, I do. That's what friends are for."

I was tired and really needed to talk to someone, but Jenn was busy, and I didn't deserve to cry on Rex's shoulder. I must have been tired, because I told him everything, including my deal with

Brett. "I'm really not looking for a solution. I signed that contract of my own free will. Thanks for listening."

"I see." His voice was gentle. "You're a good friend, Allie."

"Thanks." Even I could hear the wry humor in my voice. "I'm sorry, I got carried away. It's late and I need to let you go."

"Never apologize for needing to talk about what's going on in your life," he said. "That's what friends are for. Good night, Allie."

"Good night, Harry, and thanks." We ended the call, and I leaned back against my couch and closed my eyes. Not only was I tired, but I was also embarrassed, having shared so much with Harry. I guess I missed Jenn.

I got up, turned off the living room lights, and took my pets to bed. Putting on my comfiest pajamas, I tried not to dwell on everything. I really needed to rest.

It was important to be well rested when investigating or I'd misread a clue.

Chapter 32

Good morning, Rex texted around seven thirty the next morning. **How are you doing? How's the investigation going?**

I sat in Frances's chair behind the reception desk and studied his text.

"Good morning, Allie," Mr. and Mrs. Hargrove said as they came down to get coffee and sample the continental breakfast, I had put out at six.

"Good morning," I replied with a smile. "How did you sleep?"

"We slept very well," Mrs. Hargrove replied. "Your mattresses are the best for my old bones."

"Thanks," I said. "We try to replace them often to keep them from wearing down."

"Great idea," Mr. Hargrove said and then guided his wife to the coffee and pastry bar.

I looked back at Rex's message. Then typed, **Good morning, I'm doing okay. The investigation is moving very slow. I think I've narrowed it down to two, Vincent and Angel. I know Vincent has motive,**

but I haven't figured out yet what Angel's motive could be.

There were three dots on my phone, meaning Rex was typing something. It seemed to take forever before his reply came through. **Angel could have been upset with Matthew for not helping her with more than the one dinner.**

That sounded plausible, and very strong. **She does appear to be all about Angel, doesn't she? But why not go after Hannah instead of Matthew?** I replied, my thumbs flying across the phone keyboard.

Think about it. The killer got two birds with one stone, as they say. Matthew is dead and Hannah is going to trial. What better revenge is there?

Hmm. **Angel and Vincent were both at Angel's apartment just a half a block away that morning. Both of them had motive and means. I need to figure out the *how* and actually tie them to the murder. Right now, all I'm doing is speculating.**

What do you consider the means? he texted back.

They both had an opportunity to steal the gun, I texted. **Vincent has a key to the Joneses' house, because he used to do handiwork for them.**

Another three dots and then a long pause. I greeted more of the guests and got up to refill the pastries. I figured he was doing something else, while my thoughts went round and round on how to put the gun in Angel's hands.

"Good morning," Frances said as she got to her desk, unbuttoned her coat, and hung it up in the small hall under the staircase. She pulled her hand-knitted sweater down. Frances loved long flowy skirts, and today she wore one with spring flowers on it. "I see you were up early again."

"Couldn't sleep," I replied. "But I might have a candidate for our part-time fudge maker."

"Really? Who?" she asked as she took her seat and turned on her computer.

"Roxanne Jones," I said. "I went to visit the Joneses yesterday, and she made the most amazing tea and cookies. I asked her if she made candy and her husband, Don, said she was good at that, too."

"Hmm, I know Roxanne and she does have the touch in the kitchen, plus she loves Mackinac, lives here year-round, and is very reliable." Frances looked at me. "You'd have to teach her your recipes and how to give a proper demonstration."

"I'd have to do that with anyone we hired," I said. "I asked her to talk it over with Don and let me know."

"Wait—they do travel kind of often," Frances said.

"Yes, they told me," I said. "But I can work around it. I think you and my mother are right. I need some days off to sustain my health."

"Will you still be working on the days I have off?" Frances asked. "Because that would mean you aren't really having a day off."

"Oh no," I reassured her. "I won't work, I promise. She will work while you and Douglas are here to keep an eye on things. I'll work the weekends. It's our busiest time."

"Good plan." She greeted Mal with a dog biscuit and scritches on her head. Mal took the treat to her dog bed beside the desk.

"I'll be upstairs," I said. "I'm still looking at what

wage she should have and how that's going to fit in
my budget." I didn't tell her that I was also trying
to figure out who killed Matthew, and how adding
ten thousand dollars to the mortgage would mess
with my budget. "Call me if you need me."

"I will," she said.

I hurried up the stairs and unlocked my office.
Mal didn't follow me. She loved to keep an eye on
the guests with food, and even though there were
signs posted to not feed her, there were always a
few guests who "accidently" dropped some for her.

Once upstairs, I called Carol.

"Hi, Allie," she said. "We have an update."

"Great," I said. "I hope it's something solid.
Right now, we only have assumptions."

"We learned that Angel has picked up some
extra work for a company that offers maid ser-
vices." She sounded delighted by this.

"Okay," I said, wondering what this meant.

"Angel was cleaning two houses in the Joneses'
neighborhood the week the gun went missing."
Carol sounded satisfied. "Vincent was also in the
neighborhood doing some handiwork that week
as well. There are receipts for payment from the
homeowners. That means—"

"We can put both Vincent and Angel there," I
said. "Great, it means one or the other or both
could be the thief. Wait, I just had an idea."

"What?"

"Whoever the killer is did it in one shot, right?"

"Right," Carol said, confusion in her voice.
"And?"

"And that means that the killer is a good shot."

"Okay," Carol said. I could tell she was trying to
follow my line of thought.

"Which means they had to practice," I stated.

"Oh!" Carol finally caught on. "Whoever it was had to be a regular at the gun range."

"Yes!" I said. "And because only a portion of the ammo was taken, the killer was confident they could get it done in three shots or less."

"Oh, I get it. Any more than two shots, they risked being seen. Barry knows Tony, who owns the gun range," Carol said. "Do you want me to have Barry talk to him? Maybe call you?"

"I was thinking of calling this morning, but getting an introduction is better. My guess is that he wouldn't talk to some random stranger without at least an introduction," I said.

"I'll get Barry on it this morning," Carol said. "And call you back."

"Thanks," I said, ending the call. I sat back and thought about what I would ask the gun range owner. Then it hit me that there was another way to find out who could fire a good shot.

I turned on my computer and went straight to my search engine. I did a public search on Angel and Vincent. Unfortunately, there wasn't even a hint of them being connected to guns. Even a search of the county and state records on gun registrations came up blank. Could you rent a gun at the range? I had no idea.

Maybe I needed to widen my search. Assuming Matthew was killed by any local on the island, who was in the news as a good shot?

I called Liz. She co-owned the island's newspaper with her grandfather, Angus.

"Allie!" she answered with such enthusiasm I felt a bit guilty for not speaking to her more often. "How are you?"

"I'm good. Jenn had her baby a couple of days ago," I said.

"Yeah, the clinic notified me, and I did a nice write-up for the society page," she said. "I also heard you were seen being squired about town by a handsome man from the Detroit area."

I rolled my eyes. "Oh, please, Brett wanted me to help him with a business deal," I said. "There is no romance there."

Liz laughed. "I never said there was romance involved. But now that you protested . . ."

I felt a blush cover my cheeks. "Ugh, my mother thought I should get back together with Brett."

"Ooh, *back* together?"

I sighed. "Brett was my high school and college sweetheart."

"Why did you break up?" she asked.

"This is off the record," I said.

"Of course."

"Brett has planned his whole life around becoming the governor of Michigan and maybe even running for a national position," I said. "He asked me to marry him right before I graduated. Keep in mind he always knew I wanted to take over the family business, and that I studied hospitality and went to culinary school. He said that he would hire a manager to run the McMurphy if I was set on it. Set on it, really? He wanted to marry his high school sweetheart. It looks great on his political bio. Then he wanted to use my degrees as a way to wine and dine his constituents. As if I could ever make an always-put-together politician's wife who held fantastic dinner parties."

"Oh, no," she said. "He really thought you would?"

"My mother thought it was the perfect future for me. Even after I said no and broke up with him five years ago."

"Mothers can be stubborn," Liz said. "My own mom didn't want me to help my grandfather with the paper, but it's the perfect job for me."

"Yeah, well, guess who bumped into Brett and convinced him to bring her with him when he came to the Island to do business?"

"Ahhh," she said. "Try, try again. That's why you were at the Grander Hotel dressed to the nines."

"She dressed me: hair, makeup, and heels. Then she offered to put me through etiquette school to give me the polish I would need."

"Ouch," Liz said. "I can't believe you went."

"I kept putting her off all week. I had to indulge her on her last night. Luckily, Brett and I had lunch that day and came to an understanding. All he really wanted was for me to help him with a business deal. The outfit was my mother's last-ditch effort to bring us together. Enough about me, what's going on with you?"

"I'm the same," she said. "Reporting on the Matthew Jones murder trial."

"That won't start for a few weeks, right?"

"Yep," Liz agreed. "But I wanted to do a thorough background check on both him and Hannah."

"Can I ask you a question?"

"Sure," Liz agreed.

"Did Hannah have any marksmanship awards? Has she gone hunting regularly?"

"As far as I know, no," Liz said. "Where are you going with this?"

"I was thinking that whoever killed Matthew did it with one shot, which makes it likely they knew what they were doing and were good at it."

Liz thought about that for a minute. "You don't think it was possible that Hannah got lucky or shot him in close contact?"

"He was shot in the back of the head," I said. "I don't know if it was close range or not, but I think the shooter still had to be a good shot. The human head isn't that big a target. Also, if someone was right behind him, why didn't he turn around, and how did they leave the alley fast?"

"Huh," she said.

"I thought you might have more information about who on the island might have won an award or shooting contest or who gets the big deer during deer season."

"Maybe a hunting guide?" she suggested.

"Oh, I hadn't thought about that," I said, trying to wrap my thoughts around someone I hadn't even considered being involved.

"You're really looking for is a suspect who's a good shot," she surmised. "Does the theory fit?"

"That's what I am trying to find out," I said. "But so far, I haven't been able to prove it. Which means I'm going down the wrong path, and it could be anyone on the island who's a good shot."

"That's about eighty percent of the local residents, since hunting is popular. Okay, look," Liz said. "Give me some names and I'll check the paper's history."

I winced. "If I give you that information and I'm wrong, then it will make you look bad. What I'd like is to go through the newspapers myself."

"Oh, okay, I can respect that," Liz said. "All the old papers are on the library computer, if you want to do this by yourself."

"Thanks," I said. "I do want to do this myself. It's not that I don't trust you. I need to be open to being wrong. We already have one person railroaded for this murder. I don't want another."

Chapter 33

Coconut Fudge

Great for Easter time or any time.

Ingredients:
14 oz. sweetened condensed milk
1 cup shredded coconut divided into
    ½ cup portions
1 tablespoon butter

Directions:
    Toast ½ cup of coconut by spreading onto a microwave-safe plate and microwaving in 30-second increments, stirring after each until coconut reaches the level of toastiness you love. Cool completely.

    In a medium saucepan, combine sweetened condensed milk, ½ cup of coconut, and butter. Bring to boil, stirring constantly. Boil for about 15 minutes. Don't stop stirring or the fudge will stick to the bottom. You can test for doneness by tilting the pan. When the mixture pulls away from the bottom of the pan, it's done. It should look shiny and firm. Pour fudge into a buttered cookie sheet. Let it cool to room temperature. Then refrigerate until completely cool. With buttered hands scoop a small amount and roll into a 1-inch ball and place on waxed paper. You should have about twenty. Roll in toasted coconut or fine sugar and place in small paper baking cups. Refrigerate until completely cool, around 1 hour. Enjoy!

"Find anything?" Frances asked me as I came back for my two o'clock demonstration.

"Not anything concrete. Please thank Douglas for his suggestions at the library," I said and pulled out my little notebook. "I've made quite a few notes. Sadly, it could be anyone of one hundred residents."

"By the way, you have a visitor." She pointed to a man in a flannel shirt, jeans, and work boots.

"Who is it?"

Frances shrugged. "Go ask him."

I stuffed my notebook in my jacket pocket and walked over to where he sat, sipping coffee and scrolling on his phone. "Hello, I'm Allie McMurphy. I understand you wanted to see me?"

"Ah, yes, Brett said you were good-looking." He stood and held out his hand. "Travis McDonald, I work with Brett and his group."

I shook his hand. "How can I help you?" I asked and glanced at the time. "I have a demonstration at two and I need to get ready for it."

"When's it over?" he asked.

"It usually is done by two thirty, and the fudge sales to the crowd slows down around three."

"Okay, I'll wait," he said. "I'm going to get some lunch. Pencil me in at three thirty. We need to discuss what your duties are and next steps." He headed toward the door, put his trucker cap on, and walked out without a look backward.

Shoot. I'd been avoiding Brett's email with the presentation slides. Sounded like he sent this guy to check up on me. I hurried to the back hall, hung up my jacket, and put on a fresh chef's coat and hairnet. The demonstration started in five minutes, and I had to be focused. I didn't want anyone to have access to my notes, so I took them with me.

"What did he want?" Frances asked when I passed by.

"He works with Brett and needs me to help him go over some things," I said as I headed to the fudge shop.

"Don't tell me, you're actually going to help them with their resort," Frances said as I quickly sped to the shop.

"Why would I do that?" I hedged, and pushed the door open with my back. The glass-enclosed fudge shop was my home. It smelled sweet with chocolate and cherry and strawberry and many wonderful flavors that gave people pleasure and pride to take home.

I placed my notebook on the shelf above the sink, washed my hands, and went through the motions preparing for and starting the demonstration. Here I could be fully focused. All my concerns were on the other side of that glass door, and I was glad to leave them there, if only for thirty minutes.

The demonstration went well, delighting the crowd. I sold most of my stock and then took my time cleaning up. I guess I was avoiding the other side of that door. With no more left to do, I held the sink, bowed my head, and took a deep breath. "I would do it again for Jenn," I muttered, grabbed my notebook, and walked out of the shop.

Upstairs, I opened my office and unbuttoned my chef's coat. My phone dinged with a text. I put the jacket in the laundry, took off the hairnet, washed my hands again, then reached for my phone. It was the guy from the firing range. Barry must have given him my number.

He had introduced himself and written, **Call me as soon as you can.**

I glanced out into the hall. Mr. McDonald wasn't here yet, so I closed the door and dialed the number.

"Firing range," a gruff male voice said. "We don't have any openings until next weekend."

"Oh, hi." I stumbled a bit. "Um, you texted me? I'm Allie McMurphy and Barry spoke to you . . ." My voice went up an octave on the end as I waited for him to tell me I had the wrong number or the wrong guy.

"You must want the Hammer," he said. "Hold on." I heard him put the phone down and holler. "Hammer, call's for you."

He picked it up. "Yeah?"

I cleared my throat and tried not to be intimidated or at least keep my voice steady and professional. "Yes, I'm Allie McMurphy and someone texted me asking me to call. I believe Barry Tunisian spoke with them."

"Oh, yeah, that's me," he said. "Hang on, I'm going to switch this to my office phone." I heard a click and then on-hold commercials for things like ammo and rifles and lessons to take down the biggest deer or moose. "Okay," he said, cutting off the ads. "I'm in my office with the door closed. Barry tells me you have a killer who's a good shot with a handgun."

"Yes," I said. "They killed the man with one perfect shot to the back of the head. I was wondering if you could give me insight into anyone on the island who's a really good shot or you've seen practicing a lot in the last couple of weeks."

"Like whom?" he asked.

"I don't want to say, because it's only a theory and everyone is innocent until proven guilty."

"I see," he said. "Man or woman?"

"Do you get a lot of women who come to shoot?" I asked.

"Of course," he said. "A whole lot of them are really good shots, too. I think they could easily take a man out."

"Does Hannah Riversbend sound familiar to you?" I asked and crossed my fingers.

"That chick who was arrested for Matthew Jones's murder?" he asked.

"Yes?"

"No," he said "I've never seen her and she's not in our records as having come by. I tried to tell the cops that, but they weren't interested."

I let out a long breath of relief. "Okay, great," I

said. "Is there anyone you do think might have done it? Any rumors at the range?"

"Like Ms. Grazer?" he asked.

My heartbeat sped up. "Yes, Angel, right?"

"No." He sounded certain. "The other one. The older one. If I were looking into Matthew's murder, I'd be looking there. That woman is a champion shot. Everyone knows she came up through the pro ranks, and if they don't know, she tells them."

"Okay, um, thanks," I said, confused. Did Angel have an older sister? I hadn't even considered that. "Thanks for answering my questions."

"Sure," he said. "Call if you think of anything else."

"I will," I said and hit end on my cell phone. An older sister. Why hadn't I considered that?

Chapter 34

There was a knock on my office door and Frances stuck her head inside "Mr. McDonald to see you," she said, giving me the side eye.

"Thanks, Frances." I stood, and she opened the door to the man. He looked bigger in my tiny office. "Come in, sit down." I gestured to the chair in front of my desk. "Can I get you something to drink?" I opened my mini fridge. "I have water and pop."

"No, thanks," he said and sat. "Unless you've got something stronger."

"I don't," I said, and sat back down, facing him across my desk. "What do you need to talk about?"

"I'll get to the point," he said. "I'm the general contractor that Brett's hired to run this new project of his. I understand you're responsible for making sure we get the proper zoning and permits, right?"

"Yes, I'm under contract to do so," I replied. There was a knock on my office door, interrupting us. I drew my eyebrows together. No one really comes to see me when I'm in my office. Frances usually directs them to another time, or they text first. I glanced at my phone. No text.

There was a second knock. "Excuse me." I got up and opened the door to see Harry looking fierce. "Harry?"

"May I come in?" he asked.

"'I'm in a meeting with Brett's general contractor," I said.

"Yes, I know, that's why I'm here." He stepped inside.

I was really confused now. "Um, okay, Travis McDonald, this is Harry Winston. Harry, Travis."

The big man stood and shook Harry's hand. "Nice to meet you."

"You won't think that in a minute," Harry said and took a seat. "I bought out Allie's contract. She is no longer under obligation to Brett or his partners. You can leave."

Surprised, my mouth fell open at this news.

Travis narrowed his eyes. "That doesn't make sense."

I silently agreed. First of all, can you buy out a contract? And secondly, what?

"You should be getting a text from your boss," Harry said with confidence.

Then Travis's phone dinged. "Well, I'll be a son-of-a-gun." He looked up at Harry, who gave him a wicked smile. "I guess that's it for me here. Nice to meet you both." He stood and left the room, closing the door behind him.

I looked at Harry, still confused. "What just happened?"

"I bought out your contract," he said.

"How did you do that?" I asked. I know I was

going to return the money as soon as Hannah went free . . . but Harry? "And why?"

"It was a business decision. Something I've done many times before," he said. "I paid Brett's group cash and might have promised to do business with them soon."

I swallowed hard. "Thank you?"

"That's what friends are for," he said. "Allie, you should have come to me first. That kind of money is nothing to me."

"My parents always told me not to mix business and friendship," I said.

"I see, and Frances and Douglas aren't mixing business and friendship?"

He had a point. "How much did you pay?" I asked.

"That's not important," he said with a dismissive wave. "It's done."

"I'm going to pay you back," I insisted. "I don't want this to come between us."

He leaned forward. "Is there an us?"

"Yes, you are a dear, dear friend and I don't want anything to jeopardize that."

He sat back. "I heard Rex proposes to you all the time and you don't answer." He tilted his head and looked at me with his Chris Hemsworth–like face. Darn, the man could make any girl's heart skip a beat.

I looked down at my hands. "The timing hasn't been right."

"Maybe you aren't as in love with him as you think," he said.

I took in his words. Was he right? It was a strange

thought, and I'd have to mull it over later. "How much do I owe you?"

"You don't think our friendship can withstand a smart business move?" He sat back.

"How is this a smart business move?"

"Honey, my reputation here on the island is tied to yours," he explained. "Also, the last thing I want is to compete with an uber modern resort. So, smart business move."

I inhaled deeply and blew out a long breath. "I guess I'll have to text Brett and see what you paid to buy me out."

"Fine," he said. "I paid him fifty thousand dollars."

I gave Harry the side eye. "He went for that?"

"And a promise to do business together," Harry said. "That's worth a lot to a guy like Brett."

"Okay." I sat back. "When I find Matthew's real killer, and they release Hannah from her bond, I'll be able to pay you forty thousand dollars back. Then I'll make up the extra ten along with interest. Is ten percent too low?"

"I'd take two percent," he said.

"Five percent," I argued.

"Three percent and that's final." He leaned into me and held out his hand. "Deal?"

"Deal," I replied, shaking his hand. "Thank you."

"My pleasure," he said. "Please don't be afraid to tell me things. I promise I'll try not to step in and fix them. This was in my best interest."

"Okay," I said. "As long as you promise this is the last time, you'll do something like this without telling me first."

"Deal," he said, and smiled charmingly at me. "You could take me out to dinner."

"Yes." I smiled back. "Let's do dinner. The yacht club?"

"Naw," he said. "I have a hankering for a beer and some good old-fashioned bar food."

"The Mustang it is. Does six work for you? I need to catch up on my sleep. I thought I'd try to get to bed by eight thirty or nine."

"Six is perfect." He stood. "I'll stop by here and we'll walk over together."

"Cool." I got up and came around my desk and gave him a big hug. "Thank you!"

"My pleasure," he said near my ear, sending shivers down my spine.

"Okay." I laughed and stepped back. "Time to take a shower. I'm having dinner with a friend and don't want to arrive smelling of candy."

"It's a good scent on you," he said. "See you then." He left my office and headed toward the stairs.

What was I going to do with that man? Buying me out without telling me. I went to take a shower, breathing a huge sigh of relief.

Chapter 35

What did you find out? Carol texted me.

I was showered and changed into a sundress and sweater. **As best I can tell, Angel doesn't have any gun experience.**

And Vincent?

He has the usual hunting experience and a hunter's safety course certificate, I texted back.

Vincent must be the killer, Carol texted.

Maybe, I replied.

What do you mean maybe?

I need to talk to Monica, I texted. **On my way to see her now.**

Okay, Carol texted. **Text me as soon as you know anything. The girls and I are on pins and needles.**

Will do. I hurried down the stairs. It was nearly five when most stores closed, and I wanted to talk to Monica.

Main Street was still busy because the last ferries hadn't left yet. I power walked through the dwindling crowds, and arrived at Monica's store as she was serving her last customer. I waited for her to finish before saying hi.

"Allie," she said. "To what do I owe the honor?" She walked around, flipped the CLOSED sign, and locked the door.

"Angel came to see me the other day," I started casually. I knew I had to be careful because Angel was her daughter.

"I heard," she said and started to clean up.

"I never meant to upset anyone. I'm glad Angel set me straight."

"Good," Monica said. "Why are you even investigating this case? Hannah has been arrested and arraigned. Unfortunately, *someone* paid her bond, and that murderer is now on the streets."

I bit my bottom lip. Everyone knew what happened on the island, which meant she knew full well I was the one who paid the bond. "Jenn was in labor and needed her doula."

"I see." She kept cleaning and straightening the shelves of her gift shop. "I suppose I would have done the same thing for my friends." She turned to me and pointed her feather duster at me. "But if I were you, I'd keep an eye on her. If she runs, you'll never get your money back." She went back to cleaning. "It happened to a friend of mine when I lived in Chicago."

"I'm sorry to hear that." I straightened the shelves along with her. I'd done my fair share of retail when I was in high school and college. "Thanks for the advice."

"That girl killed her fiancé. It was cut-and-dried. Everyone knows it, you really need to accept that."

"Right," I said and nodded. "Listen, I heard one of your daughters is a handgun champion."

"You mean the USPSA Multigun Champion," she corrected me. "I only have one daughter. Angel is my world."

"Huh," I said. "It must have been Angel they were talking about."

She put down her duster and looked at me. "Who was talking about Angel?"

"Some guests at the McMurphy who went to the shooting range the other day," I lied. I wondered if she believed me. I was a terrible liar. "Anyway, they came back with tales of a female champion who lived on the island. I thought they said she was a Grazer. I know Angel's last name is Monroe, but I thought maybe you had another daughter with the same last name as you. I must have misheard." I shrugged.

"To begin with, if you must know, Angel uses her father's last name and I use my maiden name. She put her hands on her hips and looked at me with narrowed eyes. "Why are you here, Allie?"

"Well, one, to let you know that I talked to Angel, and she set me straight. And two, after I overheard the conversation, I thought I'd stop by and congratulate you." I raised my hands in a gesture of apology. "And we haven't really spoken for a while. How are you doing?"

She seemed mollified by my answer and went back to cleaning. "I'm doing good. But I'm a little sad about Matthew. He was good to my Angel. It's too bad he and Angel broke up."

"Wait, isn't she with Vincent now?"

"Yes, and Vincent is a good man, too," Monica said. "But he doesn't have as nice a job as Matthew. A mother wants only the best for her daughter."

I chuckled. "Yeah, my mother told me the same thing just this week."

"I heard you and Rex broke up. Are you, okay?" she asked and studied my reaction.

"We're not broken up; we're taking a little break. I've been working too hard, and Rex has been a little overprotective."

"How does one take a break from a relationship?" Monica asked. "In my day, you were either dating or you were broken up and free to date others."

I sighed. "Things are a little different now, and a break can really help a relationship."

"Nonsense. I blame that television show *Friends*," she said. "That's where the 'we were on a break' gag comes from and seems to entitle everyone to say that now when they want to break up but want to keep things open to getting back together."

"Huh," I said. "I hadn't thought of it that way."

We finished cleaning the store. "I should go. I'm meeting a friend for dinner."

"Uh-huh." She nodded. "A male friend, I suppose. That's going to get back to Rex, you know."

"Good night, Monica," I replied and unlocked the door. "Let's talk more often."

"Yes, stop by anytime," she said. "I can always use a hand with the cleanup."

I walked outside with more questions than answers, but I didn't dare push her further. If Angel was her only daughter, then who was the champion shooter? And Monica preferring Matthew over Vincent might be both the reason Angel and Vincent are together and why Angel tried to get Matthew back.

How's your day? I texted Rex while I waited for Harry to stop by.

Not bad, he texted back. **How was your day?**

Interesting, I replied.

How so?

I texted that Harry had helped me out with a business problem, and I was taking him to dinner to thank him.

There was a long pause and then three dots showed up on my screen. **I see**, he texted finally.

I bit my bottom lip. **I'm not seeing anyone. I'm simply taking a good friend out to dinner to pay him back for a business favor.**

Rex didn't text back, and Harry arrived. Time with Harry was always filled with laughter. When he walked me home, I gave him a quick hug and went inside.

It wasn't a date, but if I weren't in love with Rex, I would definitely date Harry. But then it might ruin a perfectly wonderful friendship. Monica's comment ran through my head. Was I stringing Rex along? Is that what Rex thought? Maybe I needed to call Rex before I went to bed.

Chapter 36

Do you have it narrowed down yet? Carol texted me around seven the next morning when I was busy refilling the coffee and pastries.

Finishing up, I texted her back. **No, the manager of the shooting range told me that a Grazer comes in to shoot regularly and has won multiple championships. I asked if it was Angel.**

Which would fit neatly into our investigation. Was it Angel?

He told me, no, the other one. I went to ask Monica about her other daughter.

She doesn't have another daughter. Carol sent a confused emoji.

That's what I went to verify. I had to be delicate about it.

She confirmed that she doesn't have another daughter, right?

I greeted a couple of guests who came down for coffee and continental breakfast, then went back to texting. **Right, and she also laughed when I asked if Angel was a good shot.**

That means she's either not a good enough shot to have killed Matthew . . .

Or, I quickly thumbed, **Monica's lying.**

But if she's lying, why? Also, isn't Angel's last name Monroe?

Yes, Monica set me straight about everything. I added a shrugging emoji. **She warned me off of Hannah, saying I was going to lose my money because Hannah was going to run.**

I wouldn't worry about that, Carol texted back. **She's a responsible girl.**

I agree.

When Frances got in, I took Mal for her morning walk. I tried calling Rex a couple of times last night, but he didn't answer. Probably served me right for asking for a break. I debated walking up to the police station and seeing if he was at work. But then I figured that checking on him at work was a bad idea.

So, Mal and I set off in the cool morning light to sniff things and to let Mal read the local news, which is what I thought of as she sniffed any place another dog might have walked or done their business.

"Allie, yoo-hoo." I turned to see Carol and Irma power walking toward me. I swear simply watching them walk made my heartbeat speed up. Also, I might feel a little guilty for not exercising like I should.

"Morning, ladies." I waved. Mal wagged her tail and sat while we waited for them to come closer. It didn't take very long.

"Oh, Allie," Carol said, breathing hard while Irma walked circles around her. "We have a theory.

What if Angel stole the gun, and Vincent made the shot?"

"While Vincent was in Don's view at the party, Angel slipped in using the key," Carol said.

"But she can't shoot," Irma said as she continued her circles around Carol. "So, she must have given Vincent the gun, and he shot Matthew, dropped the gun, slipped back into their apartment, hurriedly changed his clothes, washed up, and rushed to work."

"Not a bad idea," I said. "Vincent does hunt. The thing is, how did Angel know that the gun wasn't in the gun safe and where it was located?"

"That's easy," Carol said, leaning over to pet Mal. "Vincent was the handyman and knew where the gun would most likely be if it wasn't in the gun safe."

"Maybe," I said. "But did she have time to check the gun safe, that is opened by Don's palm print, by the way, and then go find the gun in the drawer and steal it before Don went back inside?"

"The gun safe is only opened by Don's palm print?" Irma asked.

"I'm afraid so," I replied. "Which means whoever stole the gun had insider information about where to find the gun. Vincent hasn't been close to the Joneses for a few years. He still pops in every now and then, but not lately."

"Well, shoot," Carol said. "We'll keep searching for proof."

"Thanks, ladies," I said. "I've been racking my brain. This is a tough one." One I now had to solve to help pay back Harry. The ladies went back to their power walking. "Well, Mal, do you think I'll ever be in good enough shape to keep up with those two?"

Ruff!

I laughed and we continued on our walk. It just so happened that we passed by Rex's house. Really, I should say, I had that destination in mind when we started the walk. It was a long shot that he wasn't at work, but at least here he couldn't complain that I was harassing him in front of his coworkers. Not that I would ever harass anyone.

I knocked on the door, but there was no answer. I knocked again when his neighbor, Chance Redding, popped his head out.

"He's at work," Chance said.

"Thanks," I replied, and Mal and I stepped off the porch. My heart was heavy. I wished he'd have answered my calls last night, but then again that was selfish. The only reason I wanted to talk to him after dinner with Harry was to assuage my own guilt. It was probably better to wait until he reached out to me.

Then a different idea popped into my head. I hurried toward the Joneses' house. There was something I forgot to ask Don and Roxanne. But before I did that, I wanted to see if Roxanne wanted to work part-time as my backup fudge maker.

"Oh, Allie, it's you," Roxanne said as she opened the door. "I was going to call you today. Please, come in, and your sweet puppy, too."

"Thanks," I said, and took off my shoes. It was a polite gesture on my part meant to not track dirt into her home.

"Come, sit down," she said. "Can I get you any tea?"

"No, thanks," I said knowing it would be difficult for her, and we both sat. "How are you holding up?"

Tears sprang to her eyes. "Matthew's funeral is tomorrow. It's harder than I ever imagined." She grabbed a tissue and dabbed at her eyes. "They are right when they say a parent should never outlive their child."

I stood and gave her a huge hug, and then sat next to her. "I'm sorry that the last time we talked, I didn't have any respect for your grief."

"Oh, I am also angry as heck." She looked straight into my eyes. "Your visit was welcome. I don't know if Hannah did it or not, but I suspected it was someone else. If it weren't for you, my Matthew's killer might go free."

"Is it okay if I ask you another question?"

Mal jumped in Roxanne's lap to comfort her. She absently ran her hand over Mal's soft curls. "Go ahead."

"I've been thinking about who stole Don's gun," I explained. "It seems that not only did they know where it was located, they also had to know it wasn't in the gun safe."

"Oh, I never thought about that." She sat back, continuing to pet Mal. "How would they know?"

"Do you remember if you or Don told anyone that it was in the drawer?"

"Why would we?" she said, but I could see she was thinking about it. "Oh my gosh," she said and covered her mouth in horror. "I think I did it."

"Go on," I said gently. "And remember, just because you said something does not make this your fault. It's the fault of whoever stole the gun and whoever shot Matthew."

She shook her head, tears pouring down her cheeks. I grabbed the tissue box and handed it to her. She blew her nose. "I remember, I was having coffee with my best friend, Lydia Downing, and complaining about how unsafe it was for Don to keep the gun in the drawer and not his gun safe. The next day the gun was stolen."

"Okay," I said. "Look, you spoke to Lydia in confidence. Do you remember who else was around and might have overheard you?"

"I can't! I can't remember!" She cried more tears. I handed her another tissue from the box in her lap.

"It's okay," I said. "It's okay, you don't have to remember." I didn't want to traumatize her again with my questions. Mal and I sat with her until she was all cried out. "Is it okay if I change the question?"

She swallowed. "Yes."

"I know you've got a lot going on, have you given my job any more thought?"

"I'm very excited about it, really," she replied, and wiped her nose again. "But Don said I shouldn't make such a big decision until we get through Matthew's funeral."

"That makes perfect sense." I patted her knee. "And there is no rush."

"Please don't offer it to anyone else for two weeks," she pleaded.

"Of course, I won't. If you are doing okay, Mal and I need to get home. My two o'clock demonstration is in a few minutes."

She sniffed. "Of course. Yes, I'll be fine. Please don't worry about me."

I stood and took Mal off her lap. "Good, thank

you for your help. If you think of anything else, you can give me a call or come into the McMurphy. Okay?"

"Okay." She stood and saw me to the door. "Thank you for all you're doing for Matthew."

"Don't thank me yet," I said. "I'll keep trying but I can't guarantee I'll do anything but stir up trouble." I put Mal down when Roxanne opened the door and hugged her. "Remember what I said. This is not your fault. Please keep in touch."

"I will," she promised.

I left with more questions than answers. Which coffee shop was she in when she spoke to Lydia, and who was there to overhear their conversation?

Chapter 37

"Frances, do you have a minute?" It was after my two o'clock demonstration, and the buying crowd was gone.

Frances looked up from her computer and eyed me over the top of her reading glasses. "Sure."

"Do you know Lydia Downing?"

"Yes, why do you ask?" She studied me.

"I went to see Roxanne when I walked Mal," I said. "And asked how the thief might have known Don's gun was in the drawer and not the gun safe. She thought about it for a moment and then remembered she had shared that with Lydia when they met in a coffee shop. It was just two friends complaining about the bad habits of their husbands."

"Huh," she said. "Yes, I can see that."

"She was horrified that the thief might have overheard her," I explained. "But she couldn't remember who else was in the coffee shop. I couldn't ask more questions. I felt like she was hurting enough."

"You want to ask Lydia if she remembers who was there?" Frances nodded. "Smart."

"But I don't know Lydia," I said. "I thought maybe you could tell me where she lives or where I could find her and offer to buy her a coffee and chat."

Frances gave me Lydia's address. "She works until five but is usually home with her husband by six."

"Great," I said, writing down the information in my notebook.

"Now I have a question or two for you," Frances said.

I drew my eyebrows together, unsure of what she wanted to ask me. "Sure."

Frances double-checked that the lobby was empty and patted the empty chair beside her.

"Oh, boy," I said. "That bad, huh?"

"I'm hearing all kinds of rumors about you," she said. "Mostly that you and Rex broke up and you were seen going to dinner with Harry Winston. Are you alright? You told me you were in love with Rex. What happened?"

I sighed. "I asked for a break in our relationship."

"That's a pretty big deal," Frances said and patted my hand. "Are you okay?"

"I don't know," I said with a shake of my head. "I told him I was going to have dinner with Harry, as friends."

"I see."

"He never texted back." I shifted in my seat. "I tried calling a couple of times, but he didn't pick up. Then on my walk this morning . . ."

"You stopped at his house," she surmised.

"If he was home, he didn't answer the door."

"Didn't you tell me that he has permission to track your phone?"

I swallowed my sadness. "Yes."

"Do you think he knew it was you at his door?"

"I hadn't thought of that." I looked at her. "I asked for the break in the heat of the moment. My mother was here pushing Brett on me. The only thing Brett wanted was for me to help him with a deal. And when Rex pushed me about my safety, I just unloaded on him."

She gave me a hug and pushed a wayward lock of hair behind my ear. "I'm sure he understands."

"I might have gone too far this time." I fought back tears. Then lifted my chin. "But I can't dwell on it. I have a business to run and a murder to solve." I squeezed her hand. "I really think I'm close to proving who did it."

"I'm sure you are," she said. "Please remember, you can always talk to me when you need to talk to someone."

I smiled. "Thanks. I usually talk to Jenn, but she's a little busy right now with Benjamin." I stood. "I'm going to wash up and pay Lydia a visit. Maybe she knows something."

"Good luck," Frances said.

Mal ran up the stairs in front of me and rushed in the apartment when I opened the door. Mella grumbled at the enthusiastic pup.

After I cleaned up and changed, I glanced at the time. It was only four, which meant Lydia wasn't home yet. I sat on my bed and Mal jumped up to sit in my lap. As I petted her, my thoughts were on Rex. Would we ever be able to talk openly about our feelings and expectations? Should I apologize for what I said, even though it was all true? I lay back down on the bed and stared at the ceiling. Was Harry, right? Was I making excuses not to marry Rex?

I lay there until I fell asleep. I woke up at six and sat up. I never nap, which means I must not be getting the right amount of sleep. I got up and fed my pets, then took Mal out to potty before I left for Lydia's house. I wasn't going to take Mal with me this time, I gave them both treats and closed and locked the outside door behind me.

The air was cool, and I noticed it was still light out. Spring was well and truly here. Lydia lived not far from the Joneses in a cute ranch home with early spring flowers bursting from the ground. If nothing else, I got to admire her flower beds.

I knocked on her door.

"Coming," a woman said. She opened the door, and I was surprised. She had a blond bob, flawless skin, and slim figure. The clothes she wore were all designer labels. I knew this because of my mother. Still, it was unusual for an island resident. "Yes? Can I help you?"

"I hope so," I said, and gave her my most charming smile. "I'm Allie McMurphy. Do you mind if I ask you a few questions?"

"Oh, yes, Roxanne told me about you," she said and waved me inside. Her home was immaculate, from the cream couch with the colorful, plush pillows to the soft music and pleasant scent.

I took off my shoes. She had a cream-colored carpet. Who is brave enough to have a cream carpet? Probably someone who's never owned a pet. I was suddenly glad I didn't bring Mal.

"Can I get you something to drink?" she offered.

"No, thank you." I sat down on the couch where she pointed. "Did you talk to Roxanne today?"

She sat across from me. "I did. She was so upset that whoever stole the gun that killed Matthew knew where to get it because she talked about it with me that day."

"I told her it was not her fault in any way. Everyone talks to their closest friend about things that are bothering them."

"I told her the same thing," Lydia said. "I hope she listens."

"It might take many times of saying it before it sinks in," I offered. "Also, her guilt is compounded by grief over Matthew's death."

"I was thinking the same thing." She sighed.

I scootched forward to sit on the edge of my seat and get closer to her so that she could understand how important my questions were. "Do you remember that day in the coffee shop?"

"I do," she said. "My husband had done something that got on my nerves and we were kibitzing. You know that women need to say things something like seven or more times to work through something."

"I do," I said. "If you remember that day, can you tell me which coffee shop you were in? Because there are two here."

"Oh, sure," she said. "It was the Lucky Bean."

"Thanks." I made a mental note. "Do you, by

chance, remember who was in the Lucky Bean while you were talking?"

She thought about it for a few minutes and I waited patiently.

"I can't swear to it, but I think it was the usual seniors in their corner." She pondered another minute. "I think—and again, I can't swear to it—but I think Grant Sellers and Bob Smith came in on their coffee break."

"Anyone else?" I asked, trying not to influence her with who I thought might be there. "Anyone come in who might have overheard your conversation or who was waiting for coffee and could hear you, then left?"

"Oh, my gosh," she said. "I do remember. Monica Grazer came in, ordered a latte, and stood near us. I remember because she leaned in and said after listening to us, that she was glad she was divorced. Apparently, it brought back memories of her bad marriage. We sympathized with her, and she left." Lydia stopped. "I remember feeling that it was weird that we hadn't been talking to her, but she felt the need to butt into our conversation and make it about her. Then when she left, she looked smug."

"Yes, that is weird," I agreed as my heart raced with excitement. "Anyone else that you remember?"

"I don't think so," she said. "Anyway, I hope some of that helped."

I stood. "Thank you so much, that was really helpful."

She stood as well and walked me to the door, where I put my shoes on. "Thank you for looking into this. Roxanne is a real good friend, and she deserves the truth about what happened to her son."

"You're welcome." I straightened. "Please contact me if you think of anything else."

"I will," she said.

Now I had an idea of how Angel and Vincent were able to steal the gun. The problem was proving it.

Chapter 38

Cracker Jack Fudge

This is fun for the new baseball season.

Ingredients:
- 1 cup chocolate chips
- 14 oz. sweetened condensed milk
- 2 tablespoons butter
- ¼ teaspoon salt
- 1 teaspoon vanilla
- 6 oz. caramel topping
- 2 cups Cracker Jacks (reserve toys for kids over 3)

Directions:
Line an 8 x 8-inch pan with parchment paper. In a medium microwave-safe bowl, mix chocolate chips, vanilla, sweetened condensed milk, butter, and salt. Microwave in 30 second

intervals, mixing well between each, until completely melted. Pour half of the fudge in the baking pan, smooth. Pour caramel topping over the top and smooth. Then carefully top with remaining fudge. Sprinkle Cracker Jacks on top and gently press in. Cool at room temperate for 1 hour. Cover and let set, 8 hours at room temp, 3 hours in the refrigerator. Cut into squares. Makes 16. Enjoy!

I paced up and down in Jenn's bedroom as she breast-fed Benjamin. Shane had left us alone to catch up. "I'm sorry, I know I shouldn't be bothering you with this."

"Oh, honey," she said softly and brushed a whisp of her hair, long enough to touch Benjamin's eyebrows, out of the way. "I needed to hear how it was going. Remember I'm the one who texted you, asking you to come and tell me everything."

"I wish I could figure out how to get Angel and Vincent to admit to the crime. There has to be a way to prove they stole the gun and shot Matthew. All my clues are supposition and won't hold up in a court of law."

"I'm going to change the subject." Jenn switched Benjamin to the other side. "How did your visit with your mother go?"

"My mother was . . . well, my mother." I sighed and sat down. "Did I tell you why Brett really wanted to see me?"

"No," she said and sent me a look of concern. "I thought he came to do business."

"He did come on business, but he ran into my mother a few days before and apparently she told him all about my reputation on the island."

Jenn laughed. "Your mother doesn't know anything about you, let alone how people on the island feel about you."

"I know." I rolled my eyes. "Apparently when she ran into Brett, she saw an opportunity to get us back together. Especially after finding out that he was putting together a project here on Mackinac. She played up my influence and told him I'd be happy to help him."

"Oh, that's right, you told me about that," she said.

"Sure, but I didn't expect you to remember with all that was going on at the time."

She rested her head against the headboard of the bed. "I do remember it was some nutso thing he wanted you to champion."

"Yes." *Do I tell her about my deal with the devil and what Harry did?* I decided not to tell her. She'd get upset and she didn't need that right now. "Mother tried a last-ditch effort the night before they left. She got us reservations at the Grander Hotel, and decided she was going to make sure I looked my best."

"Uh-oh," Jenn said. "What did she dress you in?"

"Remember Ashley's wedding?"

"I do," she said. "That was like five years ago."

"Yes, remember the dress I bought for the wedding?" I shifted in my seat at the memory of how short and tight the dress was.

"It was a bodycon dress, right? I remember we

went shopping together, and I talked you into buying it and wearing it because I wanted to wear one and didn't want to be the only one."

I blew out a long breath. Bodycon dresses were very tight on purpose, usually short they ended nearly at the top of your thighs and were strapless.

"Wait, you still have that?" Her eyes began to sparkle with laughter.

"I'm afraid so." I shook my head. "I had forgotten about it, and it was way in the back of my closet. She found it and told me I had to wear it."

"Oh, no!"

"Oh, yes," I replied. "She also did my hair and brought in her makeup case to do my makeup for me, to look my very best." I made air quotes as I finished the sentence.

"Wow, your mother is something else. I thought mine was bad."

"The people at the Grander got quite an eyeful." I felt a blush heat my cheeks at the thought.

She narrowed her eyes. "Wait, were you wearing it when I had Benjamin?"

"Yes, how could you tell? I had a paper gown over it."

"I was in labor, not dead," she said. "I saw you were wearing those heels you own but never wear, and whatever you were wearing under the gown was short."

"Yes," I admitted. "Thankfully, Hannah texted me to come right away, and I got to leave dinner early. But it was hard walking out of the restaurant. Everyone stared."

She reached out and squeezed my hand. "I'm

glad that more good than just Benjamin came of my labor that night."

"Speaking of that night," I said, "I didn't see any parents when I came in just now. In fact, I didn't even see Hannah, only Shane."

"Hannah is a dream. She talked the parents into going home by telling them too many visitors would upset the baby. Then she stayed another day or two before she went home. But she promised to always be a phone call away if I needed anything. Frankly, it was nice to not have any strangers in my house last night."

"On another note, Rex said he would help me investigate this one," I said.

"Really?" She sent me a look of disbelief.

"He was serious," I said. "In fact, he let me know who the gun belonged to, and helped me brainstorm on my investigation, and getting Hannah's bail."

"That guy really loves you." Jenn was very serious.

I shook my head. "All we do is argue over my sleuthing. I'd give it up, but I have to help my friends, and I'm pretty good at it." Then sighed. "Plus, Mom disapproves of a public servant who has already been married twice."

"Speaking of ex-wives, is Melanie being trouble?"

"I'm certain she is overjoyed that Rex and I are taking a break," I said. "Truth is I've been busy; I've forgotten about her. Rex told me he was done with her, and I believe him. She can do whatever she wants. I plan on ignoring her."

Jenn shook her head. "You need to keep an eye

on that one. To her, taking a break might be the same thing as breaking up. Be careful!"

"If taking a break means Rex starts dating someone else, then he doesn't really love me."

"I heard you had dinner with Harry Winston." Jenn gave me the side eye.

"I texted Rex before I went and explained what was going to happen and why."

"And was he okay with it?" She covered up and put Benjamin on her shoulder to burp him.

"He stopped replying and I haven't been able to get ahold of him since," I admitted.

"Because everyone knows Harry is sweet on you, and everyone thinks you ditched Rex for Harry as soon as you went on a break."

"It doesn't matter what everybody thinks," I replied. "I was honest with both Rex and Harry."

"I believe you," she said. "I'm not going to tell you what to do. You are perfectly capable of figuring things out on your own."

Finally, someone who believes in me. "Thank you. Now let me hold that beautiful baby."

Later that evening, Mal and I went on our nightly walk and headed to the police station. I wasn't going to be able to prove Angel and Vincent's guilt without help, and Rex said he would help. We entered the police station to find Officer Smith on desk duty. "Hi," I said as we walked up to the desk. "Is Rex in? It's not personal," I explained. "He said if I needed help with something, he would help."

Officer Smith looked at me as if trying to determine if I was lying. I wasn't, I faced him squarely. He looked from side to side and leaned in toward me. "Rex just headed home. But I'm not the one who told you that."

"Thanks!" I said and Mal and I hurried out. We took the direct road to Rex's house. Mal felt my urgency and didn't stop to smell the grass or anything.

We turned to the corner to see Rex a couple of blocks ahead, getting his mail. "Rex!" I called his name and he turned to look.

"Are you okay?" he asked when we arrived. Mal jumped up on him, asking for pets. He reached down and gave her attention. "I missed you, too," he told her softly.

"I'm okay," I said and sent him a soft smile. "Not in any trouble this time."

He straightened. "Good. What can I do for you, Allie?" We walked down his sidewalk and onto the front porch.

"I have gathered quite a bit of circumstantial evidence that both Angel and Vincent plotted to kill Matthew."

"I see," he said.

"Can I come in?" I asked. "I need your help to figure out how I can convince the DA that he has the wrong person and make it stick in court."

He opened the door and waved us in, then closed it behind him. "Make yourself at home. If I'm going to do this, then I need to be out of my uniform."

"Okay," I said, and watched him disappear into the master bedroom. Mal and I waited patiently until he came out barefoot, wearing worn jeans and a tight T-shirt that showed off his muscles. My heart beat faster, but I couldn't think about that right now.

"Do you want a beer or tea or something?" he asked.

"Do you have any flavored seltzer water?"

"Sure," he said, and disappeared into the kitchen, coming out a few moments later with a beer, a bottle of orange-flavored water and a treat for Mal. He handed me the bottle, and then put Mal through her tricks and fed her a treat before he sat and took a swig of his beer. "Okay, tell me what you've got."

I told him all about the clues that I found about Monica and the firing range. "But she didn't have a motive or a means, and I ruled her out. But Vincent had a motive and a means."

"What do you mean by means? No one saw him leave the party at all that day."

"I think that Angel could have gone to the bathroom, and stolen the gun, put it in her purse. Once they got back to the apartment, she gave it to Vincent and he could have fired the kill shot. As I said, they have motive and means. I need help proving it."

"You need a confession from one or more of them," he stated simply.

"Yes, how do I do that and stay safe?" I asked, twirling the bottle of seltzer water.

"The thing is, I don't think you can." He took another swig. "But I have a solution if you trust me to take care of this."

"I do trust you," I said.

"I'll have to get Brown involved."

"Whatever you need to do," I said. "I won't interfere. Cross my heart." I made the crisscross motion over my heart.

"Then be patient," he advised. "Brown and I will put something together tomorrow. Keep your regular activity. If the DA gets wind of this, it would be bad for all of us."

"I understand," I said. Then was quiet a moment. "You weren't answering my texts, so I came by this morning."

"I know," he said and stood. "I didn't answer. I need time to process you and Winston."

I stood with him. "There is no me and Harry," I said. "I told you why I was taking him to dinner."

"But you shared a problem with him and not me," Rex pointed out. "I thought we were a team."

"We are," I said gently. "But that doesn't mean I won't share things with my other friends as well. Jenn hears everything from me."

"That's different." He studied me with his gorgeous blue eyes ringed in black lashes. Then he seemed to shake it off. "Do you want to share it with me now? I take it that it had something to do with your deal with the devil, and the money you needed for Hannah's bail."

I broke down and told him everything "I didn't want anyone to know the details because I was afraid of what you would think."

"You should know I don't judge you. You've scared me a few times, but I trust your judgment. You need to trust me enough to tell me anything. I have your back. In fact, I was working on getting the money to get you out of that contract."

"That was a lot of money, Rex," I said. "I didn't want to put anyone else in debt because of a promise I made."

"You wouldn't have put me in debt," he said. "I was worried about the deal you were working on. But you wouldn't share the details."

"That's because I got myself in a mess and I had to get myself out."

"But you let Winston help," he pointed out, and sipped his beer.

"I did no such thing," I argued. "I was tired when he called to see how I was and in a weak moment, I told him about the contract. I explained that I wasn't looking for help, I simply needed to vent."

"He bought out your contract and you let him."

I leaned forward. "He didn't ask my permission or even tell me about it until Brett's general contractor arrived to ensure I was pushing the process forward. I never asked you or him to rescue me."

He took another swallow of beer. "I need you to trust Brown and me tomorrow. The farther away you are from this case, the better. Not because I'm telling you what to do, but because you could be arrested for interfering with a trial, or sued. Deal?"

"Deal." We both stood and I handed him my nearly full drink. "Thank you. Come on, Mal, let's go home. "I made it to the door before I turned back to see him standing in the same spot. "Good luck tomorrow and stay safe."

"I'll do my best."

I walked out into the chilly night, thinking about what he said. I wanted to argue that I didn't tell anyone what I had done. But then I told Harry. What was going on in my mind? Was Monica right? Was I really not in love with Rex? Ugh, why was I bad at relationships? Maybe I was better off alone. At least then no one I loved could get hurt.

Chapter 39

"The rumor mill is working overtime," Carol blurted. I had finished my ten o'clock demonstration when she rushed into the lobby.

I stood by Frances, going over the guest list, and looked at Carol. "What's going on that you had to hurry over here?"

Carol stopped at the reception desk and looked side to side before she leaned in. "I have the latest scoop. Rex has brought both Angel and Vincent in for questioning. He and Officer Brown picked them up this morning," she said in a stage whisper. "On suspicion of stealing Don Jones's handgun. The very gun that killed Matthew."

"I see," I said calmly.

"Why aren't you more excited?" Carol asked. "This can crack your whole case wide open. I mean, if they can get them to own up to the theft, I bet he'll get them to confess to the murder." She looked smug.

"That would be something, wouldn't it?" I asked. "Thanks for letting me know."

"Wait, aren't you going to go down to the police station and tell them what we've deduced?"

"I'm sure that Rex and Charles are professionals and don't need me to tell them everything," I said.

Both Frances and Carol looked at me, confused. "Where did this change of heart come from?" Frances asked, studying me over the top of her reading glasses.

"I wasn't able to prove anything that would stand up in court and change the DA's mind about Hannah. Maybe it's time to let the professionals do it," I said. "Carol, can I get you some coffee?" I came around the desk and walked toward the coffee bar.

"You know I will always take a cup of your wonderful coffee," she said and followed me.

I poured the coffee into a paper cup with a cardboard sheath so that she could hold it without getting burned. As I doctored it the way Carol liked it, she was silent.

"What is going on?" she asked when I handed her the coffee.

"I wasn't able to crack this one," I said. "I've decided to let the police do their job. They are wonderful, competent men."

"You talked to Rex," she surmised and narrowed her eyes. "Are you doing this because you broke up with him and are dating Harry Winston? Guilt should never run one's life." She sipped her coffee.

"First of all, I did not break up with Rex. I asked him to take a break from our relationship until we figure out what is wrong with our communication because we've been arguing and I don't like that," I said quietly.

"And second?" she asked, her expression filled with interest.

"Second, I'm not dating Harry. We're friends and I took him to dinner to thank him for a favor he did for me."

"Hmm," Carol said.

"The rumor mill is not always right," I said.

"True," Carol said and took another sip of coffee. "I do like going straight to the source to verify things."

"And I've been nothing but truthful to both men about what I want and need. For Harry that's friendship."

"And for Rex?" Carol asked, looking at me over the top of her coffee cup and taking a sip.

"That's between Rex and me," I said.

"I never did understand taking a break in a relationship," Carol said. "In marriage, sure. I mean we've already promised to stay together until death do us part. Sometimes a break is good to renew the relationship. As we got older, I told my Barry he could go on as many hunting and fishing trips as he wanted. The break is good for us both. As retired people, the last thing you want is to be stuck with your spouse every day until you die. They follow you around and ask you what you're doing all the time and then ask why. It's annoying."

"Sometimes relationships need the same thing," I said. "As long as you're devoted to each other, your relationship can withstand a break. At least that's what I hope."

"I hope so, too," she said. "I wish you only the best."

"Thanks."

"What are you going to do now that you're no

longer on the case? Better yet, what does Jenn think of you giving up?"

"I'm going to see Jenn after my two o'clock demonstration," I said. "But I'm sure she will understand."

"And Hannah? Have you talked to her lately? Is she still on the island?" Carol asked and sipped more coffee.

"I hope to go see her later today, as well," I said. "I want her to understand that I've done all I could to help her and that I believe in her innocence."

"Good girl." Carol patted my hand. She glanced at her watch. "Whoops, Irma is expecting me. Thanks for the coffee."

"You're welcome," I said as she scurried out the door. Then I noticed Frances eyeing me. "What?" I asked.

"Nothing," she said.

But I knew she had thoughts. At least she didn't try to tell me what she thought I was doing wrong, and then insisted I do things her way. At this point I didn't know what to do about Rex, but at least the killers were in police custody. I trusted Rex and Charles to discover the truth.

Chapter 40

It was a beautiful day. There was a bright blue sky and a breeze that was warmer than normal. Flowers were blooming and the crowds were happy with their purchases. The horses seemed to step higher, and everything smelled of fudge, caramel corn, and spring. Plus, Rex believed me enough to do something about Angel and Vincent.

I'd texted Jenn first, but she had asked me to stop by tomorrow. The baby had been fussing all night and now that he slept, she was going to sleep, too. So, I headed toward Hannah's apartment. It felt odd to retrace the steps that had led me to a dead body, but the weather kept my spirit lifted.

Walking past Monica's gift shop, I noticed that it was closed. I wondered if she was ill, or maybe she was at the police station waiting for Angel. I got to the mouth of the alley and took ten steps in, when Monica called my name. I looked up to see her hurrying down from Angel and Vincent's apartment. She looked furious.

"How could you?" She snarled the words as she closed the gap between us. "How could you tell the police that Angel stole that gun? You had no right to dig around and come to any conclusions. No right to convince your boyfriend to take my daughter and her fiancé into the station and question them for hours."

"You seem very upset," I said.

"Of course, I'm upset," she spit out, her fury flashing from her eyes. "My Angel is innocent! I had to shut down my shop and lose a lot of business, but I got her a lawyer who, I might add, is ensuring she goes free."

"I'm not responsible for what happens to Angel," I said. "Every action has consequences."

"And so do yours," she said and drew a gun out from behind her back.

"What are you doing?" I asked as she pointed it at me.

"I'm ensuring you have consequences," she said. "I knew you were trying to save your friend by pinning this on Angel when you asked me about my daughter at the range. Now turn around and move forward."

I did what she asked, but not before texting Rex the simple 911 we had decided on whenever I was in serious trouble. Then I hit record and slipped the phone back into my pocket.

She pushed the ticking the gun in the middle of my shoulder blades. "Raise your hands and move!"

"Okay, okay," I said, put my hands in the air, and started walking slowly forward. "Where are we going?"

"To pay a visit with your murderer friend," she said. "Move!"

I walked slowly and carefully, trying to stall her. "Vincent has a key to the Jones house, and Angel was working two houses down the day the gun was stolen." I then made up a lie. "They have Angel's fingerprints from the Joneses' back door."

"That's a lie. Angel didn't steal that gun." She sounded sure and my mind whirled.

"Of course, she did. She stole the gun, and Vincent, who was seen rushing from the alley just before I found Matthew, used the gun to shoot him."

She scoffed. "As if Vincent was that good a shot."

"Unless you lied to me, and Angel was the shooter. After all, the shooting range manager told me that a Grazer woman was a champion shot. If it wasn't Vincent, it was Angel," I said as I slowed down.

"Please, Angel has never touched a gun. Now stop blaming my baby! She didn't do it."

When we were under Hannah's window, I took a chance and turned to face her. "How are you sure?"

"Because I'm the champion shooter," she said with a tone of pride. "Besides, the shooter ran out the opposite end of the alley, that's why you never saw them."

"How do you know that?" I asked.

She narrowed her eyes. "Some great sleuth you are. Now turn around and move before you end up with the same fate as Matthew."

I stared at her, not moving. My heart raced. "You killed Matthew."

"And stole the gun," she bragged. "You might as well know how far off you were before you die."

It was like she gloated. "You stole the gun? So, it was you who planned this whole thing." I narrowed my eyes. "You lied about the argument between Hannah and Matthew."

She shrugged. "I never said it was that day. They argued the day before in front of witnesses. Stupid people assume things. I relied on that. After seeing the argument the day before, they wouldn't question my statement." She chuckled. "You didn't question it."

"How come nobody but Hannah heard the shot?"

"You'd be surprised how easy it is to silence a handgun. Look it up sometime. Oh, wait, you don't have any more time."

"I have to say, you really fooled me. I thought you were covering for Angel."

"Leave my baby out of it! She is innocent and I won't have people talk about her like that." Anger flashed in her eyes. "Now move!"

I stood my ground. "I have to know why. Why kill Matthew?"

"Everyone knows he seduced Angel the night he asked her to dinner and got her pregnant. But he wouldn't own up to it. He should have married my baby the moment she told him she was pregnant. Now all she has is Vincent, a fine enough handyman, but she and my grandchild won't have the life they deserve."

At that moment, Hannah stepped out of her apartment.

"Hannah, get in your house and lock the door!" I yelled, causing Monica to hit me hard with her pistol.

I fell to my knees. My vision blurred. She raised her gun to my head.

"Like fishing in a barrel. A supposedly smart girl like you should stick to what she does best, fudge making."

Before she could shoot, someone tackled her from behind. I sat down hard, trying not to pass out, and heard a scuffle. Then handcuffs.

"Allie, lie down, sweetheart." It was Rex. He gently pulled me into his lap, and I closed my eyes. That's when the pain hit me.

"I recorded everything. My phone is in my . . . pocket." It hurt to talk, and it came out as a whisper.

"Get EMS out here now!"

It was the last thing I heard before I blacked out.

Chapter 41

My head pounded, and my jaw hurt as I woke up slowly. My mouth felt like a desert. "Water," I managed to croak out.

"Here, sweetheart." Rex handed me a paper cup. He looked like hell warmed over.

The water felt wonderful on my tongue and soothed my throat. Strange, I couldn't remember anything but the pain busting in my head. "What happened?"

"We got her," he said. "We got Matthew's killer."

"Good."

He took the cup away and held my hand when I closed my eyes against the throbbing in my head. "Get the nurse," I heard him say. "She's in pain."

That's when I noticed Hannah was in my room. She rushed out of the door. I licked my lips. "You found me. Our system worked."

"Yes, it worked," he said softly. "Brown and I went running the minute I got your text and located you on my phone. We got there in time to see her raise her arm and pistol whip you."

"You got her." I repeated.

"Thanks to you and your recording," he said.

The nurse came bustling in and checked my pulse. Then she flashed a light in my eyes, and I winced. "What is your pain level on a scale of one to ten?"

I kept my eyes closed. "Nine."

"Okay," she said. I heard her doing something but couldn't open my eyes. "I gave you a little morphine. It should help."

Immediately I felt relief spread slowly through my veins. I was exhausted and fell asleep. Esha kept coming in and shining a light in my eyes. I grumbled because all I wanted to do was sleep. When I finally woke up, it was dark outside and the lights in the room were turned down low.

Rex slept, resting his head on the bed beside me and holding my hand. I squeezed his hand, my heart bursting with love. It woke him up and he looked at me groggily. "How are you feeling?"

"Better," I croaked out.

He poured me half a cup of water and handed it to me. "You scared me, again."

I drank the water, then handed the cup back to him. "I'm sorry."

"I love you, sweetheart," he said, looking me in the eye.

I squeezed his hand. "I love you, too," I replied. "My white knight."

He gave a short laugh. "I barely got there in time."

I reached up and put my palm on his cheek and he pressed it closer. "But you did get there in time."

Esha came in to check on me. "How's your pain level?"

"Tolerable," I said.

"Good," she replied and checked my pulse and flashed a light in my eyes. "You gave us all a scare. But you were lucky, your jaw is intact, you have two swollen black eyes that are healing, and a concussion."

"That's why my head hurt so bad," I surmised. "But my jaw hurts, too."

"You have a bad bruise on your jaw," Rex explained.

"But the doctor took X-rays and it's not broken," Esha said. "You are a very lucky woman."

"Oh."

"We were very worried about you," Esha continued, checking the bags of fluid that ran into an IV in my arm. "You've been out for three days. A concussion that bad"—she shook her head—"you could have died."

"But I didn't," I said, my voice returning after sipping the water.

Rex squeezed my hand. "No, you didn't."

"This man hasn't left your side," Esha pointed out. "He's a keeper."

"I didn't want you to be alone when you woke up," Rex explained. His expression was one of love and concern. How could I have ever questioned my feelings for him?

"Marry me," I said. "I don't have a ring and can't get down on my knees, but please say you will."

"Yes," he said without hesitation and kissed me gently.

I closed my eyes. "So tired." And fell asleep.

* * *

The next morning I woke up feeling like myself again and sat up.

"Good morning, sweetheart," Rex said and took my hand. "How are you feeling?"

"Much better. No flashlight in my eyes interrupting my sleep."

"Do you remember what you asked me?" He looked at me with puppy-dog eyes.

"I do," I said. "And in case you thought it was the morphine, Rex Manning, will you marry me?"

"Yes," he said again.

My stomach rumbled. "I'm hungry."

He laughed. "The perfect reply to my saying I'll marry you."

I felt the heat of a blush. "I'm glad you get me. I love you."

"I love you, too, and I'm glad you're hungry. It's been a while since you ate," he said and rang the nurse. She entered the room. "She's hungry."

"Good." This time the nurse was Connie. She checked my pulse and my pupils. "How is your pain?"

"Much better," I said.

"Good, I'm going to wean you off the morphine," she said. "I want you to tell me the minute your pain becomes unbearable."

"I will."

She narrowed her eyes at me. "Promise?"

"I promise," I said. When she left the room, I turned toward Rex. "I'm sorry it wasn't a fancy proposal."

"Honey, we tried fancy," he replied. "It didn't work for us."

"You have to know that I'm never going to stop

helping my friends. And, thanks to our code, I'm in no more danger than you are when you go in to work every day."

"I finally get it," he replied. "And I don't want you to change. But I think we should work together more. Bring me all your clues. I won't dismiss them."

"Thanks for taking Angel and Vincent in for questioning. If you hadn't done it, we would have never discovered the true killer."

"We make a good team," he said, his gaze filled with love.

My heart swelled. "Yes, we do."

Connie brought in my food. "You should eat soft foods for two days, then slowly transition to regular foods."

The tray held scrambled eggs, oatmeal, and chocolate pudding. "Okay," I said obediently, and dug into the eggs. Thankfully, my stomach didn't reject the food, but I filled up quickly. "Want my pudding?" I asked Rex.

"You need to eat," he said.

"I'm full," I replied. "Really." I handed him the pudding and a plastic spoon, and he dug in.

Soon my room was filled with visitors. First Jenn, Shane, and Benjamin, then Hannah, Frances and Douglas, Harry, Liz, Carol, and the rest of the book club. I had a community that cared, and it warmed my heart.

After answering all their questions and reassuring them that no matter how I looked, I was okay, I turned to Rex. "Shall we tell them?"

"Tell us what?" Frances asked.

"Allie proposed to me, and I said yes!" Rex gave me a loving look.

Everyone talked at once, mobbing the bed to congratulate and hug us both. Even Harry, who whispered, "It's about time. Just remember I'm here whenever you need me."

"Thanks," I whispered back and gave him a big hug.

"Oh, you need to have an engagement party," Jenn said, Benjamin on her shoulder and her event-planner smile on her face. "I've already got some ideas! I can't wait. We can do it next week, Friday."

"Darling," Shane said. "We need to give her some time to heal. I'm sure she doesn't want to be bruised in her party pictures."

"Hmm," she said. "How soon will the bruises fade?"

Hannah got out her phone and did a search. "Ten to fourteen days."

"Can you wait that long?" I asked Jenn.

"Sure," she said. "With that much time, I can really plan a bash."

"And so it begins," Rex said.

I laughed but it hurt. "Ow, I can't wait."

Acknowledgments

Thanks to the wonderful people at the Island Bookstore (Mackinac) for their constant support and help and to the people of Mackinac, who are graceful with the changes my books make from reality for storytelling purposes. Thanks to the readers who buy and read my books, come to my signings, and support my work.

Thank you, too, for my editor Michaela Hamilton, and the wonderful, hardworking Larrisa Ackerman, Kensington Cozy PR. Your work and support encourage and bolster me. And to all the wonderful people at Kensington Publishing Corp. who work hard to bring great stories to readers, thank you!

Fudge and Marriage

Book Thirteen of the
Candy-Coated Mystery series

"Fudge and Marriage,
Fudge and Marriage,
Go together like a horse and carriage . . ."

Chapter 1

"Allie." Brigitte Huff, head librarian at the Mackinac Island library, didn't sound surprised to see me.

"I'm returning this book and these magazines," I said. "I'm going to have a look at the interlibrary loan list to see if there's anything else I can get." I placed a total of eight books and magazines in the return pile. Thank goodness for a library card. Without it I might have gone broke by now.

Brigitte was a warm person who lived for books and loved to help patrons. She shook her head at me, her crisp gray bob swinging. "You've been checking out everything we have on weddings for the last six months. When's the ceremony?"

"Next weekend." I felt the heat of a blush that must have been five shades of red. I thought the whole island knew that I was getting married in two weeks. With my involvement in the community and the fact that I was marrying Rex Manning, the lead police officer on the island, everyone was invited. It was why we had decided on an outdoor wedding. My best friend and maid of honor, Jen Christensen, had worked it out so that everyone but family would bring their own chair if they wanted, and others could stand in the back. The reception was to be a giant potluck, while Rex and I paid for a caterer to barbecue handmade hamburgers, Coney dogs and provide savory pasties as the meat for the meal. Already the senior ladies planned a potato salad competition. Oh, and a fun band playing anything requested from its play list with a half hour break where we'll have karaoke.

June was a lovely time on Mackinac, with sweet-smelling flowers blooming everywhere. It's why I had picked the Saturday before the Lilac Festival. I would have picked the Saturday of the festival, but that was a busy day everywhere on the island, including my McMurphy Hotel and Fudge shop.

"Next weekend," Brigitte said, her blue eyes twinkling. She put her hands on her hips. "Then why are you still devouring every wedding book and magazine published since 1959?"

"There are so many details," I explained. "I'm not sure I'm making good decisions, and the books help me narrow down what I like. I never thought about getting married, let alone having five-hundred-plus people attend, and the worst part is my mother. She will scrutinize everything down to how white my teeth are. There's so much pressure."

She laughed. "You are the bride of the island. No one here expects your wedding to be a royal affair."

"If I know my mother, and I do know her, she expects a royal affair. She's been trying to convince me we should have a private reception at the Grand Hotel. Where there would be linen table-cloths on the tables, along with fine china and silver. Don't forget the cocktails and hors d'oeuvres before the meal while a trio of violins and cello plays in the background. Finally, a five-course meal followed by cake and champagne.

She laughed. "That doesn't sound like you or Rex. As for the rest of us, all we care about is that you are happy, in love, and that it lasts a lifetime. The rest will take care of itself. Besides, don't you have Jenn as your wedding planner?"

Jenn was a marvelous event planner. She shared an office with me on the fourth floor of the McMurphy, and she also had a baby boy who would soon turn one. "Yes, and I'm afraid I've been driving her crazy. She has all these suggestions and decisions she wants me to make and all I do is freeze."

"And study wedding books and magazines," Brigitte laughed. "If it makes you feel better, go on and see what's new in the interlibrary loan system, and I'll see if I can't get it here before you get married . . . next weekend."

"Thank you!" I waved and hurried to the computer. I know in my heart that marriage is what's important, not the wedding. But this was Rex's third marriage and my first—and last—wedding. With the whole island invited, and my parents and their friends coming as well as Rex's parents, people would talk about it for years. The pressure was unbelievable.

As I sat down to search the database, I noticed that the chair next to me was turned and the computer was still on the Social Security website.

Someone had been looking up retirement information and had left in a hurry or hurried to get a book from the stacks. I heard the back door close with a bump. Huh, I didn't know that the back door was open. I'll have to ask about it. Shrugging I went back to my search only to hear two women yelling. I leaned over to see if I could see who it was. I mean it was a library and although it was small, they did try to keep it quiet. But it seemed like they were a few aisles away and if I got up, it would seem like I was far more interested in a fight than my wedding and I wouldn't have that bad luck.

Audrey Davis, the associate librarian with beautiful brown skin and a welcoming personality, hurried over to where they fought, and I couldn't help but listen. "Ladies," she said in a half whisper. "Please keep it down."

"I requested the newest craft book," one woman said. "It wasn't in my reserved pile and when I got here, she had already taken it."

"First come first serve." The second woman sounded familiar, but then again, I had a pretty good relationship with all the seniors so even the first lady's voice sounded slightly familiar. "Besides, this book hog has been reserving all the new craft books and then keeping them for weeks. This time, I am going to read it first."

"I reserved it first!"

There was the sound of a scuffle.

"Ladies!" Audry used what I could only describe as a teacher's voice. "If you don't stop fighting, I will give it to the four other people who have requested it before we lend it to you two."

The fighting stopped but I could hear grumbling. Suddenly there seemed to be a race to the books for sale section, which I could see if I leaned back.

It was Velma French and Myrtle Bautista who had fought over the craft book, and now it seemed like they were grabbing new book-sale books off the top shelf. I knew both ladies through my interaction with the senior center, and I knew Myrtle was a good friend of Irma's. The rivalry between Velma and Myrtle went back decades, and no one remembers why it started. In fact, I don't think the women remember why.

I'd never seen two women grabbing up as many books as they could hold just to keep the other from finding something they wanted.

"Ha, ha!" Velma raised two books in the air and waved them in Myrtle's face. Her gray curls swung and she had a vicious smile on her face. "This is the latest Karen Dionne, and it's signed!" She hugged it to her chest and pushed the other book under her rival's nose. "And even better . . . This one is by Anissa Gray and it's a first edition!"

Myrtle looked defeated. "I've been wanting those for ages, and you know it."

"Too bad, so sad," Velma gloated, waving her books. "I got them first and they are going into my private collection."

"Until you die," Myrtle replied. "Then your daughter and son are going to have one big rummage sale. I can wait."

"Humph," Velma sniffed and turned on her heel toward the front desk so she could pay for her treasures.

Myrtle sighed and sat down at the computer table next to me.

"That was kind of mean," I said softly.

"I know. She didn't have to wave them under my nose," Myrtle said.

"I meant telling her that when she dies you're going to buy them from her estate rummage sale."

"Oh," Myrtle said, rolling her blue eyes and waving the thought away. "She knows I didn't mean it."

"Why are you fighting over books? Don't you think the only things worth fighting over would be your family and friends?"

She shrugged. "I suppose so, but you don't know Velma." Then she looked down at the computer in front of her. "Sheesh, it's just like Velma to not return the computer to the home page." She scrolled a bit. "What on earth was she doing on the Social Security site? Everyone our age knows our retirement forwards and backwards. Well, at least we should." She deftly put the browser back on the home page and stood. "She should be gone by now. Bye, Allie."

"Bye, Myrtle," I said and went back to scrolling through the list of bridal books and magazines that would get here within two weeks. I sighed. I'd read them all. I turned off the computer, grabbed my book bag, and strolled to the front of the library.

"Did you find anything?" Audry asked.

"No," I said, trying not to sound as crushed as I felt.

"That's for the best, don't you think?" she asked kindly. "Try to enjoy the experience. It only comes once in a lifetime."

"I'll try," I said with a half smile.

"Wait," Brigit said. "Here, you may need this book on slowing anxiety with meditation." She held out her hand looking for my library card. I gave it to her. "This works wonders for me when I start to over worry about details." She handed back my card and the book. "I'm sure it will work for you when you get overwhelmed."

"Thanks," I put the book in my bookbag and stepped out into the blue skies and lapping water of the nearby lake.

The library was a beautiful mint-green Greek Revival building with white columns and trim. It sat by the shore of the Straits. A boardwalk took you past the tiny, white, house-shaped letterboard with the library hours on it. But one of my favorite things was the brass sculpture of two young children enjoying a book. Thick bushes ran along the side allowing for shade so that you could read on one of the benches undisturbed by the park next door.

As I walked beside the bushes, I noticed Myrtle's precious craft book on the ground. I bent to pick it up and brush it off. As I rounded the other side of the bushes, I noticed three things at once. Velma's books were also scattered on the ground. Velma lay flat on the ground, her head turned to the side, bleeding horribly. Beside her was Myrtle on her knees, rocking back and forth and keening softly.

I rushed to the scene and bent down to see if there was any first aid Velma might need. But her skull was bashed in so deep that I knew she had to be dead. Still, I did my duty and reached for a pulse along her neck. There wasn't even the slightest glimmer of a pulse. That's when I noticed a large rock beside Myrtle. It was covered with blood and gray hair.

A man came around the corner of the library with a fishing pole in his hand. "Velma?" He asked and dropped the pole. "Velma!" He rushed to her side and started to shake her as if to wake her.

"I think she's gone,' I said.

"No! Not my Velma!" he put his face in his large, calloused hands. "My sweetheart!"

I deduced he was Velma's husband. As I reached for my phone to call 9-1-1, Irma and Carol came hurrying over.

"We heard shouting," Irma said.

"We saw Velma on the ground and Myrtle beside her," Carol said. "Is everything okay?"

"My Velma is gone," the man sobbed. "And that horrible woman killed her!" He pointed at Myrtle, causing her to cry even harder.

"Now, Richard, you can't make assumptions like that. None of us knows what happened, and it's not always what it looks like," Carol said. "This must be hard and shocking, but you are not alone." Carol comforted him by putting her hand on his shoulder. "We are here with you."

"Like you have any idea what this feels like," he snarled and put his face back in his hands.

While Irma checked out Myrtle to see if she was harmed, I stood, stepped away and called 9-1-1, but not before I saw someone watching from the bushes. They saw me and backed into the bushes quickly.

"Nine-one-one, what is your emergency?"

"Hi Charlene, it's Allie McMurphy," I said, trying to keep my voice calm.

"Where are you?" she asked. "I'm calling the police and ambulance."

"Better contact Shane as well," I said. "We'll

need a crime scene professional. We're just outside the library."

"Done," she said after a moment or two. "What happened?"

"I came out of the library and found Velma French on the ground with her head irreparably damaged. There was a large rock nearby with what I believe has her blood, hair, and some skin on it. I suspect the killer dropped it after they saw what they'd done."

"Oh, dear, Not Velma. She was always a sweet woman and baked the best cookies." Charlene sighed. "Whatever you do, don't let anyone touch that rock."

Just as she said that I turned to see Velma's husband angrily kick the rock into the lake. "Darn thing can go straight to the bottom of the ocean!" He shouted.

"No!" I yelled. All I could think about was the murder weapon in the lake being washed of all the evidence. I rushed past him and waded into the water. It couldn't have rolled far. Velma was only a few yards from the beach. I spotted it as pieces of hair and blood started to drift off as it rolled back and forth in the waves. I grabbed it and pulled it out of the water, not sure I would be able to preserve any evidence. I didn't have gloves on and neither did Velma's husband. As I turned from the lake, I saw that the scene was charged with anger and sorrow.

"That rock should be crushed and ground up to dust, and so should you!" He lunged toward Myrtle. Carol ran in front of him with her hands out while Irma sheltered Myrtle.

"Stop!" Carol shouted.

Thankfully, my fiancé Rex and Officer Charles Brown rolled up quickly on bikes. Charles dropped his bike and grabbed Richard by the arms, pulling them back and using handcuffs on Richard's wrists, then pushing on his shoulder until he sat.

"You need to cool down," Charles told him. "Sit here until we can assess the situation." Richard still looked angry, but he did as he was told.

More people had stopped to see what was happening, trampling the crime scene. I was not much better—holding the rock in both hands as well as my cell phone. I would have to take the phone out of its case and clean it as soon as I got home.

"Alright everyone, step back," Rex said with such a tone of authority everyone moved. Officer Lasko arrived and pushed the crowd back while Carol and Irma comforted Myrtle as she kneeled on the ground, cautioning her not to move until the police could figure things out. Myrtle sobbed with her hands covering her face. "Allie?" Rex turned toward me. "What do you know?"

"I think this may be the murder weapon," I said, holding out the soaked rock. There were still a few spots of blood and a hair or two.

"What the heck?" Rex looked from the rock to me.

"Richard angrily kicked it and it rolled into the water."

Rex looked up at the sky and for a moment closed his eyes. "You saved it from the water." It was a statement not a question.

"Well, I couldn't just let the evidence wash away," I said softly.

He looked at me with love in his eyes. "I'm

going to need you to hold that until we can get a big enough evidence bag or Shane arrives."

"I asked Charlene to call him, too," I said, and the ambulance rolled up, its lights and sirens running. The ambulance and firetruck were the only motor vehicles allowed on the island. Everything else was driven by horse and buggy, bicycle, or walking. I personally preferred to walk.

Rex left me to check out the scene as the ambulance arrived. Head EMT George Marron stepped out of the front seat, along with his partner of the day, Leah Harrell, who had started part-time over the winter and stayed for the summer. They opened the back of the van and hauled out their medical bags, then rushed over to Velma. We all knew, and I suspect they did, too, that she was gone. I'm not known for calling in people the EMTs can help, although I wished that wasn't the case this time.

Lasko set up a barrier of yellow tape, leaving the growing crowd to watch from afar and whisper about whether Velma was dead and who would do such a terrible thing to such a nice lady.

Carol went back across the scene and sat on the ground next to Richard far enough away that they couldn't hear the murmurs of the crowd.

Head EMT George checked her out and shook his head to confirm that there was nothing they could do for her. They blocked her as best they could from the crowd and waited for Shane, who was working back in his lab at St. Ignace. According to Rex's radio, the Coast Guard had picked Shane up by boat and would ensure he got there as fast as possible while being safe.

"Allie!" I turned to look at Carol with the rock still in my hands. "Honey, don't you have a dress fitting in five minutes?"

Right. I blew out my breath. "Thanks, Carol!"

Rex looked up at Carol's words, said something to George, who glanced at me, nodded, and produced the right size bag for the rock. Rex took the bag and strode over to me. "I'll take that," he said with a flash of love on his face. When he slid the rock into the bag, his expression was all cop. "We're going to need to collect samples from your hands. You should call Esmeralda and let her know you'll have to reschedule."

"That's what I was thinking," then I raised my hands. "But evidence."

"Yeah," he said. "Where's your cell phone?"

"In the right pocket of my jacket," I replied. He fished out my cell and held it up to my face so that it would open.

"Is she in your contacts?"

"Yes, of course," I responded. "We've been working on this dress for over six months." Esmeralda Gonzoles was the best dressmaker in two counties. While my mother wanted a large princess ball gown with three crinolines and an eight-foot veil, I had wanted something simple. Maybe something a bit bohemian. Esmeralda thought to combine the two by making the dress out of white eyelet with just enough room for one crinoline to help bring the skirt out.

Rex found her name, hit the dial button, and put her on speaker.

"Esmeralda's dress designs, how can I help you?" She had the sweetest accent from her home country in South America, even though she had come to the US when she was ten years old and her parents immigrated.

"Um, Hi, Esmeralda," I said.

"Allie, honey, how are you? Are you excited for your final fitting? Don't forget to bring your shoes."

"That's why I was calling," I said and cleared my throat. "We're on speaker and Rex is holding the phone." I glanced at him. I really didn't need more bad luck by letting him get an idea of what my dress looked like. "Listen, there's been an emergency and it could be a few hours before I'll be free."

"Oh, honey! Are you okay?"

"Yes, yes, I'm fine," I said. "Could we reschedule?"

"Of course," she said. "I tell you what, you call me when you're free and we'll make a special appointment just for you. I'm confident the dress is perfect. I'll come to Mackinac when you have time, and we'll do a fitting at your place. Unless of course the groom is . . . shall we say, around too much? It's bad luck for him to see the dress before the ceremony."

Rex raised an eyebrow at me. His deep blue eyes twinkled as he tried to keep a straight face.

"Thank you, Esmeralda!" I said. "You are a doll."

She laughed. "Take care of yourself, honey. It's important to be healthy as well as happy on your wedding day."

"I will." Rex hung up and slipped my phone back into my pocket. Lucky for me, Shane showed up, running from the special dock to the crime scene with his kit in hand. Shane Carpenter was a tall, gangly man with round glasses and an intensely smart brain. He was the main crime scene investigator and Jenn's husband. He looked as tired as Jenn did these days with a toddler in the house.

"Shane, over here," Rex waved him through the crowd. Shane lifted the crime scene tape and ducked under, then headed straight toward us.

"What do we have?" He pushed his glasses up and tried to catch his breath.

"Velma French was murdered," Rex said, his blank cop expression back in place. "What Allie was holding may be the murder weapon." Rex handed him the wet rock in the bag.

"Why'd you pick it up?" Shane asked as he put his kit down, opened it, and gloved up.

"Velma's husband was upset," I answered. "He kicked it hard, knocking it away from Myrtle. Unfortunately, he kicked it hard enough that it ended up in the lake." I sighed. "I rushed over to get it and preserve as much evidence as I could." It was then that I finally noticed how big and heavy the rock was. My arms hurt and I went to rub them when he stopped me.

"Don't touch anything!" He pulled more evidence collection instruments out of his bag. "I need to collect as much as I can off your hands."

I looked down at my wet and slightly dripping hands and silently wished him the best. "At least you have my fingerprints and palm prints on file." I tried to smile but neither he nor Rex seemed amused.

"Why didn't you tell me that what you thought might be the murder weapon was beside Myrtle?" Rex had the look he usually got when he was questioning a witness—even me.

"I didn't mean to leave that part out."

"Is this the only part of the scene you touched?" Shane asked. as he put the last swab into a bag.

"No." I winced. They both hated that answer. "I had to check what shape Velma was in when I came upon the scene. I checked for breathing and a pulse. She was definitely gone."

Shane tilted his head down and looked at me from over the top of his glasses. "Allie, I swear you touch more bodies than the ME, and it's his job to touch them."

"I can't just call 9-1-1 without any information," I replied. "If I didn't do it before, you both know Charlene would have made me do it while she had me on the phone."

"Right," both men said at the same time. I wasn't sure if they agreed with me or not, but at least that part of the conversation was over.

"I'm done with her," Shane picked up his kit and moved slowly to the body.

"Tell me everything from the beginning," Rex said as he pulled his interview notepad from his left breast pocket.

I told him everything. Starting with what I saw in the library to following the dropped books and finding Velma with Myrtle crying beside her and the rock near her.

He flipped his notebook closed. "Do you think it's an open and shut case?"

I shook my head. "You know these things never are."

Visit our website at
KensingtonBooks.com
to sign up for our newsletters, read
more from your favorite authors, see
books by series, view reading group
guides, and more!

Become a Part of Our
Between the Chapters Book Club
Community and Join the Conversation

Betweenthechapters.net